Of Arrows & Anarchy

Morgan Perryman

Dedication

To anyone who has ever questioned whether they should stand up and fight. Fight for those you love. Fight for what you believe in. Fight for who you are.

Trigger Warning

This book may contain scenes that may be distressing for some readers. On the final page of this book, I have included a list of this content. However, listing them will spoil some key events in the plot of the novel.

If you wish to seek information on these scenes, please skip to the final page.

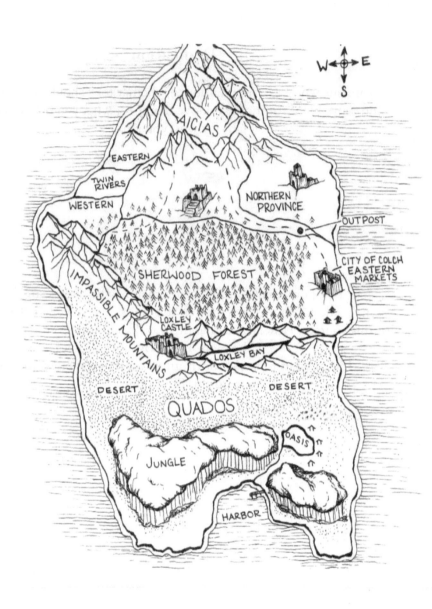

Marian

I knew the king would kill me for it, but the people of Notting didn't deserve to be slaves anymore and neither did I.

I had walked this earth for barely more than twenty years, but I would burn this morning. Lord Sampson carried the torch toward the pile of wood as I struggled against the ropes pinching at my wrists. His face was filled with contempt as he approached. The nobility gathered along the stone wall of the castle high above us.

I knew if I looked up, I would see the faces of the people I had spent my entire life trying to belong with and desperate to impress. I knew I would see the glimmering jewels of the royal family reflecting off the sunlight. I would see the face of Prince Asher—the man who was supposed to be my friend. How many of the court would cry for me today? How many would mourn my death?

Would they look away or watch me burn?

I watched the torch flicker in Lord Sampson's enormous hands. I wouldn't call to the court for aid. I wouldn't plead for my life.

Spread wide in a circle around me, hundreds of the citizens of Notting had been summoned from their beds to watch. Many of the women were openly sobbing. Their kerchiefs pulled across their noses as they wailed. Their voices called out to me despite the wrath they might succumb from the king. My crime was treason and for that the crown believed there should be no weeping.

I refused to search the crowd for the one face I wanted to see more than any other. I knew she wouldn't be there. Robyn had made her opinion known, and my actions had come far too late.

I began my journey toward death mere months ago...

The door to my bedroom closed behind me with a heavy thud. It was early morning and most of the castle still slumbered. The chill of early spring filled the corridor, bringing bumps along the sensitive flesh on my arms. The thick stone walls of the castle might be great for keeping out warring armies, but they certainly locked in the cold.

Whispers followed me through the corridors. As the king's ward, I had grown up inside the castle, but that did not stop the other ladies from hating me. Actually, they hated me *because* of it.

"If it isn't the royal pet..." Robyn of Loxley's voice sneered from the end of the hall. She stood alone as always. Her long leg jutted out, temporarily blocking my path. "Whose boots are you off to lick this morning?"

Robyn was another noble shadow—always waiting, always listening.

I rolled my eyes as I passed. I might be friends with the prince--if that's what you could call it--but I was no one's pet.

"I was under the impression that you would lick anyone's anything," I whispered back at her, trailing my gaze up from the ground, across her worn breeches, to her loose tunic. I crinkled my nose as I leaned closer to her, ignoring how the morning sun glinted from her golden hair. "Or have you finally settled on the fact that no one will allow you near them? At least not unless they were getting paid."

Surprise flashed behind Robyn's gaze. The edge of her mouth pulled up and she opened her mouth to speak, but closed it almost immediately.

"Although, I hear you are very close to your *horse...*"

I knew very little of what I said was founded. I had only heard rumors of Robyn's promiscuity from some of the other ladies. As I looked her over, I wondered again how much of it was true. How many men or women had been paid to warm her bed? How many had paid her to warm theirs?

Robyn's mouth curled upward as if reading my thoughts. She pulled her leg back, allowing me to pass. I continued down the corridor before she could respond.

As I rounded the corner, the voice inside my mind reminded me that though I wasn't anyone's plaything, I also didn't have many friends. I had only ever really had Prince Asher, and even that was strained, to say the least.

My morning rounds in the infirmary began early and I had no time to worry about petty squabbles. I could afford no distractions.

Especially distractions like self-righteous noblewomen such as Lady Robyn of Loxley.

More unfriendly faces greeted me as I entered the courtyard. I chastised myself for not using the tunnels that connected the tower to the interior of the castle. It was faster to cut across the courtyard, but I would have avoided more uncomfortable looks and forced politeness by using the healers' private pathways.

Although I was familiar with most of the nobility, having treated a great number of them for one ailment or another, new faces were pouring in from the far reaches of the kingdom every day.

A young woman dressed in a long, green, velvet gown walked by me. Though I had said few words to the new arrival at Court, I recognized Lady Rochelle immediately. Her black hair fell behind her back, reminding me of a dark waterfall.

Duke Isaac Griffiths had appeared with great ceremony to present his daughter, Lady Rochelle, only weeks before. Almost instantly, the family from the small Western River province made their intentions known. The duke had spent the last few weeks presenting Rochelle to every suitor at court—while his daughter joined the long line of ladies vying for Prince Asher's attention.

King Ruelle had welcomed them to court, though he had long ago stopped pretending to be a caring king. His subjects showed up at the gate every day, but he would only allow in those of noble birth. He would not listen to the pleas of the common people.

Today the courtyard was especially busy, and before long the uneasy feeling of someone watching me crept down my spine. A hush fell over the air as Queen Naomi approached, followed closely by the ladies currently in her favor.

The queen's long, brown hair was pulled back tight from her face, accenting her sharp and angular features. As always, she was nothing short of imperious around her subjects. I bowed low as the queen and her entourage approached, squinting as the gems in her crown and necklace cast shimmers at me.

"Good morning, Lady Marian. Off to aid the sickly?" Queen Naomi's tone told me once again how much she thought of my position at court.

"Yes, Your Majesty. Is there anything I might do for you this morning?" I raised my head, keeping my tone light. The queen had made it known plenty of times that she preferred my teacher rather than any acolytes. I had never known a time when I was not constantly under her thumb, and these days it seemed even harder to avoid angering her.

"No. However, you may have your master send Prince Asher something for all the stress he has been under lately." Behind her, as expected, the ladies murmured their praise of the prince and his excellent deeds.

"I will see to it, Your Highness."

I bowed low once again, and with the trail of her dress gliding across the dirt behind her, Queen Naomi left to visit more of the nobility trickling into the courtyard and nearby gardens.

I tried in vain to banish thoughts of the queen from my mind. Asher had told me repeatedly not to take it personally—she was simply that way with everyone. But lately, it seemed her hostility toward me was growing.

The familiar smell of the healing tinctures stung my nose as I walked into the large infirmary. Apprentices in gray robes scurried around the room, filling it with their hushed voices and scuffling feet. As I walked past the patient beds, each separated by long, flowing black cloths, I listened to the sound of angry shouting coming from the door at the other end of the room.

A great iron handle normally secured the dark, wooden door. Someone had allowed the door to remain ajar. That alone told me that things must be truly awry. All but the most-trusted apprentices were forbidden from this room. Some of the most potent remedies and herbs were stored inside.

"Foolish! That's what it is." Mistress Genevieve or Mistress Gene, as she preferred to be called, was pacing the room angrily while a couple of young acolytes cowered nearby.

Two large saddlebags and an assortment of tools were spread out on the long, wooden table. Taking pity on the two young women huddled in the corner, I waved them from the room. The blonde, who was not much younger than me, smiled timidly. A smile peeked at the corner of her mouth as she looked at me before closing the door behind her. Ignoring the flipping in my stomach, I turned toward the Royal Healer.

With the final click of the door, Gene seemed to return to her senses.

Her fiery, red hair spread wildly about her face. It looked as if the strands had been ripped from the tight bun she usually wore.

"Did the prince insist on attempting to tame another stallion again?" I guessed, remembering how furious she had been when Asher insisted on showing off his horseman skills to the royal guard.

Gene slammed her hands on the wide desk as her large chest heaved with a sigh. The stout, older woman raked her hands through her hair as her eyes fell on me.

"The king" --She spat the word out, slamming her fists on the table and rattling the jars nearby-- "has decided to host a tournament."

Sudden understanding fell over me as confusion and anger grew within me as well.

"We are low on supplies as it stands. Where will we ever amount more?"

"'The gods shall provide' was the king's only response." Gene huffed once more, turning to face the towering wall of shelves behind her.

"The city market has been dry for weeks." I looked over the gaping holes in the shelf where supplies had steadily been dwindling. Empty jars shimmered in the morning sun. Bands that normally held drying herbs now swayed loosely near the rear wall. "Even the laundresses can give us no more scraps for bandages."

"This is why you must go to the eastern markets in Colch." Gene turned back around. Her gray eyes focused on me again. The dark bags suddenly stood out, and I realized for the first time that my mentor was beginning to show her age.

I tried not to recoil under her sudden scrutiny as her gaze passed over me.

"This will be your last act as my apprentice."

My heart pounded in my chest as my breath caught. Immediately, I began racking my brain for reasons why she might so suddenly dismiss me. I knew the queen did not hold me in high regard. In fact, she often second-guessed my work or requested a different healer altogether.

"Mistress Genevieve, whatever you think I may have done—"

The old healer held up her hand. My confusion doubled as a wry smile grew across her small mouth.

"This trip shall be your last act as my apprentice." She spoke slowly, and I waited again with bated breath. "The tournament, although inadvisable, shall be your first act as Royal Healer."

My mouth fell open at her words. "Genevieve...I don't know what to say."

Once again, she waved off my words, shrugging her narrow shoulders in response. For the first time since I was a little girl, she opened her arms wide to me. Bending downward, I welcomed her embrace as she wrapped her arms around my shoulders.

"You have been through too much my child. You have studied harder than any pupil I have ever known. It is time. You have earned your place--and I am far too old for this shit. I will wait until you return, but then I will travel. There are many across Notting who need our aid—and not nearly enough healers to help them."

Hot tears threatened to spill down my cheeks as I laughed at the older woman's words, but fear filled me as I tried to imagine the Healer's Tower without her. She knew better than anyone what her words of encouragement meant to me. I was at a loss for words.

My mind scrambled to process all the new information. If the king wanted to host a tournament, we would need supplies. Colch was a two days' ride, and the road was filled with desperate bandits, eager to steal the wares of unsuspecting citizens.

Gene pulled away, smoothing her skirts as she returned to the long table. "You will have a month to prepare." I nearly choked as I realized the short deadline King Ruelle had given us.

No wonder Gene had been so furious when I walked in.

The healer's deft hands tied off the soft leather pouch, securing the items. She handed me a thin, wrinkled parchment. "This is the bare minimum we need to restock the tower. Though, bless you, if you can manage more. The king wants the tournament to launch at the end of summer."

"When do I leave?" Pounding spread across my forehead as I read over the list. Ginseng, echinacea, valerian--I knew that many of these items would be nearly impossible to find. I would have to find a southern trading vessel—something almost unheard of despite the fact that the war had ended nearly a decade ago. My palms began to sweat just thinking about everything that needed to be done.

It took me a moment to realize that Gene had spoken. My mind filled with this new responsibility. "I'm sorry, Mistress. When do I leave?"

"The royal caravan leaves within the hour."

There was barely any time at all. Inwardly, I cursed myself for bothering to even speak to Robyn of Loxley this morning. If she had not wasted my time, I might have been in the infirmary even sooner.

Robyn

The look on my father's face was positively murderous as news spread like wildfire around the court. Even here, servants already whispered about the king's decree. It had been decades since a tournament was held at court. It had been years since the kingdom could afford one--and holding one to determine which nobleman would receive extra winter rations was unheard of.

Ruel the Cruel was indeed a fitting name for our king.

As the news reached us, I was thankful Sir Johnathan, father's second-in-command, had the sense to usher us up to the tallest room of the house, away from any other ears. Unlike the rest of the nobility, while visiting the capital we lived away from the castle. The king allowed us to stay in our home near the edge of the city since Father 'assisted' Sir Godbert, who oversaw everything outside the castle walls. Though anyone who was paying even the slightest bit of attention knew that Sir Sebastion, Baron of Loxley, took orders from very few men.

Father continued his tirade for several more minutes, spearing pillows and tapestries with his daggers and sending chairs hurtling at the wall.

Johnathan and I watched the grand display, neither of us surprised at the show of emotion.

It was Johnathan who first broke the tense silence. "Someone must accompany the prince and the healer to the eastern markets. The king might be mad, but he isn't stupid. Too many troops have been sent to handle the skirmishes in the north. He cannot sacrifice any more of the royal guard so that the prince can travel to Colch and bed women."

Father and I laughed at John's candor. The prince's love of women and wine was well-known throughout Notting. There was no doubt that the arrival of the southern princess would do little to dissuade Prince Asher's more salacious personal habits.

The Baron of Loxley seemed to run out of steam as he straightened himself back to his full height. I watched in wonder as he once again became the fierce commander that Notting's enemies had dreaded for decades. His eyes were cold and calculating as he talked with his second.

"How many of our men can we sacrifice? Ruelle is not the only one with business to attend. He may ignore his people, but we shall not."

"Since the prince will have a few of his own guard, and a large portion of the duties will be monitoring the prince and assisting the Royal Healer, I suggest this be used as a training exercise for our younger men."

I rolled my eyes at Johnathan's words, certain that at least part of the reason he hadn't volunteered himself was that the older soldier *loathed* any and all cities—especially the hot, humid shores of Colch. Johnathan was happiest amongst the trees and its people. For him, the idea of spending a month shopping and preparing supplies was akin to torture.

"Yes. Some of the younger men—" I began to protest, but father cut off my words with a wave of his hand. I felt myself deflate a little at the sudden reprimand. The idea of spending a month in the eastern markets didn't sound appealing to me either.

"Despite your misgivings about the prince and his companions at court..." Father's thick brows scrunched together. His blue eyes gave me a very knowing look. "...to send only our novice men would be a great insult. Your reputation with a bow, as you keep reminding me..." I shot Johnathan a deadly glare as he covered a laugh. "...has grown immensely. If you wish to be taken seriously, you must attend to similar duties. You will act as my captain in this mission. The road to the eastern markets is not a stroll in the garden. Do not disappoint me."

Father's warm hand settled on my shoulder as he left the room without another word. Johnathan's broad chest blocked the doorway as he departed as well. John's voice called to me from the corridor. "Be quick. The others await your instruction. The prince wants to leave before the sun has reached its peak."

A long sigh escaped me as new worry took root. I had always considered it an honor to lead. I knew there were very few men who would allow a woman to lead. But Father's warning churned in my stomach. There was much to do, and very little time to prepare.

⸻

I rubbed Gold's long neck as the mare paced anxiously beneath me again. Samwell, Gawayne, and the others waited atop their mounts nearby. I ignored their impatient stares as I rode in a circle around the caravan again, inspecting the carts and other wares.

"Don't just sit on your ass!" I snapped at them all as they lazed about the courtyard. "Check those carts, your bags, and everything else is secured!" Despite the court's misgivings about a lady leading man, these men knew better than to argue. They might have grown up training in the hard war camps, but so had I. They could challenge me on the field, and they had, but they quickly learned not to do it again.

There was a flurry of movement as the men circled the wagons. Gawayne dismounted from the front of the wagon, and I watched his red head tip over and check the spokes of the wheels. I resisted the urge to smile. As a close friend, he was always one to follow orders from me without question.

I rolled my shoulders as my anxiety increased. I urged Gold around the caravan again, desperate to reign in her anxious nature as well as my own. We neared the rear of the line when a great clamor sounded from the Grand Entrance. Gripping the reins to keep her under control, I spun around toward the noise.

The sun was nearly at its apex in the sky as Marian tumbled into the courtyard. Her soft green robes from this morning had been replaced. Now a pair of stunning, white breeches wrapped tight around her legs. I recognized it immediately as the garb of a Royal Healer.

The rumors must be true then.

Throughout her long hair, a single white cloth had been plaited, pulling the loose ends back from her face. I noticed for the first time how soft and gentle her skin looked in the light, but quickly banished the thought from my mind.

Two large, brown satchels hung loosely from her arms, spilling their contents onto the ground. Clothes, water skins, and other materials spilled in a trail as I pulled up Gold. A deluge of sharp-looking instruments I assumed to be healer's tools had also fallen from a leather roll. They scattered about the ground between us.

"Shit. Now, I'm going to have to clean all these..." Marian's voice was a frantic whisper as she scrambled to pick up her belongings.

I couldn't help but roll my eyes as tension began to grow behind my brow. I noticed that several of the courtiers who had been lingering near the edge of the garden watched her with reproachful glances.

We were not off to a great start.

Swinging my leg free of Gold's saddle, I landed on the ground beside Marian and helped her to retrieve the items from the dirt.

"Will you also need assistance securing these to your horse?" My irritation was growing as I wondered again when the prince would deign us with his presence. It was, after all, his idea to leave at the hottest part of the day. We would have only a few hours to ride before making camp.

"I've got it." Marian's response was curt as she tied close the strings to one of her bags. I pulled a small, glass vial from the ground. Its top narrowed, securing the opaque liquid inside with a small stopper. Bringing it closer for inspection, I peered at the vial in the sunlight, admiring the way it shimmered.

In a flash, Marian snatched the small vial from my hand. Her eyes were large as she looked sheepishly as she checked it. "Don't. . . don't let that get in your eyes. Actually, don't let it get on your hands, or really anywhere on your body." I watched, suddenly filled with horror, and wonder as she carefully placed the small vial inside a pocket of the leather pouch padded with what looked to be cotton. Then, as if rethinking it, she wrapped a long piece of material around the pouch as well, before placing it in her bag.

I couldn't help but laugh at her peculiar behavior. I had never before considered that Marian might have it in her to be *sneaky.*

"One day, Lady Marian, you will have to tell me what's in that bottle."

Marian's brow wrinkled for a moment, as if weighted with heavy thoughts, but I noticed as the corner of her mouth rose just a bit. I ignored the feeling of fluttering in my chest

From the distance, a hostler approached with a beautiful, white mare. As the older man ambled across the courtyard, Marian abandoned her bags to the dirt, running to greet him. Again, several of the other members of court guffawed as Marian embraced him.

They walked together, nearly arm-in-arm, pulling the large, white horse toward the rest of the caravan. With a sigh, I gathered her bags again. It would not do if the king and Queen saw the healer's bags were unprepared to leave.

"Surely, Lee, you did not have to come see me off. You are supposed to be resting."

"How could I not, milady?" The old man wheezed, coughing into a faded blue kerchief. "I wouldn't even be here if it weren't for yer concoctions."

"You are sweet, but I didn't need you to saddle Marengo for me. One of the boys could surely have done it."

"Nonsense. No one was going to do it but me."

Marian's smile seemed genuine as she nodded her thanks to the hostler.

I couldn't help but admire the older man's determination. Although I did not know the hostler personally, it was well-known at court that Lee took great care with the royal stables. He only allowed the best to work with him and had recently taken on a female apprentice.

Clearing my throat awkwardly, I approached the trio. "Lady Marian, we must secure your bags."

"Yes, sorry." Marian shook her head, as if suddenly remembering where she was.

It only took a few minutes for us to secure Marian's bags to Marengo. Unlike Gold, Marengo was a bit older and stood patiently. Twice Gold came over to us, butting me in the back with her head, desperate for attention.

Lee smiled as he patted Gold's long neck. "Yer horse is young. She was born in the forest, and don't feel at home here at court. I expect you know a bit about that."

I took the reins from Lee's aged hand with a nod, surprised at how easily he had read me. Being at Court made me anxious and impatient. Every minute I spent at court was a minute I spent not helping my people. What he described was part of the reason I was drawn to the horse in the first place.

Once more, a great fanfare from the Grand Entrance had Gold rearing again. It seemed, nearly two hours late, the prince had finally arrived.

As father expected, Prince Asher arrived in the courtyard joined by only a few green-looking royal guards.

The royal troops must be spread even thinner than we expected.

Asher's eyes swept over the scene, and instantly landed on Marian. I resisted the urge to insult the womanizing pig as he approached. I had spent years avoiding court as much as possible. Thankfully, I had very few direct interactions with the royal family, but he was my prince, and today I was his captain. I had seen father fall in line to the throne many times. If he could do it, surely, I could too. At least for now.

The prince approached, several other noble men and women following close behind him. Marian, Lee, and I bowed low. Even Gold stopped her incessant fidgeting.

The silence around us was stifling, and I could feel the judgment of everyone in the courtyard leering into us. Clearing my throat once more, I straightened before the prince. "Your highness, the carts are ready, and we leave at your leisure. My men will ride on the edges, securing your company on all sides."

Asher's face suddenly flashed with anger. "*Your* men? Has your father really no one else to give me?"

"I assure you, Your Highness, we are fully prepared to protect you on the roads eastward."

"This is outrageous. We are already riding without a full company, but to send squires, and a female captain—" The prince waved his gilded hand in an arc around us. I felt my jaw clinch as I began to protest, but a soft voice rose over the prince.

"Oh, Asher. Do you think they've brought my trunk down? I've only got my saddle bags, but I must have the summer gowns." Looking back at her, I was shocked at Marian's sudden transformation from only moments before. Gone was her excited and frazzled demeanor. Replaced was a wide-eyed courtier, pulling the prince's attention away.

Asher responded immediately. His shoulders squared as he looked at the servants filing out from the Grand Entrance and back at Marian.

"Dear Marian, you know you have to command the servants to do exactly what you want, or nothing will get done." Asher snapped his finger in the air and a stout manservant appeared almost instantly. "Find Lady Marian's trunk and make sure it is loaded onto the cart with the utmost care."

My stomach rolled in disgust as the prince waved the man off.

"My silly friend, you would lose your pretty head if it weren't attached to those slender shoulders. You mean to ride, then?" Asher didn't bother to veil his compliments or hide the lustful stare as he looked Marian up and down. His gaze lingered a little too long on her white breeches. From the sudden chittering and sideways glances of the nobility behind him, it seemed I was not the only one who noticed the prince's intense stare. Just out of the prince's eye line, a young noblewoman with black hair shot daggers in Marian's direction.

Marian made no acknowledgment to Asher as she spoke, "I do. It's been so long since I was away. Will you be riding alongside me for this journey?" Marian's voice was sweet as she took the reins once again from Lee's withered hand.

The two of them shared a silent look as Marian climbed effortlessly atop her mount.

"It seems I must. You may have to aid me should our paltry guard fail." The herd of noble sheep protested behind the prince, touting his bravery and courage. Asher's cold, green eyes stared at me once more. I met his stare as calmly as I could, ignoring the insult.

"It would be safer your majesty rode in a carriage—"

"I shall ride a horse alongside Lady Marian." Asher's tone was harsh and reproachful as he spoke. I knew instantly there would be no more discussion. He was not someone who did not get his way very often.

"At your leisure, my prince." I mounted Gold, thankful that she had decided to continue to behave. Dread filled my stomach. Even without his gawdy clothes and shimmering jewels, the prince would not be hard to recognize.

"You—" The prince shouted at Lee, though the man was only inches away, having moved to hold Marengo as Marian mounted. "Fetch our mounts. I wish to depart at once."

Without another look at Marian, the older man hurried as fast as he could toward the stables. I pitied the hostler. He did not seem as if he should be running. Given Marian's worried glance as we watched the lone figure disappear, I knew she felt the same.

It would take another several minutes for the hostler and several stable workers to appear with the royal horses, and another ten minutes for the courtiers attending the prince to mount. I breathed a sigh of relief as their guards fell in alongside the royal guards--happy to add more swords to our caravan.

At the last minute, a frenzied healer appeared on horseback, clothed in gray acolyte garb. Mistress Genevieve had decided at the last minute to send an assistant for Marian. I watched warily as the red-haired girl shifted uneasily atop her horse, riding close to her new mistress.

The sun had already begun to wane when finally, the prince mounted, signaling that we could leave.

Marian

We left the safety of the inner courtyard as all manner of nobility waved farewell to their prince. Marengo bounced gently beneath me as we approached the outer wall.

The caravan passed through the crowded houses and streets of the city without incident. Though I expected more fanfare, it seemed the people of Notting had not come out to greet their prince.

Once or twice a month, Mistress Genevieve would take myself and a few acolytes into the city to provide what care we could. We would bring any supplies that could be spared. Sometimes bandages, water or even food. My heart felt heavy as I remembered that despite our efforts, it was never enough to help all who suffered in the capital.

The few faces coming to greet us were the same as every time I entered the city. Each had a familiar look of hopelessness and despair. Each had a look of hunger. Their silent gazes pleaded with the nobility to throw them coins or jewels. A feeling of guilt grew in my gut, eating at me as traveled further down the road.

I recognized one elderly woman with graying hair and sorrow-filled eyes immediately as a former patient. She waved her kerchief weakly in the afternoon sun as I smiled back at her.

Beside me, Asher was completely unaware of the silence that had fallen throughout the rest of the caravan. He had already been swallowed up by two courtiers. The giggles of the two ladies resounded over the soft thumping of hooves and creaks of the wagons.

I resisted the urge to roll my eyes as the blonde requested that Asher tell her more about his 'great journeys.' Asher and I had once been the best of friends, but he had truly become more insufferable since our time as children ended.

It had been years since I left the safety of the capital gates to journey further. Little by little, the city began to disappear around us, bringing us closer to the outermost gate.

Beneath me, Marengo trembled as our group shuffled nearer to each other, squeezing to fit through the narrow doorway. I gripped the reins a little tighter as Robyn and her horse came closer beside us.

The caravan traveled at a slow march as our guards continued to look anxiously around. A shadow fell overhead as we neared the wall. The cold stones reached high into the heavens, blocking the warmth of the sunlight. Above us, the sharp bars of the gate stretched down. They were a silent, hanging threat, urging us to push through. A shiver went down my spine as a sense of foreboding passed through me.

Robyn's golden gaze met mine across the short distance, one hand falling to rest on the bow tied to her horse. I knew instantly that she had felt it too.

The goal was to camp at the guard station marking the halfway point, but I knew before we left the city gates that we wouldn't. It took far too much time to get everyone moving, and twice one of the ladies accompanying Asher requested a quick rest which turned out to take half an hour.

I tried not to take satisfaction that others were so uncomfortable outside their carriages, but it was hard not to. Marengo and I rode nearly every day.

It was even harder not to delight in the frustration and annoyance Robyn seemed to hold back with every passing hour. She had urged the women to take their carriages, and had she been any other captain they might have actually listened.

We lost the sunlight quickly. It faded behind us, taking with it the familiar assurance that came with unending warmth. With each passing moment, we came closer and closer to total darkness. Around us, the guards pulled tighter. Twice Robyn had urged the prince to ride closer to the ring of guards or ride behind the carts--only to be ignored.

The trees around us began to fade from view, leaving only a black wall of uncertainty. I watched as Robyn shifted in her saddle again. For hours she had been slowly circling the caravan, watching her men, and riding off to look at the road ahead.

Asher and the courtiers had slowly ceased their conversations as the prince became bored with the ladies continued attempts at flattery. Despite Robyn's protests, he had fallen toward the back of the caravan to whisper at Kira, the woman who was to be my assistant—a position I would have preferred to have chosen for myself.

A sigh escaped me as I tried to ignore their whispers. Kira was certainly beautiful. Her long, flowing, red hair was inviting. The color brought out her startling green eyes and the ivory softness of her skin. I had certainly caught myself admiring her more-than ample bosom and womanly curves from time to time. It was hard not to.

Throughout my life, I had been with men and women. Although it wasn't a fact shared publicly at court, it was not entirely unheard of. Asher certainly had a reputation among the nobility for liking both sexes.

Despite everyone's assumptions about what happened between us, I didn't relish his lascivious nature. We had been friends—and only friends-- since we were babes and raised by the same wet nurse. After my mother passed away soon after my birth and the queen reluctantly took me in, we had been inseparable as children.

Every time I listened to my friend coo at a woman or flirt with her to get her to visit his bedchamber, it just reminded me of how much time had passed. Early in our teens, Asher had made many, many attempts to move our friendship to something more. Something I had never had any interest in.

I had caught more longing glances from him than I cared to remember. As we grew and flirting became more of an expectation for his behavior than anything else, our friendship changed. Asher had slowly become more possessive of my company. As the years went by I began to find him prowling outside my room, threatening potential suitors, stalking me in hallways, or doing even worse. His strange and possessive behavior continued until eventually it drove us apart.

We had been friends, but I had moved to the healer's tower as soon as the queen and Genevieve would allow. Now we rarely saw one another. I was busy with my apprenticeship, and Asher was constantly entertaining a never-ending line of courtiers looking to be his wife.

The loss of his friendship sat heavy on my heart. He had always been a spoiled child, used to getting his way, but he had also been kind. Asher and I had grown together running the halls of the castle and swimming in the lakes on hot, summer days. But from the first time I said no when he tried to kiss me, and rejected him, something dark had taken hold of him. Something twisted by greed.

Kira's voice reached out again, describing for the prince what life as a healer was like. The way she described our tower, and the life of an acolyte was full of intrigue and grandeur. I smiled to myself at the girl's attempts at bravado. Kira was certainly intelligent, but not more so than any other acolyte in the Healer's Tower.

Why Gene had thought I could use her on this trip was beside me.

The moon was high overhead, casting its white glow on us all. The silence around the caravan began to grow until there was only the crickets serenading us, and the whisper of the wind through the wall of trees.

Like a phantom from my nightmares, Robyn returned. Her hooded cape fell in long waves across the back of her horse, shielding her face from the moonlight. She urged her mare along the right side of me, positioning herself between the silent guard to my right.

"Eyes up, Samwell." Robyn's voice was curt as she nudged at the guard with the tip of her bow.

When had she untied it from her mount?

Robyn dropped her hood, and in the darkness, I could see the anxious look in her eyes as she glanced around me toward the prince.

"Your Highness. There are steep cliffs along the road ahead. It would not be easily defensible. We should wait to pass between until the morning when it is safe. I believe we should make camp."

"Perhaps," was Asher's flippant reply as he walked his black gelding alongside Marengo. "Right now, I am enjoying watching how stunning Lady Marian looks in this moonlight…"

Asher's words caught me off guard, but I did my best to smile politely back at him. Something itched at the back of my mind as I stared at Robyn with her bow. I stretched slightly up in my saddle, trying to see the road ahead. There was nothing but darkness.

As if sensing the change in us, Gold and Marengo both shifted uneasily.

"Isn't she lovely, Robyn? Surely even you cannot deny it, though I know women seldom truly compliment one another." Asher's voice crooned as he leaned over toward me, dragging my attention away from the road. His gaze drifted up my body, settling on my chest as I bounced in the saddle.

"You are too kind, Asher." I gently pressed against Marengo's round belly with my heels, inching her away from the prince and his horse.

My leg bumped gently against Robyn's, and it was then I noticed her eyes drift over to me. For a moment, I watched her silent appraisal. Her golden eyes reflected in the moonlight as they too traveled up my body before meeting mine with their curious stare. It was harder this time to resist the urge to smile back as warmth spread through my body and my heart raced in response.

I did my best to ignore the way Robyn's stare, so different from Asher's, made my breath catch. I did my best not to squirm beneath her silent appraisal, but my body did not listen. There was no reason I should begin to wonder how her strong thighs that guided her horse so gently might feel entangled with mine, but my curiosity was piqued as I stared at the way her breeches clung to them.

The sound of the prince's voice dragged my thoughts away once more, and I was thankful to for the distraction from the sudden flush of heat that had overcome me.

From my periphery, Robyn straightened in her saddle. Her keen eyes were once again watching the road ahead. Around us, the night seemed to change. The wall of trees faded away, giving way to steep cliffs ahead that nearly blocked all moonlight.

"Your Highness, we are nearing the cliffs. I really must insist we stop—"

Again, Asher ignored Robyn's urgent words.

Not appreciating the sudden closeness, Robyn's horse lunged its head angrily at Marengo, forcing us to shift abruptly into Asher's horse. Cursing, Asher pulled hard on his reins, forcing the gelding backward.

As Asher leaned back on his horse, the shrill scream of an arrow filled the night air. I watched in horror as Asher was knocked backward. His scream broke the silence around us.

The long shaft of an arrow protruded from his shoulder.

Chapter 4

Robyn

The prince nearly fell to the ground as the arrow pierced his shoulder. At the last second, Marian reached for him, gripping his tunic tight and pulling him back on the horse.

Chaos reigned around me, threatening to take over as arrows continued to fly into the trees.

"To the prince!" The command left my lips before my first arrow was even knocked. There was a commotion and a flood of movement, but the men knew that meant to create a tighter circle around our noble charges. "Do not stop!" I urged Gold forward as Marian did the same with Marengo.

My heart pounded in response as I scanned the cliffs above for enemies. I aimed the tip of my arrow high, ready to strike as I fought to calm my panic. The rock face's rough surface looked down around me, mocking me with its hideouts and crevices.

Gold knocked into Marian's horse again, as Samwell pulled tight against my other side. I looked at the man beside me for just a second. His bow was in his hand as well. He waited for my command as he too watched the sky.

"Asher, hold tight to your horse!" I yelled over Marian and the sounds of screams coming from the nobility around us. "Do not stop!"

An arrow landed alongside the caravan, missing our horses by several feet. Confusion filled me. *Why weren't there more?*

It took me two heart beats to process as I scanned the terrified party around me. It was so dark it was almost impossible to see the others. Then, the prince's hands glittered against the moonlight. One hand held his reins, the other gripped the shaft of the arrow in his shoulder. Each of the jewels along his fingers had become a beacon, guiding the enemy to their target.

"Cloaks!" From the open bag on Gold's side, I whipped the extra cloak out, spreading it across Marian's shoulders. For a single second I looked at her, expecting to see terror. Instead, she looked up at the hood now covering her, then back at me. What I saw could only be described as trust. Then, like a candle blowing out, the enormous fabric settled, and her long, golden locks and her stunning, white horse disappeared. "Do not stop!"

The sound of fabric whipping through the air filled my ears as my men and every member of the guard pulled their cloaks out, spreading them in a wide arch around their horses. A royal guard draped the cloak I had given him earlier over the prince's bent form. In the darkness I heard a sharp, female gasp. The ladies had been covered as well.

A calm swept through me, despite the pounding of my heart. Any glimpse of our party from above had just disappeared.

Now, it was time to get the hell out of here.

Our party had slowed, but I gave thanks to the gods, we were still moving.

The sound of a twig snapping split through the night air, resounding over the trample of hooves and the heavy breathing around me. Just as I suspected, this had been their plan. Our enemy meant to distract us with their lone archer, forcing us to stop so the others could pounce.

I whipped to the side, releasing my arrow as I spotted the shadows growing around us. "Behind!" I warned the others, pulling another arrow from my quiver and releasing it into the night. The royal guard drew their long swords, turning their horses to face our foe. The metal of each sword glinted menacingly in the moonlight like deadly stars.

I continued releasing arrows as more filled the air, headed for the shadows quickly approaching. I knew the others were from Samwell and Gawayne. Each arrow hit a shadow, producing a thump, and then the shadow did not move again. "Keep moving!" I yelled to anyone who was still listening.

Never before had I been in a battle that was so quiet. The thought chilled me to the bone. These were no wild bandits, desperate for food or a few pieces of gold. These attackers were far too silent. Their moves were far too calculated. They stalked through the night, making almost no sound, even as they met their deaths with my arrows.

These were assassins.

"Run!" A voice in my head told me we couldn't be more than a few miles from the royal outpost. It was just beyond the cliffs. *We could make it.*

The noise grew around me as everyone urged their horses to a run. I knew the ladies were inexperienced riders, but hopefully, their guards would aid them. Their shrills screams rent through the air and the men around me grunted. Our circle spread further apart as the horses ran through the night. I prayed to any god that was listening none of them tripped or stumbled as we raced between the cliffs.

My prayers were answered as the prince's horse gathered speed. Marian's cloak billowed behind her, filling with air and revealing her white mare, but there was nothing to be done about it now. Gold raced beside her as we neared the back of the cart. Behind her cloak, Marian's eyes lit up like fireflies.

In seconds, a rift developed in our circle. Despite the horse's best efforts, the cart was falling behind. My heart skipped a beat as I watched the circle close again. Gawayne's hood had fallen, and his red hair stood out in the darkness as he urged the horse and cart onward.

Behind him, half a dozen pairs of eyes glinted in the distance. The sound of hooves echoed off the walls around us, and I knew he wouldn't make it. The assassin's horses were bred for speed and endurance.

I had only seconds to decide.

"Samwell, to the prince." I waited a split second for the squire's nod that he understood, then pulled on Gold's reins. The horse reared as it struggled to stop. I held tight, squeezing with my legs to stay in the saddle.

Gold didn't miss a beat as we ran from the others and headed for Gawayne, even as the arrow grazed his side, slicing open his sensitive hide. Fury filled me as I felt the horse flinch.

In front of us, the squire had changed tactics. The horse and cart had been brought to a halt. Gawayne was trying desperately to free the panicked creature, cutting and hacking with his sword at the leather straps holding it to the cart, while wrestling the frightened horse under control so he could ride.

The shadows in the distance were thundering toward us now.

It felt like a lifetime before Gold closed the distance between us and the cart. The sound of hoof beats shook my chest like cannon fire as one assassin pulled away from the rest. In the moonlight, I watched the sash he wore around his face ripple in the wind. His horse was the darkest creature I had ever seen, blending in with the air around us in a way that was unreal.

I shot an arrow at him. Shock filled me as he dodged it like one would ignore a leaf falling from a tree.

I jumped from Gold, stumbling across the ground to maintain upright. There were only seconds before the assassins came upon us.

The carthorse was positively frantic now as Gawayne tried to hold it steady. My heart pounded in my chest, threatening to burst. The horse and rider were nearing the back of the wagon. The assassin drew his curved blade. When the steel of his weapon glinted at me, I knew it would be the last thing I ever saw.

From the corner of my eye, a white flash appeared. I was dumbstruck as I watched Marian appear, throwing something at the assassin's face.

The walls echoed with the sound of shattered glass as a strange, sizzling noise filled the air. For the first time all night, our enemy cried out in pain. Ten feet behind him, the others stopped as well.

Bile rose in my throat as the smell of burning flesh filled the air.

"Let's go!" Marian's voice rang out, pulling me from my shocked stupor. I watched as Gawayne mounted the horse, nearly sliding off the other side. They took off together into the night.

Gold pounded anxiously at the ground nearby, desperate to follow Gawayne and Marian's horses. I pulled myself onto the saddle, gripping desperately as the horse gained speed.

The familiar sight of torches and tents greeted us as we finally brought the horses to a halt. Beneath me, I felt Gold shudder.

My limbs were boulders as I dismounted. Exhaustion wrapped around me as my heart and breathing struggled to settle. All around us, men called out to one another of our arrival. A young boy I didn't recognize came and took Gold's leads from me.

"Be careful. She is wounded." I rubbed the horse gently as they faded into the background. Several men patted my back. Their voices all blended together, and I struggled to decipher their words.

"Thank you…" Marian's soft voice cut through the uproar as another younger boy assisted her in dismounting. Her black cloak fell to the ground around her like water rippling in a pond. Her brow was damp with sweat, giving her skin a soft, shimmering aura.

I was not the only one who noticed. Several of the men had quieted. They looked at her with awe as Marian ran a comforting hand down Marengo's long neck. Annoyance rose inside me once more at the men's strange behavior.

It was true that there were not many women with the fair skin and lighter hair like Marian's in Notting. I watched as she moved around the front of her horse. Her long, slender fingers glided across the creature's hide. It shook beneath her touch.

Beside her, a young boy watched Marian too. His mouth seemed to fall open as he shook his head a bit. After a few seconds, the boy cleared his throat, waiting for her permission to leave. The soldiers around us had not moved either. They looked at Marian like she was some fantastical creature that had sprung from the woods. Some sort of fey that could disappear into the trees at any time.

Didn't they have anything better to do than gawk?

The thought shook me from my stupor as the weight of what had happened fell over me once more. News of tonight would travel very far very fast.

"Where is the prince?" I immediately chastised myself for not asking the moment we rode into camp. *If Asher were…*

I couldn't let myself think it. I may not like the prince, but I also could not allow his death to be on my hands.

Marian's head shot up, as if she were remembering too. Guilt flashed across her face as she grabbed her leather satchel and ran toward the light in the distance.

Without a word, an older soldier with gray and white speckled hair guided us around the tents. Men were seated around small fires everywhere we walked. The green cloth of their uniforms was worn and threadbare. The royal insignia of a soldier who couldn't be much older than me was frayed and nearly torn off completely. Most of the soldiers in the camp kept their eyes downcast. Those that watched as we passed held the familiar horrors of battle and hunger behind their gaze. Silence hung in the air like an unseen visitor. It told me everything I needed to know.

The older soldier led us to the center of camp, and the sound of sobbing shattered through the silence. Marian went through first. Her shoulders squared as her chest rose. I knew she was preparing herself for whatever was to come.

Half a dozen pairs of eyes fell upon us as we entered the tent.

"Where the hell have you been?" It was the prince's voice that screamed at us first. The inside of the tent had been lit with torches. Their light flickered across the canvas, giving the prince a crazed look as he winced. Beside him, Marian's assistant wiped Asher's brow with a wet cloth.

Marian did not miss a beat as she knelt beside the prince. For once his eyes didn't linger on her, instead, he turned his murderous gaze toward me.

"You left me to *die*. Then, you took my healer with you."

Marian was silent as her deft hands examined the wound.

"It's not too deep. Just barely in the skin. It seems to have missed most of the muscle. We should be able to remove it and bandage it."

Commander Nicholaus next to me exchanged a look with his comrade, a captain by the name of Raoul, and I wondered if they had surmised the same thing. The prince cried out again before Marian had even touched his shoulder. Tears streamed down his cheeks as he prayed loudly to the gods.

"Please, Marian. Do not let me die." His voice was pitiful as he spoke to the healer. I shifted uneasily, embarrassed at such a pathetic display from someone who was to one day be my king.

"You are not going to die, Your Highness." Marian removed the arrow before anyone could blink, staunching any blood flow with a clean cloth from her assistant. "You may need a few stitches though." Her voice was kind as she helped Asher to lie back on the cot. This time he ogled at her chest as she leaned over him and helped him get comfortable.

"Would you like to do the sutures, Kira?" Marian looked the other woman over, as the redhead sat up in surprise.

"Truly?" Kira looked at her master with new appreciation as Marian removed several long needles from the leather roll inside the satchel.

The commander beside me shifted uncomfortably. He began to step toward the door, grabbing my arm and dragging me along as he walked.

Fury rose in me at the audacity. He may be a commander, but I was a captain in the king's army, not some servant to man-handle in a dark hallway.

"Excuse me, sir!" I wrenched my arm from his grasp as we walked away from the tent and the sound of the prince's moans of pain.

"What the hell happened out there?" The commander's voice rose, and I was suddenly aware of the hundreds of listening ears in the camp around us.

"We were riding. I suggested we make camp before reaching the cliffs—"

"I don't give a damn what you suggested. This was *your* charge. They were under *your* command."

My heart raced as anger flushed through my cheeks. "The prince did not want—"

"The prince is injured because you didn't make the dangers clear. The ladies traveling with him are *hysterical,* and I'm sure the king will receive word by morning of everything that happened. You'll be lucky if they let you command the pageboys in how to muck after the horses after this! Letting yourself get ambushed by some wild folk."

"Commander, these were not just some roadside bandits. These men made no sound. They never cried out. They were on us in seconds."

"It's true...sir." Gawayne appeared like a phantom beside me. His red hair was slick with sweat and he still wheezed uncontrollably.

The commander looked down at us. His face was full of anger and disgust, but for the first time he seemed to be considering my words. "What are you saying?"

"These weren't bandits. They were the Silent Ones."

"Southern assassins in Notting?" The commander's voice was incredulous, but he didn't argue. His face became pensive as he turned back toward the tent. I wondered if perhaps the commander knew something that we didn't.

Gawayne pushed his red locks back from his face again as the commander disappeared into the tent. My fury continued to build as everything from tonight settled over me.

"I'm sorry, Robyn." Gawayne's look of pity sent me over the edge as shame built inside me.

"How many times did I say we needed to stop?" I struggled to keep my voice down, as a pain began to throb inside my head. "How many times did I try to get him to listen?" I threw my hands in the air angrily, stepping away from the prying ears inside the tent.

Gawayne nodded as I fumed. His hands crossed in front of him, waiting for me to continue.

My face warmed once more, sweat pooling on my brow. The ache in my temples was nearly unbearable as images of flying arrows, the prince with an arrow sticking out of his shoulder, and Gold's hide being torn open flooded my mind.

The angry, panicked memories clouded my vision, which is why I did not notice the tent flap open once more.

"We all could have been killed, all because the prince wanted to play with his *pet*. I hope it was worth getting us killed just so the prince could have one more woman to warm his godsdamned bed." I turned on my heel to face Gawayne once more, but someone different was behind me now.

Marian looked at me through the dim light of the torches. Her face was pale and tired. Her long hair hung limp against her shoulders. A look of pain fell over her, and I knew she had heard me.

"Commander Sampson says he has prepared a tent for us nearby, but feel free to sleep with the horses." Marian marched away between the tents and into the dark. I felt my shoulders slump as I watched her disappear.

I should have forced the caravan to stop. I should have been more commanding. Prince or not, the safety of everyone in the caravan tonight was my responsibility and I had let them down.

Chapter 5

Marian

The scream of the assassin filled the air around me. I watched in horror as he crumpled to the ground at my feet before dissolving completely into a pool of blood.

My body awoke from its slumber as the air changed. Sweat poured down my brow as I shook off the nightmare that had sent my heart racing. The morning sun peeked over the horizon. Each long ray stretched more warmth across the tents. With each passing minute, the air became thicker, and the blankets atop me became sticky and unpleasant--as if the air itself were pushing me from my cot, urging me to wake.

Peeling back my thin blanket, I placed my feet on the grass, letting my heart ease and shake off the terrible nightmare. To my dismay, even the ground had begun to heat. As my vision struggled to adjust, the emptiness of the tent truly hit me. Neither Robyn nor Kira had returned to the tent the three of us were meant to share.

Though I was fairly certain I knew who Kira had spent the night with last night, I had left a wide berth between my side of the tent and Robyn's.

Across the small space, the grass was undisturbed. No blankets or clothes or even a clothing bag littered the floor. A sharp pain filled my chest at the implication. She had been truly furious with the prince last night, but part of me knew it was more than that.

Robyn had urged Asher to stop—and he had ignored her. No doubt because she was a female captain. As much as I hated to admit it, I could imagine how that might feel.

I ignored the voice of reason growing inside of me as frustration filled my chest. I remembered her words, "…if the prince had not been so eager to play with his *pet*…" With each shove of my items into the thin leather of my clothing sack, my fury grew. If I was supposed to live for the next month with Robyn as a constant annoyance, the thought of it nearly made me spit in anger, then she needed to understand that I was not some simpleton she could push around.

Throwing back the heavy tent flap, I began my trek across the camp. I played through every word I would say to Robyn as I stomped across the ground.

Prince Asher's tent was nearest the center, and two weary-looking guards nodded to me as I passed. A small fire had been erected in the center of camp. Smoke wafted from the embers, the smell greeting me as I walked by. Men on thin bedrolls littered the ground before me. Although I checked each slumbering face as I walked by, something told me that Robyn was the kind to wake before the sun.

With every step I felt my anger grow. As I continued to check each sleeping form I pictured finding Robyn and stomping hard on her stomach. If she was a man, I might have aimed my kick lower, but a good, swift kick in the stomach would have to do.

The horses and wagons had been stationed at the bottom of the shallow ravine, near the edge of the trees. A shallow creek ran along the edge of the thicket, allowing the horses to drink their fill. As I tip-toed around the sleeping men, the familiar sound of a horse's neigh drifted across the morning air.

"You're being ridiculous!" Robyn's angry voice sounded in the distance. Her declaration was met with a shrill screech, and the thumping of angry hooves into the ground.

Images of last night, and the assassin's face as I threw the vial at him flashed across my memory. My stomach rolled in response, and though I had not eaten yet, I thought I might be sick.

Shaking myself of the image, I watched a few more moments as I walked down the small slope toward Robyn and the horse.

A smile spread across my face as I watched Robyn approach the mare. A long, brown wrap draped from Robyn's arms as she approached the enormous creature. The vindictive part of my mind whispered that I hoped the horse gave Robyn a good kick, but I did my best to ignore it.

I had done enough harm last night, and healers were supposed to harm no one.

"If you do not allow me to change your bandages, you are going to get an infection!" Robyn reached for the mare's hindquarter again, but the horse was too fast. It danced out of reach just as Robyn began to place the bandage.

Laughter burst from me as the horse shook its long, golden nose back and forth. It sneered and chomped its white, flat teeth—barely missing Robyn's shoulder as she ducked out of the way.

The sound of my laughter brought the attention of both horse and rider. Two pairs of big, golden eyes watched me across the distance. Not failing to miss the opportunity, the horse lunged for Robyn's short hair again. She flinched, once again ducking out of the way. The long cloth floated to the ground—where the creature promptly stomped on it. I could not help but double over in laughter.

My breath caught in my throat as I clutched at my sides, laughter spilling from deep within me. Beside Robyn, the mare danced on its front legs, further grinding the cloth into the mud. Robyn crossed her arms, eyes darting back and forth between me and the creature as we laughed at her.

"If you two don't *mind...*" Robyn's voice was filled with disdain as she retrieved the dirt-covered cloth from the ground. She let out a deep sigh as she inspected her make-shift bandage.

I was suddenly reminded why I had sought her out. Annoyance built inside of me, bubbling over like hot stew.

"Actually, I don't mind. It seems that I was wrong--" Robyn eyed me suspiciously as I approached "--not even your horse likes you." I stepped down the shallow ravine, approaching the two of them warily.

Robyn didn't bother to respond. She inspected the thick gash along the horse's muscular flank. The horse's long tail flicked angrily as Robyn held the strip of cloth up again.

My eyes fell to the gash again, remembering last night. The smile fell from my face as I neared the horse.

"Hello, you beautiful, brave creature...." I crooned as I walked along its side. Careful to avoid any nips or kicks, I watched the mare warily from my periphery. "You were so brave yesterday. We should find you all the treats in the kingdom."

The horse's warm nose butted my shoulder in agreement as I inspected the gash.

"You shouldn't cover this yet. Let's gather some herbs for it first and I'll make a salve for the creature—"

"Her name is Gold." Robyn's voice interrupted my thought as I circled to the other side, looking for more scrapes or cuts.

"Gold..." I tried to keep the irritation from my voice, "...needs something to stave off infection. I'm no hostler, but I think I could find us some herbs for a paste. We can use that until we get to the duke's castle tonight."

Gold's wide nose butted against me again, drawing my attention. I ran my hand the length of the horse's neck, patting the dirt from her coat. Beside me, Robyn gave a huff of indignation, rolling her eyes as the mare nuzzled against my chest.

"Fine." Robyn drew out the word, crossing her arms tight across her chest.

I tried my best to ignore Robyn's contemptuous glare as we trekked upstream. Like the cool waters around me, I tried to let my anger and frustration wash away.

It wasn't Gold's fault that her owner was so insufferable.

The morning sun cut through the branches of the trees overhead as the water around us glistened. It reminded me of morning rides with Marengo, and afternoons spent in the stables. Lee had taught me so much, and it was a debt I could never repay.

"What exactly are we looking for?" Robyn whined as she trampled through the underbrush.

"It's a white flower with a red center."

We continued in awkward silence for several more minutes. Gold followed behind at a slow, steady pace, startling the birds from the trees overhead. Despite their feud, horse and rider seemed to have called some unspoken truce. Robyn's irritation seemed to soften as she rubbed a loving hand across the mare's long nose.

The sounds of camp stirring to life sounded in the distance. The caravan would be ready to move at any time. As the wind pushed through the underbrush, I finally spotted it.

Soft, white petals reached out at me as I plucked them from the earth. Robyn and Gold watched in silence as I ground them on a nearby rock. With a few scoops of water from the stream, I began creating a thick paste. Gathering the paste in my hands, I walked slowly toward the wound.

As I reached out, Robyn's hand rested atop mine. Her brows were scrunched, and her features were heavy with concern as she looked between us. "Are you sure it won't hurt her?"

Time seemed to stand still for a moment. I knew the stream

trickled, and the birds chirped, but I could only focus on the pounding of my heart against my chest as I looked at our hands joined together.

We had never stood so close before, and I found myself once again studying her. Rough calluses rubbed against the back of my hand, but Robyn's grip did not hurt. The smell of pine greeted me as she stepped closer. At first I thought it might be the trees around us, but after a second I realized it was her.

Robyn smelled like the forest after a storm, and it was intoxicating. My body seemed to respond to her presence without bothering to ask permission. Though the sun was barely visible in the horizon, I suddenly felt very, very flushed.

My throat constricted as I struggled with the words. I pulled my hand from her grip, trying to ignore the pulsing sensation spreading through my body. "Despite what you may think of me, I am not so horrible as to let an animal suffer needlessly. I've seen Lee use this exact herb on horses for years. It shouldn't even sting."

Robyn released my hand, which I took as her acquiescence. To my surprise, Gold stood still as I rubbed the herb into the wound. I repeated the process three more times before I was satisfied that it was thick enough.

I looked again at the strip of cloth that the horse had ground into the dirt.

It would be almost another full day before we could get her to a proper hostler, and the wound would need to be covered while we rode so that it wouldn't fill with debris.

The soft breeze blew through the oversized tunic I had been given last night. Marengo had been carrying my medical supplies, but none of my bandages would be long enough for a horse and most of my clothes were still atop the abandoned cart. Asher had instructed the commander to send men to retrieve it at the first sign of daylight, but Gold couldn't wait that long.

As the breeze tickled at my skin, an idea suddenly occurred to me. "Do you have a knife?"

Robyn's quizzical stare returned, but she leaned down and slipped a small blade from the side of her boot without question.

I watched her dumbfounded stare as I sliced through the thin cloth of the tunic, right below my breasts. I continued to slice and tear the fabric in a circle until I could reach no further.

"Do the back." I handed Robyn back the knife as she approached me warily. She was a bit taller than me and leaned down close as she took the small knife to the fabric. Her breath fell against my back, tickling my sensitive skin, and I jerked in response.

"By the gods, do not *move.*" Robyn's voice was filled with frustration as she moved in a slow circle around me.

Finally, we had cut the entire bottom of the tunic, creating enough bandage that we could secure it around Gold. Robyn said nothing as I passed my end of the cloth over the horse, but her stare was incredulous as she gaped at my exposed stomach.

We looked over our handiwork again. The mare must have approved, since she did not try to bite or kick us.

Robyn and I stood for a moment in silence, but we were quickly interrupted as men had begun to trek toward the stream.

"How's she doing?" I immediately recognized the man, Gawayne, we had saved from the cart only hours before, followed by the guard who had ridden so silently behind me last night. Robyn had called him Samwell.

Gawayne stopped short on his journey down the hill as he looked at me for the first time. Behind him, Samwell also stared now. Though Samwell did not stop walking, nearly causing the two of them to topple down the hill.

Robyn huffed next to me as the two men righted themselves. "Gold is faring better than you two it seems."

Both men nodded to me as they approached, but it was Gawayne who spoke first. "My lady, I did not get to thank you for last night." His shoulders fell, as his thick, red brows pulled together. "I owe you a debt for coming to my aid."

Gawayne's sudden declaration filled me with unease. Though my patients were often beyond grateful, the idea of someone owing me a debt was never something I intended or desired.

"It was nothing." I shifted uneasily under everyone's sudden attention. Samwell's eyes seemed to linger on my exposed midriff. A fact Robyn seemed to notice immediately as, to my relief, she cleared her throat in his general direction.

"Do you know if the cart has been recovered?" I asked the question, hoping to distract from the awkward energy hanging between us.

Gawayne nodded. "I will take you to it now…if…if you prefer." He stammered, sweeping one hand out toward the top of the hill.

"That would be excellent, and perhaps we could procure breakfast."

With one last look to assure myself that Gold's bandage was secure, I moved to follow Gawayne back up the hill. Just as I turned to leave, Robyn's hand once again reached for mine.

"Thank you for helping Gold." Her voice was thick with emotion. I nodded to her, grateful to be putting some space between us. I hadn't forgotten what she had said to me last night, or that she had refused to even share the same tent with me. Hopefully though, this meant we could at least tolerate each other's presence.

"What a great morning to wake up to—" Samwell's words were cut off by a soft thump. I did not turn around as Robyn huffed loudly again.

Whispers and stares followed us as Gawayne and I walked through camp. Thankfully, it didn't take long for us to find the cart. It had been brought to the center of camp and already several of the ladies from court had their trunks open and had begun pulling gowns out and clutching them to their chests like the dresses were babes separated from their mothers.

I recognized the woman in the dark-green dress as the same one flirting with Asher all day yesterday. Lady Rochelle was a few years older than me or Asher, but it didn't stop her from trying everything she could to win his affections. Her long, black hair was currently tied up around her head like a crown. It was a clear declaration to anyone who looked at her that she already thought she was royalty—despite the fact that her family owned one of the smaller provinces in Notting.

Her cold, green eyes grew wide as they looked over my disheveled appearance. Gawayne had asked me the color of my trunk, and he heaved it out from the masses. I thanked him, moving to open the lid, as the sound of a familiar voice greeted me.

"Lady Marian. What has happened to you?" Asher's face was stunned as he looked me up and down.

"I assure you, Your Majesty, it could not be avoided." Heat flushed through my face as I bowed before him. Asher cleared his throat but motioned for me and the other ladies to continue.

I buried my head in the trunk, suddenly desperate to find

anything but the shirt I was wearing. Gawayne stood silently beside me as I pulled out a white, healer's chemise.

A shadow loomed over me before Asher knelt beside me. I cringed as his mouth came disturbingly close to my ear. "Perhaps this is a look that shouldn't be avoided in the future. I believe you have the attention of every man in my camp."

I said nothing as Asher stood and walked away. I felt the heat of his gaze linger on my skin like something too sticky and sweet to wipe off.

Once my new clothes were gathered, I thanked Gawayne for his help and made my way toward the tent.

Despite my attempts at dismissal, the large red head appeared beside me.

"Perhaps, I can guard the lady's tent while she gets ready? I will keep anyone from disturbing her." Gawayne gave me a knowing look, and I knew immediately who he was willing to protect me from.

"Thank you," I whispered before walking into the tent.

When I emerged a few minutes later, I was relieved to find that Asher and his flock had disappeared.

"Perhaps you might do me the honor of dining with me this morning?" Gawayne's smile was surprisingly reassuring, and I found the unsettled feeling in my gut dissolving.

"That would be excellent." I couldn't help but smile as Gawayne led me to the edge of camp. We walked for a few minutes, before approaching a small fire near the edge of the trees.

Samwell and a few other men crouched near the small fire pit. A small kettle hung over the pit, sending smells of something sweet to my nose. Gawayne leaned down, retrieving a small bowl and handing it to me. I thanked him, trying my best to smile reassuringly as I followed him to a nearby log to sit.

One of the men, with a toothless smile and a nose that had obviously not been set back in place correctly watched me from across the fire. "Heard ye felled a man last night, I'd definitely say that earns you breakfast."

I nodded into my cup, drinking up the sweet porridge while trying to banish the images and memories of the assassin's scream from my mind.

"The nightmares will get easier if you talk about it," Gawayne whispered to me, and I was startled at how quickly he had guessed.

There was silence for a few minutes, and I knew the men were giving me space to share if I needed to. Something in me struggled against the idea, and I stayed silent, drinking my porridge.

"What we really need to know, is what was in that vial you threw at him..." Samwell slid over closer to me, wagging his eyebrows.

"And how do we get more of it." The toothless soldier added, with a mischievous grin.

My face warmed as I blushed under their sudden scrutiny. "It's just something I made by accident. I thought it could be used as something to clean an area before and after treatment, but it seems to have quite the negative effect when it touches skin..."

"Well, I'd say!" Gawayne burst into laughter, followed by the rest of the men. I couldn't help but join, suddenly comforted by the fact that I had found people who would not judge me for the horrendous act I had committed.

Samwell filled my cup again, and I felt myself relax for the first time since the arrow had pierced Asher's shoulder.

Robyn

I waited anxiously next to the prince. The outpost commander had lent us twenty extra guards, but after what happened last night, I was determined not to let Asher out of my sight until he was safe behind castle walls again.

That might be harder than I thought, as his royal highness had not stopped whining about his shoulder a single second since we all gathered. If it would not have cost me my life, I might have jabbed him in the other shoulder just to shut him up. Even worse was the catering to his royal whines by the noble women.

If the prince had allowed it, the one with long, black hair would have literally pulled the prince from his horse and clutched him to her bosom like a wet nurse.

Gawayne and Marian appeared just as the caravan was beginning to gather. Marian had changed clothes, and her bare stomach was once again covered. As I watched her walk nearer, I was reminded of the sharp curve of her hip this morning, and of the steep V that had flowed seamlessly into her breeches. Her skin was flawless, and it had been hard not to gawk.

As Marian and Gawayne approached, it seemed the two of them had reached some new camaraderie. Her smile was wide as she walked toward our group, but it faltered as she looked over at the prince and me.

To my surprise and confusion, Marian followed Gawayne toward the cart.

"Lady Kira has been instructed to take Marengo with her." Marian's voice called to me. I nodded, watching as Gawayne helped Marian into the front of the cart.

After a few minutes, Kira appeared on her own white mare, pulling Marengo on a lead rope. I watched as she tried to ride closer to the prince, but Asher ignored her presence.

"It seems the prince has once again satisfied his curiosity." Samwell kept his voice low as he rode up from behind me. "Rumor is his shoulder was not the only thing Kira attended to last night."

I rolled my eyes at Samwell's lewd words, though I was not surprised. I watched as Kira sat atop her mare. Though the prince seemed to have cast her off, she showed no signs of disappointment at his behavior. Her gaze was steel as they stared ahead, ready to go.

We rode the second half of our journey without incident, arriving just as the sun was beginning to set. The faint lights of torches began to glow ahead of us as we crested a large hill that would end at the field before the city gates. The steep journey would be the hardest on Gawayne and the cart, who would have to keep the horses at a steady pace as we descended.

Without needing an explanation, Samwell took my place closer to the prince as I rode Gold up to the side of the cart. We would block the way should the horses decide to spook. I focused on the two brown geldings pulling the cart up the hill. The horse pulling the cart yesterday had been too shaken to pull it again, so these two would have to suffice. As we reached the crest it was Marian who startled me with her loud gasp.

I watched her delicate hand move to cover her mouth immediately and turned my focus toward the horizon. On the field before us, hundreds, maybe thousands, of tents had been erected. Almost a city on its own, thousands of Notting's citizens looked up at their nobility with worn and weary faces.

Silence spread around the caravan as the prince and his miniature court stared at what was ahead.

"Where are they from?" Lady Rochelle's voice shook with emotion.

"From everywhere." The sight did not stun me as it had the others. Father and I had known of the meandering masses on the edge of the city for months. Though I was unaware of just how large it had grown. The plight on the crops had spread across the northern provinces, decimating villages that depended so heavily on them. The king had been sending troops into the northern provinces as the skirmishes with the tribes of Aicias were growing worse.

It seemed rumor had spread of the wealth of Colch and its

markets. Out of desperation, people had traveled from the far reaches of Notting, hoping for something better.

The cart horses were cool under Gawayne's tight control as we made our way down the center of the camp. Faces began to appear between the tents, and though I expected that none of the people had even enough strength to hurt the prince, I gave the signal for the guard to tighten around our charges.

The soft murmur grew louder as the people cried out to their prince.

"Do something!"

"Help us!"

The faceless voices called from the distance. Prince Asher stared straight ahead, but again it was Marian who caught my eye. From the front of the cart, tears streamed down her face as she emptied her purse, throwing coins into the crowd. A pained, puzzled look filled her face as no one moved to retrieve them.

"It will do them no good." Samwell shifted in his saddle next to me. His gaze was pure anguish and fury. "The duke will not allow them inside the gates to spend their coins. Instead, they must barter with each other for the rations sent by the crown."

"They're lucky to receive that." Asher's words were ice, and only a nudge from me kept Samwell at bay. His face was red as he seethed.

There was a deafening creak as the city gates swung open, allowing us through. No one spoke as the royal caravan trudged through the city streets. The faces of hundreds more of Notting's citizens greeted us. These faces seemed to fill with hope as they waved and greeted the man who would one day be their king.

Asher and his entourage smiled brightly back at the shadowed faces, the sights of the camp behind the gate quickly forgotten. I scanned the faces of my men, Marian, and Lady Rochelle. A pallor had fallen over them, like the light behind their eyes had suddenly been snuffed out.

We climbed the hill to Duke Inglis' castle overlooking the sea. Every window and doorway were lit up for our arrival. Candles and torches twinkled against the darkness, beckoning to us as we entered the courtyard.

The caravan slowed to a halt just shy of the steps where the Duke and Duchess waited to greet us. Safe in the castle walls, the guards parted to allow for the prince to approach. Both the duke and duchess bowed deep, a young girl popping out behind them to demonstrate her curtsy as well.

To my surprise, Asher bowed low to the child, taking her small hand and kissing the back delicately. Behind him, all the ladies—except Marian—smiled at the show of affection.

"Greetings and welcome to Colch, Your Majesty." Duke Edward's voice boomed through the courtyard. "I was infuriated to hear of your incident on the road. We have already dispatched troops to find the culprits responsible."

"Thank you, Duke Edward. Though, I fear they may evade you. Our scouts were unable to find any trace—even the body of the man felled by our healer was not recovered."

Marian bristled beneath the prince's words, and I watched as she squirmed under the sudden scrutiny of the Duke and Duchess.

"We are so thankful to you for coming, Lady Marian." The duchess' smile was warm as she held a hand out for Marian, motioning the healer to come closer. "We hope to learn much from you in our short time together."

"Mother is our healer. She helps everyone." The child reached her tiny hand for Marian, who immediately smiled in return.

"Eva is correct. Duchess Elsie selflessly helps all the people of Colch and the nearby villages. We would love to share in your knowledge."

"I would be delighted to help." Marian's voice lit up in a way I hadn't seen before, and I knew she truly meant it. "I'm sure there is much I can learn from you as well." Marian swung Eva's arm in a circle as the child squealed in delight.

"We have an extensive collection of medical books, purchased from tradesman from across the land, in our city library. We would be honored for you to take a look."

Marian's mouth fell open a little as she nodded in delight. The nobles descended further into the main hall, and I took a steadying breath as I turned to oversee the unpacking. Finally, we had arrived.

Now the real work would begin.

The morning came far too quickly. It had taken hours to unpack and deliver all the bags and trunks from the caravan. By the time I had fallen into my bed, it was only a few hours until sunrise. Despite my fatigue, years of training had instilled in me an unnatural internal clock, and I woke before the first pink light of dawn had stretched across the sky.

Shaking off my stupor, I rose, placing my feet on the cold floor. Familiar aches from days on the road spread throughout my back and legs.

This morning I would accompany Marian and the other nobles into the city marketplace. It was not a chore I welcomed, but it must be done. At least traveling into the city would give me a chance to connect with others in my father's employ--and to assess the situation with the citizens outside the city gate.

Like most mornings, I dressed quickly. A sigh escaped me as I realized that the duke and duchess would be dressed in formal wear for the prince's royal tour. I would be expected to do the same.

My trunk was much smaller than the ones kept by most nobility. Its edges were a simple polished cherry and not lined with leather, like most. I unlocked the massive box, retrieving a replacement for the breast wrap I had dirtied with days on the road. Once it was secure, I pulled the soft fabric of the tunic which had the least number of holes over my head. The soft leather of my boots greeted my cold feet as I slipped them on.

Beside the head of the bed, I had tossed my assortment of weaponry. It took a few minutes to secure the twin daggers in my boots, but soon I had nothing left to gather but my sword and bow.

The familiar weight of the weaponry settled against my muscles like a child with a favorite blanket. Once outside my room, the corridors of the castle were eerily quiet. I walked alone for several minutes before finding a servant to direct me toward the soldier's mess hall. As I expected, it would take a bit of a walk.

When I finally arrived at the large outbuilding near the rear of the castle, I was unsurprised to find it deserted. Though at the capital I was expected to dine with the other members of Court, I preferred to sit with my men whenever I could manage.

Three long rows of tables spread the length of the room—a testament to how many soldiers the duke kept ready to protect

Notting's coast and largest harbor. Noise began to fill the hall as more and more soldiers emerged from the barracks.

"Good morning, Captain Loxley." A petite brunette greeted me as she brought me a plate of gravy that resembled soup and rolls which fell to the table like rocks. Beside me, several of the men grumbled. It seemed the duke had not served meat to his men in weeks.

The girl's smile was warm and inviting as she leaned the curve of her hip against the table. I smiled politely, too tired to indulge in whatever she might be offering. She lingered for several minutes, murmuring something about having never seen so many royal guards before. She ran a finger across the back of my hand before skittering back toward the kitchens.

A deep laugh resounded behind me as Samwell sat on the bench to my left. It was Gawayne who laughed, walking around to the other side of the table. To my surprise, Marian was once again at his side.

Today she wore a white gown that hung just above the ground. The thin fabric along the shoulders had been trimmed for easy movement and fell along the tops of her arms. Throughout her long, blond hair she had once again plaited the white ribbon.

"I swear, Robyn has more luck than I do." Gawayne inclined his head toward the brunette.

"Gawayne, there are *priests* who have more luck than you do." Samwell ducked as Gawayne lurched across the table toward him.

I could not help but roll my eyes at the two of them.

It was much too early for their bullshit. I turned my attention instead to Marian, who had a sour look on her face as she watched me across the table. *It was also much too early to be disappointing the nobility.*

"Perhaps I should find a better way to spend my mornings than listening to the two of you whine." I looked pointedly toward the brunette, who had reappeared, balancing several plates on her long arms. She passed one to each of my new companions, ignoring Samwell's attempts for her attention. I winked at the brunette as she walked away, elbowing Samwell as she smiled in return.

Samwell's shoulders slumped forward, but it was Marian whose face flashed with anger. I balked at the judgment written clearly across her face as irritation filled me.

"I hear there is a brothel somewhere in the city. We should ask the guards. If we're going to be here a while, we may as well enjoy our stay. Prince Asher certainly will."

Samwell and Gawayne both looked up at me. They knew I wasn't normally the one for such suggestions. I looked at Samwell and I could see his excitement immediately. To my surprise, Gawayne merely looked disappointed.

I did my best to ignore it.

Marian's brows furrowed together, and once again I got the distinct feeling she was assessing me, trying her best to figure out if I was being sincere.

"Shouldn't you be dining with the prince? You will miss your chance to drop grapes or other morsels into his awaiting mouth." I asked her, before shoving the first bite of the disgusting gravy in my mouth.

"How sweet of you to be concerned about the prince's mouth, when you clearly don't care what goes in yours." Marian's words were curt as she cocked her head to the side. She rose one brow and jerked her head toward the brunette who was once again disappearing into the kitchens.

Gawayne and Samwell both failed to hide their laughter as they buried their heads in their plates.

"I have a feeling he won't miss my presence nearly as much as he seems to miss yours. Though I'm sure he will appear at your chamber any night now."

Silence fell over the table, and I immediately regretted my words. Last night Gawayne had shared some of his suspicions about the prince's disturbing behavior and Marian's response to it.

My chest grew tight with guilt as Marian hung her head over her plate, taking a small bite of her gravy before pushing the dish away. Her nose crinkled in disgust.

A sour feeling grew in my gut, deepening as Marian rose from the table. The desire to apologize gripped at my chest, but I stumbled over the words.

I knew what it was like to be constantly harassed, to have to show the world how hard your skin was so that none may touch it.

In a flash of white, before I could say anything, Marian disappeared out the door. Suddenly, the room seemed a little darker.

Marian

I welcomed each breeze as it swept over my damp skin. The morning had grown hot, and the air was thick by the time everyone had mounted. Sweat dripped down my brow as the duke's gate was pulled open. Each thunderous clank was a shock to my system, waking me and forcing me alert.

Today's venture would be a short one down to the city markets, and I had opted to ride side-saddle, knowing a dress might provide more breeze. Next to me, the duchess discussed the various preparations made for the southern princess' visit with several of the other ladies. On the other side of Marengo, Eva and her nursemaid played some silent game on the back of a wide, brown mare. I wondered if the young girl was still learning to ride, as the horse did not shift or stomp like the other impatient horses around it.

I listened half-heartedly to the conversations around me, smiling and commenting when absolutely necessary. The list of things I would need for the tournament played over and over in my mind, making me restless and edgy.

My hope for today was the duchess and other nobles would satisfy their curiosities about the city and then leave me in peace. As Asher and the duke approached on their stallions, I knew my hopes were foolish.

"You all look stunning, ladies. Surely Princess Madawi will be envious of our ladies' fashion and demand her seamstresses to mimic your beauty." Asher's blue eyes sparkled at the group of women as they approached.

"Even her finest seamstresses may try but they will never find such beauty as the ladies of Notting." Duke Edward leaned forward to greet his wife, and I felt my frustration ease a little as he kissed her hand. The fact that the duke and duchess loved each other was obvious, and they were clearly not afraid to hide it.

The ladies smiled, some feigning blushes and waving the men off for the sake of modesty — all but Lady Rochelle. I watched her face fall in dismay at the mention of the princess' impending arrival. It was no secret that Queen Naomi intended for Asher to propose at the earliest possible moment.

Did she truly think bedding him would win her a crown?

I thought back to how she had reacted when we first came upon the camps outside the city. To my surprise, she seemed truly distraught by the sight. For the first time, I wondered if the people of the Western River were faring much better than the rest of Notting. Perhaps that was why Duke Griffiths seemed so desperately eager to marry his daughter off to a wealthy suitor.

Asher and Duke Edward rode to the front of our caravan, and the riding party took it as their cue to leave. There were fewer guards around us today, though far more than needed. I looked around at the stern, serious faces of the men — surprised I didn't find more I recognized.

"So kind of you to loan us your men this morning." Asher spoke to the duke. His voiced carried over the soft clacks of hoof beats on the brick road.

"It is no trouble, Your Highness. Captain Loxley and her men came to me this morning and explained that they had business to attend."

Asher visibly squirmed at the duke addressing Robyn so formally. Realization struck me. Guilt grew in my gut at the mention of her title. Like the others, I had been addressing her according to what we wanted her to be — what we expected her to be — and not as she was, which was an Officer in the King's Guard.

I would have to address her correctly the next time I saw her.

A different feeling overcame me at the thought of seeing Robyn again, making my heart race and my stomach flip, but I did my best to ignore it.

The trip to the markets was not far, but I marveled at the city's structures as we went along. Each building was crafted carefully of polished stone. Their walls were not very high, but the base was enormous. At the bottom of each outer wall, small holes about the size of a hand had been carefully constructed.

Duchess Elsie noticed my curious stare almost immediately. "Our craftsmen have tried many types of homes designed to withstand the rage of the sea. We learned quickly that the taller structures fall quickest when the winds come." Her tone was somber as she continued her explanation. This time, I did not have to feign interest. "If it got too bad, we may not be able to get everyone out in time. Our hopes are that once the flood waters begin to recede, the holes will allow homes to drain faster."

I nodded toward the duchess, but her gaze was trained on her daughter. I could almost see the weight the duchess carried with her. I had lived through many storms, but none such as the ones the sea gods could create. I reached out, grabbing her hand gently.

The duchess smiled back, squeezing my hand before releasing it.

"What about mice?" Lady Rochelle's question startled me. Not only because she had never spoken so forcefully, but in all the weeks she had been at court I had never heard her make any sort of inquisition. I chastised myself again for not realizing the depth of the woman's intelligence.

I have been letting the intrigues of the castle get to my better judgment.

Duchess Elsie let out a roar of laughter. "Actually, that is quite a story. Our craftsmen had not considered what else the holes might allow in. Our citizens scrambled for a solution. Thankfully one was found quickly. The homes throughout our beautiful city have suddenly filled with some rather fat cats."

For the first time in a long time, I joined in the ladies' laughter. When an orange and white cat, with the most enormous stomach dragging the ground, crossed lazily in front of our line of horses, the laughter began anew.

The sun was not quite at its peak as we arrived at the crowded market. All around us the sunburned faces gawked and bowed at their Prince. Asher and the duke dismounted first, each hurrying to help with women from their saddles.

Asher ran to my side, and I had to force myself to smile as he reached for my hand. His hands slid quickly up my waist, making me instantly thankful the hem came down as far as it did. He smiled at me, and I knew he was trying to get me to see the boy who had once been my friend, but that time had passed long ago.

As if sensing my discomfort, Asher nodded his head toward me. A slight frown appeared from the corner of his mouth, but in a flash, it was gone. His charming grin was replaced as he moved from lady to lady, helping each to the ground. To my surprise, Lady Rochelle did not wait her turn. Instead, she dropped softly to the ground. Her long, black hair floated around her. Seconds later, she disappeared into the crowd—leaving nothing behind but her horse.

Neither Asher nor the duke and duchess seemed to notice Rochelle's departure.

A young girl appeared beside me, bowing low before asking for my reins.

Immediately, I noticed the splotches of pink and red across her arms as she grabbed the reins gently.

"I could be wrong, but does your mother wash your linens in the sea?"

The young girl looked shocked, but she nodded. I pointed at her arms. Immediately, the girl held her arms up, allowing her sleeves to slide back and expose the tender skin on her wrists.

"Wash your linens in fresh water, if you can. The salty water of the sea is sometimes too much for the skin. It should ease your itching too."

I smiled at her as she nodded enthusiastically before pulling Marengo and Rochelle's black mare to the stables nearby.

"Lady Marian." I looked back to find Duchess Elsie staring at me inquisitively. "I have some local shops I'd like to show you. I believe they may aid in your search for supplies."

Slight relief filled me as I realized the duchess did not mean to blindly follow Asher and Duke Edward all day.

Perhaps I would get more accomplished than I thought.

It quickly became apparent that it was not unusual for the people to see Duchess Elsie or Eva in the marketplace. Many stall merchants smiled as they arrived, pulling out items they knew would be of interest.

Elsie drifted from stall to stall, inspecting wares and commenting on the types of goods available. None of the merchants were hesitant to barter prices, and though she wasn't swindled the duchess also would not allow anyone to cut her a deal or offer less than what was deserved.

In only a little while, I had given a number of merchants the lists of supplies I needed, with a promise to return to see what they had gathered. Though it wouldn't be official until we returned, many of them already referred to me as 'Mistress Marian,' the title I would use once I was the Royal Healer.

I wrote each merchant's name and the list of what they promised in my small, leather parchment book. I looked over the list again.

It wasn't everything I needed, but it was a start.

All this Eva watched, gripping her mother's hand, as they continued along. We eventually followed our noses to a local bakery. The shop was small and the air stifling with heat from the wood-burning ovens in the back. Once again, the owner attempted to provide Elsie with free lunch, and once again the duchess denied.

"I know the cost of flour has gone up. The mills have nothing to provide when the grain up north has died so quickly."

The baker, an older woman with salt and pepper hair and worry lines across her face, nodded appreciatively at the duchess's words. The baker's eyes were full of unshed tears as she looked at the empty shop window.

"The southern sugar traders want so much for a sack of sugar these days."

I purchased a handful of some bright-red candies from the shopkeeper. Following the duchess's lead, I paid twice what the store was asking.

The duchess handed over the coins from her pouch, and the woman pulled Elsie in for a tight hug. We headed back out to the street, but not before the baker had passed Eva what looked to be a treat dripping with sweetness. I pretended not to notice as the little girl stuffed her face.

Out of the corner of my eye, I watched the duchess set two more gold coins on the wooden table by the door. When the duchess looked at me and winked, I knew she too was pretending not to notice the sweets falling from her daughter's mouth.

"The library now?" Eva's small hand wrapped around mine, then latched on to her mother's hand too.

"If Lady Marian wishes, but perhaps we should retrieve the horses?" Eva's nurse maid, who I had learned was called Calla, asked quietly.

Duchess Elsie's knowing eyes reached out for me, and for some reason I felt as though I was being tested by the two women.

"I am enjoying walking and seeing the sights of your beautiful city." Else's smile widened, and once again Eva ran forward. Her feet left the ground as she clung to us. "Besides, I have ridden enough these last few days."

We swung the little girl between us as we walked down the street. Calla pointed to house after house, describing the stories she knew of each denizen. Most were fishermen or craftsmen. Some had young children, or elderly. It was not uncommon for many generations to live in the same home. Calla's face fell as she spoke of the ones owned by widows whose husbands or sons had died in the skirmishes up north and were now left alone.

The noise of the marketplace faded away. My legs began to burn, and I was regretting my choice not to take the horses. After a few minutes, I realized we were nearly back to the castle. Up a steep hill, just beyond the wall of the castle, stood a wide, stone building. It had to be the highest point in the city.

Eva ran ahead of us, Calla following closely behind her.

Two wide double doors were opened by a pair of footmen as we approached. The smell of the books waiting inside hit me, and I couldn't help but smile as we entered.

"To the back, you will find many books about healing, herbalism, and many of the sciences. For a hundred years, since before even the war, we have gathered stories from sailors from every corner, every country." The duchess spoke with pride as we walked between the high shelves. A rainbow of colors reached out to me. Leather-bound tomes stretched high above us, and rolled scrolls were tucked tight into square sections on the lower shelves. We walked along the strange shelves and I realized no item was placed lower than my knee.

"In case of flooding?" The duchess gave me a wry smile as she nodded.

"Lady Marian, if you will forgive me, I must find my daughter. Eva likes to wander and can sometimes be too much for poor Calla. I also suspect you too may want to get 'lost' in some of these books."

I laughed. Duchess Elsie had most definitely read my mind.

"You may bring whichever books or items you need back to the castle. However, in the southern wing of the castle, usually kept for when the royal family visits, there is a beautiful library. The rooms are taken by Prince Asher and the other guests, but I have a feeling the library may be quite empty. You may find it to your liking."

I had no words at the duchess' generosity. It was far more than I expected, and I was beyond grateful. It would be a relief to find a quiet space for myself.

"Thank you so much." Just like the bakery owner, I found myself hugging Elsie's small shoulders. The older woman squeezed me in return, before disappearing to the other end of the library.

I ran nervous fingers through my hair as I puzzled over which topics to explore first. Although we had some books in the healer's tower, it was nothing compared to this. I had to force myself not to run as I headed toward the back of the enormous building.

Robyn

We had not traveled far into the forest for this meeting, just far enough to be certain that we would not be overheard. The young messenger with the long, black hair disappeared back between the trees. His job was over. The message had been delivered.

Gawayne had lit a small fire, and I crumbled the parchment before tossing it into the flames.

Father's plans were moving faster than I expected, but the truth was the people of Notting needed our help and they needed it now. The tents sitting outside the city gate were certainly proof of that.

The cries of my people trying desperately to get the attention of their prince echoed again in my mind. Fury filled me once more.

"We need to get supplies out of the city." Gawayne's words mimicked my thoughts, and I was reminded why he was my second.

"Rumor has it that the order not to allow the people from the camps inside the city came not from the duke, but straight from the king. The city was to be secured for the arrival of Princess Madawi." Samwell picked at his nails from the other side of the table. I had no doubt the rumors were true, and not just because Samwell had a tendency to gather information from many different sources at very intimate times.

"And I suppose once the princess has arrived and left for the capital the king will allow the gates to be thrown wide open and welcome in his subjects." My furious, forced laughter disrupted the quiet of the trees.

Neither Samwell nor Gawayne bothered to reply. We all knew the answer.

I pulled at the ends of my hair, trying to find a solution. "Talk to our merchant contacts in the city. See what they're willing to give. It seems with the number of court members in town we should surely be able to find a few *loose* purses that have fallen to the ground. Make sure every noble finds the price of goods in the marketplace *very* high. The extra coin will compensate for what the merchants send outside the gates."

It wasn't a long-term solution, but it was something for now. Gawayne doused the fire, making sure all traces of the parchment had turned to ash. We would reenter the city at different times, each making sure they weren't followed.

I wondered again how things could feel as though they were changing so fast and simultaneously feel like they weren't moving at all.

The sun was setting by the time I entered the rear gate of the castle. A gentle breeze swept across my brow, and I breathed a sigh of relief. I would never get used to the thick, humid air penetrating the sea—nor the way it forced my clothes to cling uncomfortably to my skin.

In the distance, I heard the clash of swords and the distinct grunts followed by loud swearing. Samwell's colorful language could only mean he must be sparring—and by the sounds of it, he was losing.

Samwell losing was not something that happened often. I followed my ears, curiosity instantly piqued.

A small group had gathered around the fence marking the edge of the ring. Prince Asher, the duke, and several of the prince's other comrades watched eagerly. Their cheers got louder as I approached. None of them seemed to be cheering on Samwell.

"I told you not to underestimate her." The duke's laughter sounded over the cheering crowd.

I neared the edge of the ring, surprised to find Samwell sword-to-sword with one of the most beautiful women I had ever seen.

Sweat dripped from her brow. Her thick, curly hair was pulled back into two tight braids along her scalp and tied high on her head with a leather band. Her dark skin shimmered in the fading sunlight. A sheen of sweat spread across her skin as she bobbed and weaved with a grace I had seen few warriors possess.

"He's not doing bad—for a man, at least." The woman darted at

Samwell, who eagerly dodged the attack. They danced around each other for several minutes, each assessing their opponent.

"Captain Sagar is not someone I would cross swords with lightly..." The duke's voice filled with pride. "That is why she commands my men."

Recognition filled me at the name—Captain Danyeil Sagar. I had heard talks of the warrior from Aicias. Orphaned after her parents made the passage from Notting's southern neighbor, she had enlisted just a few years after me. It was a wonder we had not met before.

Danyeil and Samwell danced around each other. I watched Samwell's keen eyes focus on the movement of her lithe hips, tracking her and trying desperately to predict what she might do next. True to form, he blew kisses and sent lustrous looks at her as they continued.

I couldn't blame him. She was certainly attractive, but I knew better than to take his actions as anything more than an attempt to distract his opponent. Samwell might be one for flirtations and frivolity when it came to the bedroom, but he was something else entirely on the field of battle.

His bravado was a ruse. Something to keep hidden his true concern.

Samwell was an excellent swordsman—the best I had ever seen. If Danyeil had him this worried, then there was something we all could learn from this match.

So fast I wasn't sure how it happened, Danyeil spun low. Her leg swept out—knocking Samwell to the dirt. He rolled as he hit the ground, but she was already there. Before he could recover, Danyeil had the tip of her sword against his throat.

A cheer of applause came from the duke and several of his men as Samwell dropped his sword onto the ground in surrender. A grin spread across his face as Danyeil reached her arm down to help him to his feet.

"You are a blur! The fastest feet I have ever seen." Samwell clapped Danyeil's shoulder heartily as they walked to the edge of the field.

"I would be happy to show you some tricks while you are here." Danyeil smiled at him, hitting him playfully with her hip. I knew she did not just mean tricks in the sparring ring, and judging from the heat suddenly scorching out of Samwell's brown eyes, he did too.

"Perhaps we should allow the women to spar." Asher's snide voice washed over my skin.

The training yard grew silent, the men waiting for either Danyeil or me to respond.

"It is getting late, perhaps we should retire and wait for another time—"

"Nonsense. It seems Captain Loxley could certainly learn from your beautiful Captain Sagar." It was the first time Asher had addressed me properly, but I knew it was not out of respect. The prince named my title like someone would name a child. From the look on Danyeil's face, she knew it too.

"I fear I must retire." Danyeil bowed to the prince as she approached. "However, the prince is correct. I have heard of Captain Loxley's skills and would certainly be honored at the chance to learn from her. If she should like to accompany me, I train every morning. I would be happy to share skills with such talented warriors." Danyeil turned her head toward me. Her eyes danced with mischief. "The legend of the Great Sherwood Archer has reached all shores of Notting."

I stood still. My mouth fell agape at Captain Sagar's blatant refute of the prince. Somehow, she managed to say he was correct while directly contradicting exactly what he intended.

I could not help but smile in return as Asher's brows furrowed. He was clearly struggling to figure out what had just happened.

"It would be my honor to improve your archery skills, and to build new skills from such an excellent swordsman." I nodded toward Danyeil, trying desperately to keep the smile from my face.

"My prince, should you wish to attend we typically start our mornings a few hours before sunrise. If you should wish to join you are of course welcome."

Asher's face soured, his lips pulling tight together. Suddenly the idea of getting up so early—something Asher had certainly never done in his life— wasn't worth the effort just to see two women spar.

"We shall see." The prince turned on his heel without another word. The duke and the others were close behind.

Laughter erupted from me as soon as Asher was out of sight. Danyeil and Samwell quickly joined. I shook my head, running my fingers through my short hair.

My stomach rumbled, reminding me that I had not eaten since breakfast this morning. "Shall we see if dinner is edible?" Danyeil rolled her eyes as she sheathed her sword. Beside her, Samwell nodded heartily as he did the same.

We walked in silence toward the large mess hall, Samwell and Danyeil each stretching and pulling at their sore muscles. I tried desperately to ignore the furtive glances they shot toward one another.

A strange feeling sat in my gut as it had this morning. Though Gawayne had teased me this morning, it was Samwell who seldom slept alone. I envied the ease Samwell had with women.

Laughter filled the night air as we approached the door to the mess hall. Confusion filled me as we entered. Several of the tables were empty, but men were crowded around the center table. A flash of red and a flash of blond sat hunched together, dozens of men leaning in eagerly toward them.

"Alright. So, if you had to guess a number, how many do you think you have seen?" One of the duke's men leaned toward Marian as we approached. He pressed tight against her shoulder and wagged his brows at his lap.

"More than you can imagine…" The men all chortled at that, but Marian continued with a knowing look in her eye. "But I'll tell you, every time someone makes the same joke about 'making sure I don't hurt myself with it,' it's usually that man who doesn't impress."

The whole mess hall roared with laughter. Soldiers walked back to their tables. Their curiosity had apparently been satisfied. Beside Marian, Gawayne shoved the man pressing against her. I watched as the soldier walked away dejectedly.

"Ey. They've something edible tonight. It seems Marian supplied the kitchen with some herbs and spices for the soup." Gawayne beamed, shoving a spoonful into his mouth.

Marian's face fell as she looked at me, and the guilt became a boulder in my gut.

I did not want to be the one wiping away her smiles.

Once again, Samwell and I crossed to the other side of the table. Danyeil looked between us all curiously, waving to a few of her men as she sat. Bowls were brought out immediately, probably due to the presence of the duke's captain at our table.

Steam rose from mine, bringing with it the smell of spices.

"Hello. I'm Marian." Part of me was disappointed to see that Marian's smile had returned as she stuck her hand out to Danyeil. It seemed it was reserved for everyone but me.

Danyeil greeted Marian, returning the smile as she introduced herself.

"Marian has become the hero of my troops it seems." Danyeil nodded approvingly at the light-hearted atmosphere of the mess hall. It was certainly a change from the somber breakfast this morning.

"I've found that men are easy. They only want for three things—feed them, bed them, or mend them." Marian stated it as a matter of fact. Her delicate shoulders rose and fell as if she had just declared the simplest of equations.

I nearly choked on my soup, as did Samwell and Gawayne beside me. Gawayne's heavy fist pounded the table as he fought for breath. We all erupted in laughter. Samwell knocked his spoon, sending it flying.

Marian smiled into her lap, and my heart skipped a beat at her sudden blush.

Eventually, our laughter died, but I was relieved to see the gentle lift of her mouth remain.

"I have brought you all something. I didn't want to give it in front of everyone else, but I thought it would make an excellent dessert."

Marian slid a small pouch from her side, gently untying the short string and spreading it on the table. Inside were a dozen small, red candies.

Samwell grabbed one eagerly, earning a disapproving stare from Gawayne.

"Thank you, Marian." Gawayne retrieved one of the sweets, passing it to Danyeil before getting one for himself.

I hesitated, doubt filling me. After my foolish words this morning, perhaps Marian did not intend for me to have one. It was what I deserved.

There was a moment of awkward silence, and for the first time since sitting down, I truly looked at Marian. Her long, blond hair had been taken down. It fell loose around her shoulders. To my surprise, her sapphire eyes stared back at me. She bit her thin, delicate lip—as if debating on whether to speak.

My heart pounded in response, but I found I could not look away.

Her lips were supple, and I could see the tint of the red from one of the candies she must have already eaten. A strange thought occurred to me then—if I tasted her lips right now, she would be sweeter than honey.

This was not the girl I had detested as simply another noble at court. She was witty, kind, and not at all what I had thought. The realization struck me, and for some reason, I felt like she could read it on my face.

Marian reached down, grabbing one of the red sweets. She stuck her hand out for me, and I felt something between us shift. She was giving me a chance toward kindness—perhaps the last chance I would get from her.

I held my palm open, and she dropped it into my hand. The rush of sugar melted in my mouth.

"Thank you." I cleared my throat, suddenly desperate to control the throng of emotions overcoming me.

"The pleasure is mine," Marian whispered the words across the table, and they seemed to reach out and caress my skin, sending small bumps up my arms. I found myself longing to find out what other pleasures she enjoyed.

Marian

It had been nearly two weeks since we arrived at Duke Inglis' castle. I had made the trek to the market each day, bartering and collecting the supplies on my ever-growing list. Tonight I had stayed until well after nightfall, waiting eagerly in the harbor for the ship carrying my latest supplies to dock.

After assuring myself that my wares would end up at the capital like they were supposed to, I finally trudged back up the hill toward the castle.

Everything was chaos as the duke and duchess, and everyone else in the castle, prepared for the arrival of Princess Madawi. There was to be a grand ball in her honor shortly after her arrival, and food was already being brought in from every corner of Notting.

Guilt filled me every time I spent a single coin in the markets. I wondered how the thousands of people just outside the city gates felt watching food be brought in from across the kingdom and supplies being sent right past them.

An ache spread through my temples as I walked between the gates. I had walked down the hill to the markets and back up to the castle so many times in the last few days that my legs screamed in protest.

My feet were heavy, and my mind was tired. The thought of climbing all the steps to my room was almost unbearable. What seemed like hours later, I finally turned the corridor toward my room.

The candles in the sconces gave the stone an eerie glow, casting flickering shadows along the walls and floors.

A shadow rested against the wall, and even from where I stood I could already see the glint of jewels.

Asher's brown hair fell into his eyes as he pushed off the wall. I approached him warily. His gaze seemed unfocused and clouded as he swayed on his feet. The smell of rum was thick in the air.

I did not bow as I approached. This was not my prince before me. Nor was it the sweet boy I had played with in childhood. No. This was the man I had found perched on the edge of my bed. The man who had roused me from my sleep with his heavy hands exploring my body.

Bile rose in my throat at the memory. It had been almost a year ago, but I could still feel the terror that had gripped me that night. I had fled my room, careening down the hall. Shame had gripped me, keeping me from screaming. Who would believe me over the words or the prince? I had finally stumbled into Genevieve's office—the only room in the healer's tower with a lock.

I had barely escaped that night, and whether he was my prince or not I would not go through that again.

"Mar-ian. Where have you been?" Asher slurred his words, and I steeled myself as he approached.

"I was gathering supplies for the tournament, but I am afraid I am rather tired. I must go." The smell of the alcohol increased as Asher closed the distance. I ducked under his arm as it reached for me but quickly realized my mistake.

My back was to the wall now—just out of reach of my door. Asher's smile was lopsided as he looked from me to the thick door frame. He had realized it too.

"You could invite me in…"

I dodged him again, searing pain burned across my brow as I scraped my head against the hot metal of the sconce. I placed my hand on my head, but it blinded me to my foe.

Asher did not seem to notice. He leered at the bounce of my chest. I had begun wearing only a corset and my healer's attire to fend off the heat of the markets.

"Asher. You are drunk. I will send you a tincture for the headache, but you should rest…" I kept my words sweet, trying my best to back away, but, even drunk, Asher was quick on his feet.

His hands reached for me, grabbing at my wrists. I wrenched back, but his grip was tight.

"You could invite me in. Why won't you invite me in?" His breath was hot against my face, and I had to resist the urge not to vomit.

"Let me go, Asher." I pushed against him with my free hand, but it only made him squeeze tighter. He leaned his hips against me, pinning me against the wall. Between us, I felt his erection throb.

Panic filled me. A scream rose in my throat, but Asher placed his free hand over my mouth. Something snapped in me, and I fought with everything I had. One of my legs slipped free, and I brought my knee to his groin.

Asher released a cry of pain and crumpled to the ground. I took the opportunity to put as much distance as I could between us.

The door next to mine came crashing open, and I ran for it blindly. Tears fell down my face, and my heart threatened to burst from my chest.

It didn't matter who came out that door, only that Asher and I were no longer alone in this hallway.

Robyn's golden eyes passed back and forth between me and Asher. She looked me up and down for a heartbeat, before shoving me inside her room. The room around me swayed a little as I gasped for air. Panic was taking over me now, and it was all I could do to stay standing.

Fury seethed from Robyn as she stepped slowly into the hall. Her face was red with rage as she walked toward the only other door in the corridor. Her fists pounded on the heavy wood.

After a few seconds, Kira poked her head out. Her red hair was disheveled, and her mouth agape as she looked at the scene before her.

I watched through my blurred vision as Robyn took a deep breath.

"Samwell," Robyn spoke his name slowly. "Take Prince Asher to his room. It seems he has *fallen.*"

A few seconds passed, and there was a soft shuffling from behind Kira's door.

In the dim hallway, I watched Samwell emerge from the bedroom and approach the prince. A look of confusion crossed Samwell's face. Then the horror donned on him as he saw me cowering in Robyn's doorway. Samwell grabbed at the hilt of his sword, but Kira quickly rushed toward him. She placed a firm hand on his chest, and I watched something pass between them as he looked down at her.

Samwell closed his eyes, taking a deep breath—just as Robyn had.

"I will see Prince Asher safely back to his room" —Samwell looked at me now, and I felt myself cringe away from the pity written clearly across his face—"and I will be sure he stays there tonight."

Kira stepped back, allowing Samwell to walk toward the prince. There was a soft groan from Asher, who still had not moved from the floor, as Samwell grabbed at the prince's arm.

Robyn crossed toward me, blocking me from the sight. "I will stay with you tonight." It was not a question, and I did not argue. "Do you want to stay in your room or mine?"

I thought it over for a second. I believed Samwell would stand guard over Asher, but the idea that Asher might come back and know where to find me was too much to bear.

"Yours, please." Shame filled me at how much my voice shook. I silently prayed that Robyn would not notice.

Robyn closed the door behind us, and I was relieved to see the heavy lock slide in place. The room was warm from her small fireplace, and a candle had been lit on the desk that was littered with papers. Some part of me realized she had been up late, reading.

My shoulders shook as I realized what might have happened if she had not been...

I sat on the edge of the bed, staring at my hands and praying for the tremors to stop. Robyn paced in front of the fire, but I could feel her staring at me.

"You did what you had to do." Robyn paused in her pacing, and I nodded in response.

I dropped before the small fire, desperate for its warmth. Something cold and dark had taken root in me, and for a moment I wondered if I would ever be warm again. Would I ever stop feeling the touch of his hands on my skin? I wrapped my arms tight across my chest, rocking my body back and forth. I needed it to stop. I needed to try to get the shaking to stop.

There was a heavy silence. I tried to control my breathing, but it came out in short, quick bursts.

Robyn knelt on the floor beside me. She did not reach out to touch me, but I found myself looking at her anyway.

"This is not the first time," Robyn whispered. Her golden eyes were sad as they looked up at me from the floor. I nodded weakly.

"I—I woke up about a year ago, and he was in my room. His hands were on—on my body..." Robyn stood and began pacing back and forth again. I felt my heartbeat slow, like it was connected to the soft thump of her boots.

I took a breath before continuing. It was the first time I had ever spoken the words to anyone. "I pushed him off. He must not have expected it, because he fell back, and I ran from the room. Genevieve let me sleep in her office for weeks after. Then, we finally put a lock on my door..."

Bile rose in my throat, and I tore at the skin along my arms, digging in with my nails. I remembered the feel of his hand underneath my blanket, and the crazed look in his eyes when I awoke. Once again, I stared into the bright flames of the fireplace.

It was what I had done that night too, and every night for weeks and months after. I built the fire in my room until it was stifling, and then I would sit and stare into its light. Sometimes I wondered if the only way I would ever feel clean, feel whole, again was if I succumbed to the flames.

Robyn dropped to the floor before the fireplace, startling me out of my memories. I watched in confusion as Robyn took a pair of knives out of each boot, then violently pulled at the heels. She hurled each boot toward the other end of the room.

"What are you doing?"

Robyn did not look at me. She ran her fingers through her short hair. A long sigh filled her chest again. "I hate the feeling of the cold on my feet. So, if I take my boots off maybe I will not charge through this castle and shove one of my knives through the prince's throat." As if imagining doing just that, Robyn grabbed one of the blades from the ground and threw it across the room.

The knife flew through the air, landing perfectly in the heel of one of her boots. Awe filled me, but when she made to throw the other, I crept closer, moving right beside her. I reached out my hand.

The unspent anger fell from her face. She looked at my hand, and then up at me again.

"Could I have that tonight? To help me sleep?" The words came out before I could stop them, but Robyn handed me the dagger.

I stood, gripping the handle tight as I walked to the bed. My legs felt shaky, but I finally made it. I placed my head on the soft pillow, but I could not stop staring at the door. I wiped my palms against the fabric on the bed before pulling my knees tight against my chest.

Terror still grew inside of me. Terror that Asher would come back. Terror that he might be angry enough to punish me.

Would he call the guards? Demand that I am whipped or worse?

Robyn crossed back in front of me. She had retrieved the desk chair and now placed it between the bed and the door. I watched her lean down and pick up her bow and quiver from the bedside.

"Marian." She said my name and my breath caught in my throat. "No one will come through that door tonight. *No one.*"

There was a promise in her words, and I considered them for a moment. I watched the door, digging my nails into the sensitive skin on my thighs.

"Why should I trust you?" The question hung in the air between us. Yes, she had saved me, but she had also tormented and teased me. She had made it perfectly clear numerous times she was not interested in my friendship.

"You shouldn't. You shouldn't trust anyone, Marian. That is why I gave you the knife—so you could protect yourself. When you wake in the morning, I will teach you how to use it."

I considered her words. As a healer, I never considered that I might have to hurt another human being. In fact, I had vowed not to.

Could I do what she said? Could I learn to protect myself if it meant killing someone else?

I had killed the assassin on the road, but that was in defense of someone else. I considered her offer, the sting of my scalp throbbed painfully, and my skin crawled thinking back to Asher's hands against my body.

"I will not allow him to hurt me again."

"He will never have the chance." Robyn's words comforted me in a way I didn't expect. I finally looked away from the door, and I could see the determination in her eyes. Her back was rigid, and she had placed her sword between her knees.

Finally, my breathing seemed to slow, and I knew my exhaustion would win eventually. Soon my eyes were too heavy to keep open.

I repeated the words again and again until my body forced me to succumb to sleep.

No one would get through that door as long as Robyn guarded it.

I woke with a start, as I did most mornings. My heart raced, and my mind struggled to remember where I was.

The contents of the room seemed to shift back into focus, but it only added to my confusion. The desk nearby was not mine, and the trunk at the foot of the bed wasn't either.

"Do you want some water?" Robyn handed me a small glass, and I drank it heartily.

"I think you will need some burn salve for your head. I have some here." She handed me a small vial. She opened the contents, and I crinkled my nose at the sour smell.

"Yeah..." —Robyn scratched at the back of her head and then quickly secured the stopper—"I figured you might have something better."

"You should dump that out. I will bring you something better." I smiled as Robyn moved to put the vial on the desk. She shuffled across the room, which was when I finally noticed her feet.

"What are you wearing?" I bit my lip, trying desperately to control my laughter.

Robyn ran to the end of the bed, sliding across the smooth stone. She nearly toppled into the heavy frame as she hastily pulled the colorful socks from her feet.

The heavy lid of the trunk closed with a thud, and she stood beside it quietly. I waited for an explanation, giving her my most pointed look. Robyn ignored my stares, retrieving her blade from the bottom of her boot and then slid each onto her feet.

"Fine. Gawayne's grandmother has these sheep. They live high in the Impassable Mountains, where almost no one can reach them, except for her. She shears them once a year. Last year for the winter solstice she made us all socks. They are wonderfully warm and soft."

Robyn shrugged her shoulders, and I smiled in return. It was odd to see her so relaxed—so calm.

"You did say you hate when your feet get cold."

"Yes, and I wasn't quite calm enough yet to risk putting my boots on..." Her words trailed off, sucking all the air from the room.

She wasn't calm enough to not go after Asher.

I hung my head in my hands, memories of last night threatened to overwhelm me.

"I instructed the servants to bring lunch to your room, but you're welcome to stay in here if you prefer."

Robyn's kindness touched me. I knew she was trying to make me comfortable by giving me control. Part of me longed to stay locked in her room all day, but the other part knew if I didn't leave now I never would.

"I appreciate everything you have done, but I won't hide."

I walked to the door, trying not to let my legs tremble. I turned to glance at Robyn, surprised by the look in her eye. Her chin was set, and a smile rose at the side of her mouth. Unsure of the meaning of this look, I suddenly realized that in all this time I had not given her back her blade.

The stone hilt had warmed in my hands, and I moved to pass it back to her. Her smile widened as she pushed my hand away. "Keep it. I let you sleep through training today, but I won't do that tomorrow.

Robyn

Although I knew it was silly, I felt the need to walk Marian safely to her door. She was silent as she disappeared into her room, still clutching my dagger tight to her chest as the door clicked in place.

I waited for a moment, resting my head against the cool wood. I had spent all night and early morning silently praying that perhaps while escorting Asher to his quarters Samwell had somehow failed to save the prince from a tumble down the stairs. The longer the morning went on and no wails or cries of the prince's untimely demise filled the corridor, the more disappointed I became.

It wasn't quite late enough in the morning for the prince to rouse—not with the amount of whiskey he must have consumed last night.

It was time to make sure he had arrived safely to his quarters.

The halls were a bustle of noise. Princess Madawi's impending arrival was causing near-panic and hysteria inside the duke's castle. Yesterday two guards were whispering over dinner about how one of the ladies asked the duchess if somehow the castle could be made a shorter walk to the docks. She was apparently distraught that they could not somehow shorten the road.

The wing where the prince slept was deep in the castle, tucked away safely in case of invaders. Only two royal guards kept watch at his doorway. As a captain of the guard, they did not look at me twice as I entered the prince's suite.

*What fools...*I smiled to myself.

The room was vast, with several other rooms connecting to it. When the queen was present, she would stay in the adjoining room at her leisure. I peered through the darkness, looking for my first target.

Samwell jumped from the chair. His eyes were cold as he watched me cross the room. The queen's room would have no one in it, but Samwell walked to stand before the door anyway. I grabbed the large chair he had vacated, pressing it firmly before the second door which led to the footman's quarters.

With a jerk of my head, I motioned to the door. Samwell did not need to be a part of this. He did not move, and I waited to be certain. Samwell crossed his broad arms in front of his chest, and I knew he was there to stay.

I calmed my breath as I stalked toward the enormous bed. Hanging off one edge, like he had been thrown there, slept Prince Asher. His clothes reeked of vomit and his mouth hung open.

The soft bed sank beneath me as I leaned down. Asher did not stir as I retrieved the twin dagger of the one I had given Marian from my boot. Within seconds, I had secured his hands, twisting the sheets around them, and using the weight of my body to hold them in place.

Images of the burn on Marian's head floated through my mind. Her look of stark terror last night had been almost unbearable. Rage filled me again, and I struggled to choke it down.

With a noise that I found immensely satisfying, I brought my hand across the prince's face.

Asher's eyes opened immediately, but he was at least smart enough not to yell for help as I pressed the tip of the dagger against his throat. His face filled with rage, and he struggled to free his hands. But, as I predicted, he made no moves against me.

"Today, Prince Asher, is about *listening*. Do you understand?"

Asher's face paled a bit, but he nodded just slightly.

"You seem to be under the impression you don't need to listen. You don't need to listen to the cries of your people, the directions of your guards, or to women who do not want to sleep with you."

I watched as Asher's mind, muddled by alcohol, tried to piece together my words and why I was here.

"You have failed to listen, and for that, I should kill you, but I have other plans for now. For now, you're going to learn a valuable lesson. You. Will. Never. Force. A. Woman. Again." I poked the tip of my dagger into the prince's delicate skin with each word, watching tiny cuts open on his pampered skin. Anyone who saw it would simply assume that the prince's groomer had done a shit job while shaving.

"When I leave, you could run and tell the guards I attacked you. You could tell them I threatened you, but you won't."

Asher's brows furrowed together in disbelief.

69

"You won't because it's not just me who is tired of having nobles who don't listen. There are thousands of us out there. Your guards. Your servants. Your people. They are waiting for you to crack. They are waiting for you to fail—which is exactly what it will look like if you start accusing one of the oldest families in all of Notting of treason."

We stared at each other, and I did not look away from the prince's sapphire eyes until I was sure he understood.

"Choose your actions wisely. If I go down, another will simply take my place. It might be a guard who was paid off, it might be a servant. But, rest assured, we are watching. You will not see my arrow before it strikes you down."

I moved the blade away from Asher's throat. My heart pounded in my chest as I waited to see what he would do. The prince sat up in the bed, pulling the covers tight around him.

I looked at the prince one more time before crossing toward the door. He seemed to shake with terror as I slipped the blade back into my boot.

We left the room, and I breathed a sigh of relief as the guards did not immediately come chasing after us.

Samwell's face was pale. The reality of what I had just done settled over us. My stomach churned, threatening to spill its contents onto the floor.

"Your father is going to be pissed..." Samwell clapped me on the back as we headed up the stairs.

Marian

It had been a week since the incident with Asher, and each morning I found a different trinket outside my door. It was a desperate plea to try to win back my affection, but each present only soured my mind against the man who used to be my friend.

The first morning a maid had delivered an enormous ruby necklace in a cloth-lined jar, then earrings, then bracelets. I smiled wickedly to myself, remembering the price I had gotten for each piece at the jeweler's shop. It had been more than enough to cover the extra coin I needed to buy supplies for the people outside the gate.

An assortment of glass jars and vials littered the desk before me, waiting to be filled. I had spent days reading through the books borrowed from the city library, desperate to create some tinctures and cures to add to my list of supplies.

The sad, desperate faces of the people called out to me in my dreams, and I knew I had to do something other than drink tea with the duchess—lovely as she was—and avoid Asher and his adoring entourage.

In the nearby fireplace, I had begun boiling water to add to a healing remedy. The medicine would help to slow infection. My thoughts whirred through the list of tasks to be done before we returned to the capital.

I pulled the large pot from the fire with the hook, internally measuring how much echinacea I could get if I bartered with the kind trader I had met the day before.

The heavy pot threatened to splash its molten contents onto my legs, and I placed it down hastily as I suddenly remembered that I had also commissioned cloths from the local seamstresses for bandages.

A small, brown parchment book was spread across the desk. I searched the floor for the quill I had been using, only to topple the small jar of ink.

"Shit. Shit. Shit." I cursed myself as I mopped at the ink with the cloth napkin my breakfast had been wrapped in.

The ink spread over my hands, staining my skin as I panicked. The smell of smoke hit my nose. I looked over to see small tendrils of fire spreading across the sheets. Some of the coals from the pot had latched to the bottom and now ignited the thin fabric.

Panic filled me, and I wracked my brain with what to do first. Running to the head of my bed, I ripped the sheets off, sending the pot to the floor with an ear-splitting clang. The flames hurtled onto the floor with it, and I immediately folded the sheets over the embers, dousing them completely.

I truly had no response as Robyn came bursting through my chamber door, her face full of alarm and her sword drawn.

She scanned the room for the perceived intruder before her gaze fell on me again.

"What the hell are you doing?" Robyn bit her lip and covered her mouth with one hand--as if holding back laughter.

"I have so much to do!" I rubbed at the pounding in my temples and began lining the edge of the desk with empty vials from the crate I had secured at the market. "I need enough supplies for the tournament, but I also want to take some...elsewhere..." I caught myself, looking over to Robyn. She most assuredly would not permit me to wander beyond the city walls. Robyn cocked her brow at me suspiciously as I continued, "...and now the duchess has requested I teach a class to her assistants in the evening."

In the last week, whether her, or Gawayne, or Samwell, I seemed to have an escort everywhere. True to her word, she had arrived at my door every morning to take me to train with her, the two boys, and the captain of the duke's guard. They worked harder than I had ever dreamed. The morning started by running up and down the steep hill to the marketplace, followed by body workouts, before finally practicing some basic sparring moves in the training ring.

Watching Robyn spar with Captain Colet was like nothing I had ever seen before. They were a perfect match. Each woman moved and lunged around the ring like highly trained, deadly, dancers. Danyeil was more swift footed than Robyn, but Robyn had an ability to predict her opponent's moves that was uncanny.

My first attempt at sparring had been an absolute disaster. I could barely hold the heavy, wooden sword, and tripped twice over my own feet. Not once had any of the others laughed though. Each of my newly found friends had stood where I was, and I was grateful for their guidance.

I hoisted the heavy pot onto the desk, careful not to bump the glass vials. There was a soft clink as I dipped the vial into the pot.

"It's empty. Remember, you spilled it?" Robyn motioned to the damp floor between us as I remembered.

"Shit. I need to start over." I sighed, kicking the edge of the desk in frustration. Pain shot up my toes, and I fell to the ground. I did not have shoes on.

Several of the vials tipped, but I was grateful none of them fell from the desk on top of me. Hot tears welled behind my eyes, but I refused to let them fall.

Robyn was next to me in seconds. She squatted across from me on the floor, pressing our knees close together. I hung my head, still trying to control the rush of emotions overcoming me.

"I just...need to get all this done." I gestured to the desk and all my materials.

To my surprise, Robyn grabbed my hand gently. Her face was kind as she whispered, "You don't have to do all of this on your own. You are allowed to ask for help. Actually, it's expected of you to need help."

My chin quivered at her sudden kindness and understanding. She squeezed my palm as she continued, "Mistress Genevieve sent you with an assistant. Perhaps it is time you let her fulfill her role. Being a leader means knowing how to use the strengths of the people under your care. Kira seems to be quite...friendly." —We both laughed at that.— "Perhaps she can teach the classes or go to the market for you."

"That would help immensely." I sighed. Robyn's advice was so simple, but it gave me a newfound appreciation for who she truly was.

Captain Loxley, Leader of Men. I stared at her for a moment, thinking about all I had seen her do. She had led the caravan to safety, saved Gawayne, and stood up to Asher that night in the corridor. My heart

raced as I remembered the way she had burst through the door just
now, and the way she had watched over me that night.

The morning after the incident with Asher, Robyn had personally
overseen three new locks were installed on my chamber door. If I had
not forgotten to lock them when I came in, she would have struggled
greatly to burst through as she had.

As she sat across from me, the muscles of her forearms bulged
beneath her tunic, sending flips through my stomach. All week I had
watched her carefully, desperate to learn more so I wouldn't find
myself helpless again. Every day, it became more and more difficult to
ignore how stunning she was.

Every time she picked up a sword or drew her bow, I watched her
lithe muscles flex. When a bead of sweat dripped from her brow, I
found my eyes tracing the droplet's path down her throat. Suddenly I
was wondering what Robyn might look like beneath her tunic.

"I think, Marian, what you need is time away from this dreadful
castle…" My heart lurched threefold at the look of mischief in Robyn's
golden eyes. She helped me to my feet and her smile widened. She
picked up the cloth I had been using. Her touch was delicate as she
dabbed at the ink on my neck.

Despite the fervor and ferocity I had seen from her in the sparring
ring, she was gentle now. Her touch was delicate as she continued to
clean the ink now dripping onto my collar bone.

I felt my breath quicken as she wiped the last droplets off my
chest. I swallowed hard, trying to calm myself. Warmth spread
between my thighs, and I found myself filled with an ache that was
hard to ignore.

"What did you have in mind?"

Robyn spent three more hours helping me prepare the tinctures for
the people in the camps. It seemed that she had guessed my plans
quite easily.

She was hesitant to help at first, and when she did, she was always
double and triple-checking each step. "You're sure this is okay to
touch, right?" she asked every five minutes.

I assured her repeatedly that none of the ingredients would melt her skin like the vial I had thrown at the assassin. I laughed as she lifted a jar of wild raisin to her nose, making a face of absolute disgust.

"This one has gone bad. It smells like Gawayne's boots." Robyn thrust the small vile toward me, violently shaking her head.

"It's not gone bad, it's just not necessarily pleasant to smell. Though it will heal anything from a sore tongue to a high fever."

Robyn's brows raised and she made a distinct noise of approval.

"The berries are quite sweet though." I dumped a few into my palm, holding it up to show her. Robyn eyed it suspiciously before taking it from my hand. I bit my laughter back as she inspected the tiny bulb.

With a sigh, I popped one of the berries into my mouth. Her face was still full of doubt, so I stuck out my tongue at her, the small red berry balanced on the tip.

Something passed behind her eyes, and I felt a rush of warmth in response. I swallowed the berry. My face flushed as I poured the rest back into the vial. Robyn did not eat hers, instead, she dropped it back into the vial again.

When we finally finished, I began the clean-up as Robyn excused herself for a moment. My excitement grew, and I could hardly contain myself as I changed into my healer's garb. The white, leather pants Genevieve had given me were a bit tighter than they had been when we first left the capital. The cloth clung to my thighs like a second skin. It seemed that between my daily walks to the market and the week training with the others my muscles had begun to change and tone a bit.

The air inside the castle was already thick and oppressive. During one of the duchess' afternoon walks in the garden, she had given me a special corset. Unattached to a dress at the bottom, it would allow for easier movements while traveling or treating patients in the field. The stunning, pearl color would also signal my role as healer, notifying anyone nearby that I was there to help.

I slipped the top over my chest, before reaching around to tighten the long strings in the back. The fit was snug against my small breasts, pressing them together. Near the large armoire where I stored more of my formal clothing, stood a tall mirror. I adjusted my bust in the mirror, suddenly feeling insecure at the heavy dip in the front.

A soft knock at my door told me Robyn was ready. Except for this morning, she had not once entered my chambers without permission.

"Come in." I walked toward the desk, trying to figure out how I would smuggle all these vials out of the castle. Duke Ingles still had not allowed supplies to be sent to the camps, nor allowed any of the people into the city to purchase supplies for them. My heart ached at the thought.

How had they survived so long?

I began to gather my supplies in the center of the desk. I had a few boxes for supplies sent to the capital, but those were always marked by the duke's men at the gate, and then added to the next caravan headed out.

How would I keep these boxes from the guards?

The door clicked behind me, startling me from my thoughts, and I turned to ask Robyn for her ideas.

Robyn's thick, muscled arms held a long box, about the length of her torso, before her. Her golden eyes grew round, traveling up my body, over my pants, and finally resting on my corset. I watched her take a deep breath as she approached.

"I...have something for you." Robyn cleared her throat as she hurried to place the strange box onto the barren bed. Her face turned a deep red as I came near, and she did not raise her gaze from the floor.

I opened the box hesitantly, confused by her strange behavior. Two thick, leather straps hung from the edges of the box, they splayed out from the corners in a loop, like arms. I opened the latch, removing two more buckles and straps holding the lid on.

Inside the box were dozens of pairs of tiny straps secured to the interior. Each had a small buckle on one side. It took my mind a moment to puzzle out their purpose.

My breath caught as I looked at the vial in my hand. I placed the glass inside the box, securing it in place with one of the buckles.

"It's to transport vials." My mouth fell open as I hurried back toward the desk to get more.

Beside me, Robyn seemed to ease.

"Yeah. I had it made for you after I saw how you stored the scary vial." She grabbed some of the containers, securing them in place alongside me. "The inside is leather, so it can be easily cleaned, and the box is made from trees from Sherwood that are known for their durability."

I didn't know what to say as we continued filling the box. All of the tinctures I had made this morning fit easily inside, with room for more.

Robyn locked the lid, lifting the long box before me. I threaded my arms through the leather, securing the box in place along my back.

"I wanted it to be small enough and light enough to fit under a cloak." Robyn shrugged her shoulders as we looked over her gift. "Plus, if you're going to carry something that might melt someone's face, it should definitely not be tucked inside a roll of clothes."

I nodded in agreement. It was truly the best gift I had ever been given.

"This is…amazing. Thank you so much." I wrapped my arms around Robyn's broad shoulders in a tight hug. She tensed beneath me, and I released her. Embarrassment spread warmth across my cheeks.

The edge of Robyn's mouth curled upward again, and she ran her long fingers through her hair. We stood in silence for a moment, before Robyn finally spoke, "Now, let's go grab Marengo and Gold."

Robyn

It didn't take long for us to retrieve the horses and head for the outer gate. Dozens of faces turned toward us as we rode to the edge of the city.

Women and men alike waved at Marian as she rode by. It seemed she had developed more than a few relationships inside the city wall. More than once, someone stopped to gawk at her, and I had to keep myself from joining them.

Looking at Marian as she rode through the streets atop her white mare was like looking at the sun for too long. You got lost in the moment, dazzled by the beauty, and found your vision suddenly out of focus.

She knew what we were doing was directly against the crown's orders, but she risked their wrath anyway.

The guards nodded to us as we approached. I had worn my uniform for exactly this moment. These might not be my men, but they wouldn't question us.

A young, brunette soldier signaled to someone nearby, and the loud clanks of the gate began. Marian went still beside me--as if she were holding her breath.

We rode through beneath the gate and were almost immediately swallowed by the noise of the camps. Families were huddled at the canvas entrances, while young children scampered across the road.

Even from atop Gold, the tents seemed to stretch on toward the horizon. Marian guided her horse next to me, and I watched as she chewed her bottom lip in worry. For the first time, I was hesitant. It was one thing to send my father's men out into this, or to go out myself--if something happened, they could handle themselves. Marian was a different story.

Anxiety began to eat at me, but I reminded myself that this was her choice to make. Still, the more people who suddenly took notice of our presence, the tenser I became.

"Where would you like to begin? I think perhaps we should stay close to the main road in case of trouble. People from the capital are not always welcome among the camps."

Marian's frown grew as she looked around. In one, fluid motion she dismounted. Dust stirred around us as I followed suit.

Just ahead in the road was a small divot where a group of children played in rain water. Marian walked toward them, pulling Marengo gently by her reins.

"Hello. My name is Marian." Marian's voice cooed at the children, who looked up at her with wide-eyed expressions filled with curiosity.

"I have some very special sweets, and I was hoping you might tell me if you know any children around here who would like some...." The children's faces immediately filled with delight, but Marian took a step back.

"To get the sweets you must do two things first." I watched each child nod eagerly. "You must go ask your mommy or daddy or whoever takes care of you to come to see me so I know it's okay, and you must let me and my friend give you a check-up."

I laughed at the brilliance of Marian's plan. In seconds the children darted off in different directions. Marian approached Marengo, unstrapping the blanket roll she had secured to the horse earlier.

She draped the blanket across the rough ground, right in the middle of the main road. Together we started unloading the rest of the supplies hidden amongst our bags. In only a few minutes, piles of food and supplies were spread across the blanket. My mind filled with awe at everything Marian had managed to bring.

Without a word, she sat in the center of the blanket and waited for her first patients to arrive. I stood behind her, wary of every murmur, as more people began to take notice of our little display.

I knew that the eyes of the crown were certainly on us. The guards posted along the wall would surely report everything.

It didn't take long for the children to return. Many of them held tight to the hands of their parents—dragging the adults from all sides of the camp.

It seemed word had spread quickly. New, curious faces also appeared from all sides.

"Hello. My name is Marian."

Several of the children held their hands out eagerly as Marian whispered 'not yet' to them. Something warm spread through my chest as she winked at them playfully.

"I am the Royal Healer, and today I would like to help those who need it."

"Everyone in this camp needs help, or we wouldn't be here." A young mother spoke from the crowd. A small boy held her hand, and another babe hung from a makeshift sling across her shoulder.

Marian shuffled her feet on the ground, and I knew she wasn't expecting resistance.

"We know the unfair restrictions placed on you. We are here to help." I walked to Marian's side as I spoke.

"Leave the supplies and let us be. The crown doesn't care for us." An older man with a grizzled beard and a crooked back spat at Marian's feet.

I gripped the hilt of my sword, ready to defend us if necessary, but Marian grabbed at my hand. She shook her head calmly, and then she looked out over the crowd that had gathered.

"I'm not here on behalf of the crown. I'm here on behalf of what is right. You are citizens of Notting. You are human. You deserve to live with access to the same care as any other person—and for that, you deserve the best treatment I can give. If you wish to take supplies you may. If there is an illness or ailment I can treat, I will gladly help."

The road filled with an awkward silence, until finally, the young mother approached.

"My daughter cries when she takes to my breast, and her mouth seems swollen and sore." Marian nodded, leaning toward the babe nestled in the hammock.

She rinsed her hands with the water cask at her side, before gently opening the babe's mouth. The people around us watched warily, and I felt again that we were being somehow tested.

Marian searched the pile behind us, grabbing a small vial from the box. She opened a small leather pouch and began scooping a bit of the white substance inside into the vial.

"This is just salt." The woman's brows drew together. "Mix it with some warm water and rub it along the babe's gums three times a day. This should reduce the pain and cure the sores." The young mother stroked the babe's hair, taking the vial from Marian's hand.

"Can I look at him now?" Marian leaned down toward the boy. "Can you jump really high? As high as my horse?" The boy nodded excitedly before bending down and leaping toward the sky. "Can you take a deep breath and hold it like you are under water?"

The boy's face turned pink, and Marian told him to release it. I couldn't help but smile as she ran him through a number of other tests. I recognized them immediately for what they were, ways to determine the boy's reflexes and growth.

"Great job. If mom says it's okay, you can have a sweet." The boy's chin began to quiver before Marian had even finished speaking. It sent all of us into a fit of laughter.

The tension along the road seemed to ease. The boy and his mother disappeared among the sea of tents, and more children began lining up for their turn.

It wasn't until nearly an hour later that we realized we hadn't even begun to put a dent in the crowd. Marian had smashed the candies to pieces to help them go around, but there were more than just children to attend to here.

"We need a better system," I whispered to Marian as more people began to fill the edges of the road.

Marian nodded, and I watched calculating each face around us. She looked over the horses, and then back at me. Her gaze lingered on my bow for a moment, and I watched an excited grin spread across her cheeks.

"I need an assistant," Marian yelled to the crowd. "Someone who knows everyone and can help guide us to those who need the most care."

There was a murmur among the crowd as they all turned to face one another, pointing and urging different people forward.

Finally, an older man limped forward. He ambled toward Marian, several members of the crowd nodding at him in recognition. The man's thick, salt and pepper brows were drawn together. He looked Marian over with a frown spread across his wrinkled cheeks.

"Hello, sir. Could you help me with something?"

"My name is Lawrence. No one has ever called me 'sir' before. Don't know why you would want to now." Again, the man looked skeptically toward Marian.

"I believe leaders should be rewarded with a title. Sometimes they earn that title... sometimes they don't." Mari whispered the last part, giving the old man a sly wink. "You have obviously been nominated by these people as their leader..." She swept her arm across the crowd and her meaning was clear.

He seemed to chew on Marian's words for a moment, running his frail fingers through his long beard. "Yeah alright, Ma'am." —Marian and I both chucked as he returned her wink— "What is it you need?"

"We need a clear way to discern which tents need care first. I need to be able to spot the tent a ways away, and to be able to send my assistant or others there if necessary."

Marian looked at me, and I nodded in approval.

It seemed she had taken my suggestion to begin using Kira for more than flirting.

"Like a sign or a note?" I thought back to the notes father had been passing me these months.

"Not everyone can read." Lawrence shrugged his shoulders, and I immediately realized my mistake. Sometimes I forgot how fortunate my upbringing had been.

"What you need is a flag." Lawrence pointed to the pole at the center of the nearest tent, hoisted high above our heads. A piece of the patchwork had come loose and flapped in the gentle breeze. "I dunno how you would get it up there without taking the tents down though."

Marian rubbed at her temples with her hands, and I knew she was devising a plan. She turned toward me, and I shrugged my shoulders.

"Robyn will do it."

Marian's eyes swept across the ground, and she knelt, tugging at the thick blanket under our supplies. Her chin jutted outward, and her brows pulled together when she could not get it to tear.

A breeze swept through, stirring dust up around us. As it left, Marian patted down her thick braid as it rested against her shoulders. Her head shot up excitedly and she immediately released the leather tie from the end. As always, a long, white ribbon had been plaited through her hair. It was just another symbol marking her as a healer.

The ribbon continued to unravel, and I realized I had no idea the true length.

My chest swelled with pride as she retrieved from her boot the knife I had given her. Marian began cutting and tearing strips of the ribbon, each about half the length of her forearm. A small field of fabric littered the ground around her when she was finished.

Marian stood, carrying one of the strips clutched in her hands. She held it out to me.

I cocked my head, unsure of her intent. Lawrence seemed just as baffled. Marian looked between us like she truly didn't understand why we were so confused.

"Robyn will attach this ribbon to the arrow and shoot it at the center pole of each tent. This way I know which tents need help the most and the tents are marked in the future when we come back."

Lawrence laughed, clapping his hands as he went to retrieve the shreds of ribbon. Once again, the crowd around us began to murmur.

I pulled an arrow from my quiver and then took the fabric from Marian's hand. She smiled up at me so confidently and it was hard to ignore the feeling in my stomach when our hands touched.

"Ay! You're a bunch of fools. We can't have arrows flying down from the sky when she misses." It was the older man who had spit at Marian that spoke now.

My blood began to boil, and I turned to yell back at the man. Once again, it was Marian who stopped me. My heart nearly skipped a beat as she placed a warm hand on my chest, stepping in front of me.

"If you have a better idea, by all means, contribute something other than fluids." I held back my laughter at her words. Lawrence did not. His cackle filled the air as he gathered more ribbon in his hands. "Your fear of injury is unnecessary. Robyn does not miss."

My mouth fell open at her words. Though I may be confident in my skills, it wasn't something I had expected to hear from someone I had insulted so many times.

Marian looked back toward me, and I was unsure what to say.

I speared the tip of the arrow through the thin fabric. First I balanced the weight on my fingertips, and considered how the fabric changed the feel. I could feel the eyes of everyone watching, but especially Marian.

The center poles in each tent might vary a bit, but each towered over us. The sun warmed my skin and the breeze brushed gently against my hand. I took a breath as I knocked the arrow into place on the bow. The ribbon danced lazily across my arm.

My knuckles touched gently against my cheek as I pulled the bowstring tight and adjusted my aim. I took another breath as I released it.

You cannot disappoint her, played over and over in my mind as the arrow whizzed through the sky. There was a loud, satisfying sound of the tip splitting into the wood before I released the breath I had been holding.

I spent the day following Lawrence around from tent to tent. Although we intended to start in one area, it quickly became apparent we would be marking tents all across the massive field.

To my astonishment, Marian never tired. She continued on to each tent, hardly stopping to eat or drink, until well into the afternoon. Once the people began to trust her the requests came out in droves. Marian looked at every boil and every sore. She gave tinctures for cuts and infections on every man, woman, or child who asked for her aid. Lawrence and I ran out of ribbon quickly, and instead began marking down the supplies that people begged us to gather.

Marian washed her hands again in a water flask someone had graciously given us. The blood and dirt washed away, and I noticed the exhaustion in her gaze.

"You don't have to do it all today. You have done so much. Let's return to our horses."

The supplies, and the blanket, were gone when we returned to the horses. Marian seemed to look down the road again.

"How can I be this weary and still feel like I have done so little?"

I considered how to respond for a moment as I climbed onto Gold's back. I looked out at the white ribbons flapping in the breeze.

An idea struck me. I realized that I could do it. I could show her the truth of what we had been fighting the crown so hard for.

"This is only a small portion. I have been all across Notting. I have fought against the tribesmen from Aicias and seen the plight on the land first-hand. You have no idea how many are out there. You have no idea how many sick and injured and starved are spread amongst the land and the trees." My throat constricted as I struggled with the emotions suddenly choking me.

"Could you show me?" Her sapphire eyes looked up at me from the ground. She had been toiling all day to save people she didn't even know. Her delicate, white, healer's garb once glowing in the morning light was now covered in the blood, dust, and debris from the day.

My breath caught in my throat as I stuck my hand out for Marian.

"I have been waiting to show you." My heart beat wildly against my chest. Part of me worried about what might happen if I truly showed her what was hidden in the woods. The other part was terrified of what might happen if I didn't.

Marian's hand gripped mine as I helped her onto the back of the saddle. Her smile dazzled me, sending flips through my stomach. Her arms wrapped tight around my waist, settling just below my breasts, and I knew I would remember the feel of her against me for as long as I lived.

I moved the horse through the camp, and before long we were back on the road. In the distance, the branches of Sherwood waved at us, beckoning us onward.

Marian

We rode atop Robyn's horse for a while, pulling Marengo behind us. The trees of Sherwood grew larger before us. We approached the tall branches as their shadows stretched across the field. The light behind us was dimming, and I knew we would have to make camp soon. Whatever Robyn had to show me would have to wait until the morn.

Trepidation filled me as I squeezed Robyn tighter. The trail around us grew narrow, almost indecipherable from the brush against the ground.

"Should we dismount?" I whispered against the back of Robyn's slender neck.

"The horses of Sherwood are born in the wood. Even the mares used for Castle Loxley are taken into the woods to give birth." Robyn leaned forward as she spoke, patting the long, roan neck of her horse. "She knows where to go."

Indeed, as we traveled into the dark woods, the horse seemed to lead down the narrowing path. To my surprise, Marengo seemed to follow comfortably as well. The crickets sang us their songs as we trudged along. From the boughs overhead the birds called to each other, settling for the evening.

"I have missed these trees." Robyn whispered, and I wondered if she meant for me to hear it at all.

"I have always loved the forest and the fields." I looked around us, truly marveling at the forest life. The breeze swept over as we rode low against Gold's back.

"My family has looked after Sherwood for hundreds of years. It is said they were the first settlers of Notting, back when the people were one with the trees and well before any king came to make his claim."

Robyn's words were low and thoughtful as she spoke of her family's history. Some part of me knew that what she was saying was treason. No one but the king owned the land. His subjects only worked the land for him. But another part of me whispered not to interrupt. Robyn spoke with calm reverence--like she was sharing a secret not many knew.

I remembered the maps I had studied during my lessons when I was younger. Sherwood was vast. Its branches stretched hundreds of miles, from one coast of Notting to the other. The southern edge butted up against The Impassable Mountains—where Castle Loxley was said to hide amongst the clouds.

Not many in the kingdom had been to Castle Loxley. It took weeks, sometimes months, to traverse the harsh forest terrain. It was said it was easy for visitors to get swallowed by the forest. Many were never seen again.

I looked around at the dense woods. Each trunk, each piece of brush suddenly blended together, and my heart quickened in response. It would be very easy to get lost here, and no one would ever find me again.

"What is it like?" I asked the question before considering that Robyn might choose not to respond.

In front of me, she drew in a deep breath, as if considering my question and whether or not to answer. I knew she had secrets. She had been disappearing for hours at a time for weeks just after breakfast.

But this secret seemed different, maybe even more personal. I was asking for something much more personal than just who she was sneaking off with. This was her history. Her people's history.

We traveled in silence for several minutes, until I had resigned myself that even more of my questions would go unanswered.

"It's stunning." Robyn lifted her head, looking off into the distance as if she could see the thing she pictured in her mind. "Castle Loxley was built hundreds of years ago, but you'd never know it. The stone was worked and worked until it shined. The castle is nestled against a spring that flows high into the mountains, and the water deposits into a lake that looks like it is made of glass."

She turned to look over her shoulder at me now, and I leaned my head forward to show I was listening. "In the winter, when the lake is frozen, we host contests to see how far we can make it across the frozen water without falling. Men actually ride their shields down the hill and across the lake. Father holds the record."

Robyn chuckled softly and I found myself laughing with her. I had not met her father, but I couldn't imagine any nobleman slipping and sliding across the ice without laughing. "Truly?"

"My mother used to say he was so good at it because his big head kept him balanced, and his gut gave him a push. He holds the record for the longest and furthest trek through the Impossible Mountains." Her laughter filled the forest around us, startling the birds from the trees. I laughed along with her, suddenly envious of her adventures.

"I miss her." Robyn's body went tense again. Her laughter faded and was replaced by something else. "She was the first one to place a blade in my hand."

"What happened to her?" I rested my cheek against her back as we rode. Although I wasn't sure why, I desperately needed to comfort her.

"She fought in the great war until my father and her met. They married, and she stayed behind. No one has ever breached Loxley's walls, due in large part to her." I listened to the pride in Robyn's voice as she continued. "She got ill when I was seven. I was away training. Father and I both were. When we returned, she had passed. It had been months since we'd seen her." At her waist, Robyn's warm hand draped over mine.

She cleared her throat, and I knew that was all she would say on the subject for now. "What about your family? How did you become the king's ward?"

It was my turn to be silent. Listening to Robyn talk about her family and their traditions opened old wounds I had fought long and hard to forget.

"All I know is that my mother died during childbirth. She never told anyone who my father was, but she and Queen Naomi were close, so the queen took me in and raised me in the castle."

I breathed in the cool air of the forest around me, as a familiar heaviness sat in my chest. Robyn said nothing, and I realized she was waiting for more.

"My mother had money when she passed, and it was overseen by the king and queen. They told me when I was finally old enough to understand that it would be used to pay for everything until I was of age. Each year I received a letter, detailing the costs of my clothes, my food, and everything else it cost to stay in the castle. I realized when I was about eight that it would be gone well before I was old enough to live on my own.

"I moved to the healer's tower the year I turned ten. Three years younger than most acolytes do. The queen had made it known, in no uncertain terms, that I would be thrown out of the castle at the first sign I couldn't pay."

Robyn shifted in front of me, startling me from my melancholy thoughts. Her rough fingers intertwined with my own, bringing warm tears to my eyes. It was the truest sign of friendship she had shown me.

"I remember the day you were presented at court." I smiled a little at the memory.

"Do you?" Robyn's tone was sharp as she responded.

"I remember how your parents stood beside you. They looked so proud, but you looked like you would rather be anywhere else..."A soft chuckle shook from Robyn, and I knew we were both remembering that day. "Then, Prince Asher took your hand to give it a kiss, and you spewed purple vomit all over his arm."

I tried not to, but I couldn't hold back the laughter. Robyn's roar spilled from her, startling the birds from the trees.

"Do you know that was Samwell's fault? He gave me some berries he'd picked on the journey, only moments before we walked in the throne room. I was sick for days!"

"I remember that, and I remember how absolutely furious Asher was. They never got the purple out of his favorite shirt."

Robyn's laughter died at the mention of Asher, which seemed to bring the revelry to a complete halt. Robyn dropped my hand as she adjusted her hold on the reins.

We rode in awkward silence until the sun was barely a distant memory in the sky. As we entered a small clearing, Robyn pulled Gold up short next to a shallow, trickling creek.

I could feel that our time of sharing secrets was coming to an end, and I knew I couldn't ignore a question I had been wondering ever since that morning when the young woman had flirted with Robyn at breakfast.

"Robyn...Did—did you ever find that brothel?"

I regretted the words as soon as they were free from my lips. It really was none of my business, I reminded myself again. Why should I care who Robyn did or did not bed?

"Ha. Actually, I'm not a fan of them. I've only ever been once, to celebrate with Samwell and Gawayne the three of us coming to age. Apparently, there are many who assume I enjoy the company of women, so I must enjoy the company of anyone."

Robyn shrugged her shoulders, but I could tell that it bothered her much more than she let on. Guilt filled me as I remembered that though I knew better, I had allowed the Court gossips to warp my opinion.

The world seemed to fall away around us as we made camp. The familiar sounds of night began to sing through the trees. Crickets and frogs filled the air around us, as I spread out the bed rolls and Robyn dug a pit for the fire.

"If you're going to hang about, you should at least bring some wood over and make yourself useful." Startled, I whipped my head toward Robyn as she spoke loudly. Her voice carried, and from the distance, there was the sound of laughter. My confusion multiplied as two men emerged from the tree line.

I recognized them at once. As suggested, both Samwell and Gawayne crossed the clearing, each carrying armfuls of tinder.

Samwell dropped his logs in a heap on the ground, joining me instantly on the bedroll as we watched Robyn try to light a small pile of tinder with her flint. Her frustrated grumbling grew as she leaned closer.

After setting his pile on the ground, Gawayne disappeared back into the tree line. He emerged a few seconds later, pulling the reins of their horses and settling them next to Gold and Marengo.

Robyn continued to try lighting the wood in the pit as Gawayne came to stand over her. My new friends seemed to share some knowing look between them. Robyn grew more agitated as she breathed onto the pile. Tiny wafts of smoke drifted toward her, but there were still no flames.

"Robyn is shit at lighting fires...." Samwell's attempts at whispering in my ear only brought him a death stare from Robyn.

After several more minutes, Robyn tossed the flint angrily into the pit, and I had to fight to suppress my laughter. Neither Samwell nor Gawayne bothered hiding theirs.

"It's too gods-damned wet." Robyn declared, before stalking off, muttering about "checking on the horses."

"Watch this…" From beside me, Samwell nudged me with his elbow as Gawayne leaned down into the shallow hole. With only a few strikes, he had flames. By the time Robyn came back carrying more bedrolls, the clearing was bright with the light of the blaze before us.

"You were telling her wrong earlier. Robyn is shit at telling stories too." Gawayne laughed as he rested near the fire. "They're the 'impassable mountains', not the 'impossible mountains.'"

I realized for the first time just how long the two of them had been following us.

"No. My mother always said it was 'impassible.'" Samwell argued as he added wood to the fire.

"Perhaps it is both?"

The two men looked at me strangely, as if they had never considered that before.

Near the edge of the forest, I noticed Gold picking at her bandage.

I searched the box of tinctures, finding one that would soothe her tender skin. It took only a few moments for me to change the bandage out. I crossed back toward the fire just as Robyn reappeared from the tree line ahead.

"Asshole," Robyn muttered as she watched Gawayne's fire come to life. With a sour look, she tossed each of the men their bedrolls.

"You know what, Cap?" Gawayne's deep voice was filled with laughter as he spoke, "For that, you can keep the first watch."

"Yeah, because you were going to volunteer." Robyn rolled her eyes as she circled the fire.

Next to me, Samwell had once again placed himself along my side. The rough wool of his blanket overlapped with mine as he splayed out on the bedroll. I couldn't help but smile.

"Are you afraid of the dark?" It was my turn to tease him, nudging his backside with my knee as he turned over. One arm was tucked under his head as he pretended to snore.

The long day of helping those in the camps and riding through the thick forest began to settle over me as I lay under the blankets. Between the fire and Samwell--who I quickly realized emitted nearly as much heat—I began to feel just how tired I had become.

"Better watch out, he's a snuggler…" Gawayne whispered from his bedroll on the other side of the fire. Not failing to miss his opportunity, I felt Samwell scoot closer to me, just a bit.

"Samwell, you have the second watch." A low whine sounded behind me. Robyn rounded the fire once more before coming to sit just above my head. "And you get to dig the latrines." A longer whine followed.

Just as sleep was about to take me, I glanced one last time toward Robyn as her intense, golden eyes scanned the tree line. The wood of her bow glinted off the firelight as it rested in her lap. She turned the long shaft of an arrow between her fingers, and I knew she could probably send it through her target before any of us so much as stirred. A breeze swept through her short hair, pushing it away from her face, which instantly became aglow against the night sky.

I fell asleep more warm and more comforted underneath her trees than I ever had in any castle.

Robyn

I awoke Samwell for his watch only when I could no longer fend off sleep. Just as Gawayne had predicted, Samwell had to peel himself away from Marian's sleeping form.

All night I had paced the fire, relentlessly inspecting the trees, stoking the embers to keep us warm, and avoiding the very bedroll I now longed to crawl into.

Something foreign and irritating grew in my stomach whenever I looked at Samwell intertwined with Marian. Even through the blanket, I could see where their bodies met.

I had allowed the fire to die down, leaving only the embers for heat. A chill fell over my skin, and I knew that I should retrieve my bedroll from the horses, but the thought of the warm blankets beckoned me, and my weariness won out in the end.

I tried to push the image from my mind as I crawled into the roll behind her. Unlike Samwell, I didn't tend to seek company in my sleep. I didn't tend to sleep with company at all.

Though it wasn't forbidden, there were very few female soldiers in the king's Army. Being constantly outnumbered by men made it easy to become the target of lustful stares and attracted far too much attention than I wanted. I'd learned quickly that the easiest way to settle an annoying man persistently inviting you to bed was with a blade pressed firmly against his throat.

A sigh escaped me as the warmth of the blankets settled around my shoulders. The cold of the ground underneath sent shivers down my spine, but I forced myself not to crawl closer to Marian.

Watching Marian today had been so much different than I expected. Though the Loxleys were one of the oldest noble families in Notting, Court had always been a kind of chore. It was a necessary evil that I shied away from well before I enlisted in the king's Army at eight.

The day my mother and father presented me to court was one of the worst of my life. We arrived with a small caravan. Gawayne and Samwell had accompanied me. We all were to stay at court for a year until our formal training began.

Though some children began attending court as young as four or five, Father had waited until I was nearly seven to bring me. Leaving Castle Loxley was not easy. Only the most highly skilled captains could make it through the inlet out to the sea, and even then, only smaller vessels made the journey more than once. The safest way to the king was through Sherwood Forest, and that took nearly a month by horseback.

Mother had spent hours after our arrival combing my hair and adjusting my gown. I hated that gown, though I would wear similar ones for years to come. It wasn't until the end of my first year of training that I vowed to never don the oppressive cloth again.

Even at such a young age, I knew what was expected. Father had fought for the late King John, who had led our armies to victory over the north. I always believed I would fight for King Ruelle and, when the time came, Prince Asher too.

I had no idea how much would change in just a few, short years.

I hadn't expected to spend my first three days at court in and out of consciousness, much less with my head in a bucket. Though the berries had left me weak and defeated, I finally recovered.

Mother and I spent the days walking the gardens, and the evenings reading and enjoying each other's company. When she left a week later to return to Castle Loxley, it was the last time I would see her.

Heaviness sat in my chest like a stone as I remembered the way she had waved to me all the way to the outermost gate. I spent that night crying in my room. Father was already away on business for the king, and I was truly alone for the first time in my life.

Within seconds of spreading out on my bedroll, sleep pulled at me. Samwell stoked the fire nearby, trying to bring warmth back to our little camp.

As if sensing my presence, or perhaps seeking my warmth, Marian's sleeping form turned over. Her long arm fell across my chest as the rest of her tucked in tight against me.

One of her legs spread over me, and I did my best to ignore the way the warmth of her thighs felt against mine.

In the back of my mind I imagined what it might be like to feel her really grind against me. I imagined how warm she would be in my hands. An ache grew deep in my core, and a throbbing sensation settled between my thighs until it was almost painful. I drifted to sleep before I remembered I should push her away.

The smell of lavender floated through my dreams. I ran my hands through the warm waters of a stream, letting the current slip through my fingers like strands of silk. The sun was peeking over the treetops. Long, beautiful rays shined through the branches.

The sound of laughter came from somewhere in the distance. I peered past the trunks, desperate to see its source. The undergrowth was soft beneath my feet as I approached a tree with a trunk as wide as my arms could stretch. On one side of the trunk rested a hand with long, delicate fingers.

I reached out to grab it. I wanted desperately to hold that hand with my own. Just as I reached for it, the hand was gone.

The sounds of feet shuffling on the ground stirred me into consciousness. Though my back instantly reminded me I had slept on the cold, hard ground, the next thing I felt was the peaceful warmth enveloping me.

An unfamiliar, but oddly comforting, weight clung to my chest. I gathered my thoughts, struggling to pull myself away from the peacefulness of sleep. Though my toes had grown cold, my fingers were surprisingly warm.

"Have you ever seen Robyn sleep past sunrise?" Gawayne's gruff voice whispered somewhere nearby.

"Never thought I'd see the day." It was Samwell whispering now. "Can't say I blame her though. I always sleep in when there's a woman on my arm. Now, if you *really* want to sleep in try one on each—ow!"

There was a soft thump, and I knew Gawayne had smacked Samwell on the head--as we both had many, many times before. "Shut up, Sam. It's too early to hear about your wayward tavern nights."

Samwell's words brought me crashing back to reality as I realized the weight resting against me was Marian's sleeping form. Exhaustion might have overtaken me last night, but with the clarity that daylight brought, I was forced to remember the truth.

I might know a little more about Marian's history now, but that didn't change who she was. She was another noble woman. As Royal Healer she would cater to the exact system we were trying desperately to change.

With a sigh, I began to gently lift Marian's arm. Her long, blond locks had fallen over my other hand. I pulled my arm out from underneath her.

My heart nearly leapt from my chest as Marian jolted upright. Her hair fanned out around her as her hands searched the ground. She was frantically searching for something.

I sat up immediately, watching for a second at her panicked, unfocused stare. I recognized it immediately. I'd seen that look plenty of times on men who came back terrified of the horrors of war haunting their dreams.

"Hey. Hey!" I grabbed Marian's shoulders tight, shaking her gently. She seemed to look past me for a second, before her gaze finally came back into focus. She shook her head gently--as if casting away some nightmare.

Beneath my grip, Marian shivered. Her breath came in quick bursts, but I watched her come back to herself as she pulled away.

"I—I am sorry." Marian stood abruptly, looking out over at camp before walking slowly toward the stream.

My first instinct was to chase after her, but as I stood Gawayne's broad hand fell to my shoulder. "Give her a minute," was all he said as we watched her walk away.

We broke camp in silence, loading the horses back up with our meager supplies. Marian said nothing as she checked her bags. I did one last check of Gold, surprised to find that Marian had at some point changed the horse's bandage.

Tension hung in the air between us as Samwell and Gawayne mounted their horses.

"Marengo seems to follow well. You can ride her if you prefer." Marian still didn't speak, though she nodded in acknowledgment before mounting.

The village was only another hour's ride. We followed the narrow path one at a time until the trees began to thin, giving way to a grand opening where a dozen small houses had been built.

"How do they survive?" Marian's voice was filled with wonder as she rode up beside me.

"They get a lot of their game from the forest, but they also barter and trade with other villages." Gawayne's voice was full of pride as he spoke. "This is Hazo. There are villages like it throughout Sherwood, though you could look for years and never find any of them."

Marian's brows scrunched in confusion as Gawayne spoke. We neared the edge of the village, bringing our horses up behind one of the houses. Gawayne continued while we began to dismount.

"These people have lived for generations in the safety of the trees. Many of these villages have survived because the forest is so thick and wild that they cannot be found, except by those who already know their location."

"We are not all that mysterious as these three make it sound." A short elderly woman rounded the corner of the house as she spoke. Her gray eyes were full of joy as she approached Gawayne.

"Keata!" Gawayne wrapped his broad arms around the old woman in a tight embrace. Samwell approached, just as Gawayne released her before he too hugged Keata.

Beside me, Marian laughed as the older woman snuck a kiss on Samwell's cheek. I joined the fray, Keata's arms squeezing me gently.

"You have brought me gifts, I assume?" Keata's toothless smile beamed at me as she peered at our horses.

"Only for the most beautiful woman in the village would we trek so far." Samwell crooned as he began to unpack the small hoard of supplies from our horses.

"You have brought me more than gifts this time." Keata hobbled toward Marian as we all watched nervously. Villages were notoriously hostile toward outsiders, even well-meaning ones. Keata's gray eyes seemed to inspect Marian. I watched her gaze trail over the dirt-stained pants and the leaves embedded in Marian's hair.

Tension rose in the air between us all. Samwell and Gawayne passed me anxious looks. We all knew Keata was an influential elder in this village, and her opinion would determine whether others would accept Marian's aid.

"Even in the villages, we have heard of the healer who comes from the castle. She trudges city streets, walks among the camps, and seeks out those most in the castle think are beneath them…" My heart rose to my throat. Keata grabbed Marian's hand, bringing it closer. "We have heard of your kindness, and we welcome any help you may give."

Keata wrapped her arm around Marian's before leading her through the village. Samwell, Gawayne, and I released a collective breath.

Hours passed as every manner of villager came to greet us. Once again, I watched Marian disappear into the throng. Eventually, we brought a large worktable and chairs over from one of the nearby homes. It wasn't as clean or sturdy as some of the healer's tables at the tower, but it would do.

Villagers of all ages began to form a line toward Marian as she waited at the center. Just as with yesterday, she never seemed to tire. Though her supplies quickly depleted, between her and Keata—who also served as the village herbalist— they managed to find cures or remedies for nearly everyone.

Gawayne and Samwell hovered nearby, bartering and trading their supplies to the local merchants. I brought both women cups of water as the day went on, which they eagerly drank. Though it took all three of us to convince the women to stop and eat, Keata was the first to retire. She sank back in her rickety chair with a sigh as Marian continued.

The same, strange pride filled me once again as I watched Marian work. More than once I had to step away from the sores or pustules— something my stomach couldn't handle. But she was content to lance, stent, or treat any malady.

As the sun began to wane in the sky, the last of the villagers disappeared. Until, finally, there was only one woman, I had never seen before, left behind. The young woman's long, brown hair was plaited behind her and swayed as she approached. Though her clothes looked worn and a bit tattered, they were tight over her swollen belly.

Marian never missed a beat as she brought the chair around the table, offering the pregnant woman a place to rest.

"Thank you." The young woman let out a deep breath as she rested back in the chair.

"Anya here is my apprentice." Keata rubbed the young girl's back as the two women smiled at each other. "She's the fastest learner I've ever seen. Never has to be told twice."

I watched as Marian smiled before leaning down to feel the underside of the woman's stomach.

"My last one barely made it out. She came out all twisted..."Anya's words trailed off as if they were too painful to even finish.

"We nearly lost them both." Keata's voice was solemn. Her shoulders slumped forward with worry.

"When you are near the end, make sure to get lots of rest, and eat anything in sight." Marian smiled up at the other woman. "Keata can give you some herbs for your nausea. I wish you were closer to the tower, where one of our midwives could help you better. I've seen them work miracles when babies come out stubborn."

Anya seemed soothed by Marian's words, but I could see the familiar look of concern behind Marian's gaze.

"Perhaps we will journey there before we get too close to the end." Anya rose from the chair, Marian and Keata reaching out to assist her.

"If you are as good as Keata says, I would happily give you a job in the tower."

Anya's eyes lit up at Marian's words. "Truly?"

"Absolutely, and then you could bring some of this training back to the village and pass it on to help others."

Anya nodded in agreement. A few minutes later, she walked off with a new sense of purpose, followed closely by Keata—who declared she wanted to see the girl home safely.

Beside me, Marian released a long, weary sigh before dipping her hands in the wash bucket. The sun was beginning to set as the day's work was finally over.

Gawayne rose from his perch along the side of the well, stretching his wide arms. "As much as we might not like to, perhaps we should ride back to last night's camp? I know Keata would allow us to stay, but it seems better to not impose."

Marian, Samwell, and I nodded our agreement.

Night had begun to grow in the trees as we entered the path again. In my weariness, I did not notice the silence as it spread through Sherwood.

Marian

Night had fallen around us by the time we arrived. Marengo and I were the first into the clearing, with Samwell and Gawayne close behind. Robyn pulled up behind her men as we all began to dismount.

My body was weary with exhaustion, but my thoughts still reeled with everything I'd seen. There were so many in the village that needed aid. *If Robyn was telling the truth about the other villages throughout Sherwood, there was still much, much more to be done.*

As my stomach rumbled angrily, I was reminded of Anya's swollen belly and my promise to her. Perhaps if she were truly to come to the tower to study, we could fill the hole that Notting so desperately needed. Perhaps, if Anya was willing to learn, there were others who would be willing to learn as well. Each of the noble families had healers who served them. *Why shouldn't there be healers in some of the villages as well? Robyn seemed to know the villages better than anyone, maybe she had an idea of what could be done to help them.*

"Rob—" A rough hand fell over my mouth as I spoke. I grabbed at Robyn's hand as my anger rose. Her finger moved toward her mouth, silently warning me. My heart leapt to my throat as my mind struggled to catch up.

Then the realization hit. All around us, the forest was quiet. There were no crickets to greet us. No curious squirrels or chipmunks skittered nearby. Even our horses had a look of alarm. Gold's ears perked, and Marengo stomped the ground behind me.

A hush had fallen through the trees. Signs of a predator nearby.

Robyn lowered her hand from my mouth to my shoulder, pressing my back against Marengo's warm side. Like the well-trained unit they were, Samwell and Gawayne posted themselves on either side of Robyn. Their swords were drawn at their sides.

Silence stretched around us while I forced myself not to panic. I scanned the tree line, trying desperately to see whatever was coming.

Robyn retrieved her bow from Gold's saddle, before silently drawing an arrow from the quiver at her back. I crouched, keeping my eyes toward the trees, and retrieved Robyn's small blade from the inside of my boot.

Without making a single sound, six silent figures in black hoods appeared from the brush, before fanning out around us. I knew immediately they were the same who had attacked our caravan.

"Six." Robyn's voice broke through the silence. "Not seven Silent Assassins. I wonder what happened to your comrade." Her voice was positively evil as she sneered at the figures before us. Memories of the assassin I had killed sent shivers down my spine, but the other attackers did not react to Robyn's obvious taunt.

My heart beat so hard in my chest, I wondered how it was possible that the others did not hear it. I watched Robyn and the others scan each hooded face before us. Unlike mine, their fear was not as evident.

Robyn's eyes were cold and calculating under the moonlight. We stood in stunned silence for several heartbeats before the tallest figure stepped forward. His black gaze met mine as he pointed his gloved hand directly toward me. He crooked his finger, ushering me forward. Bile rose in my throat.

He had made his point clear. *They are here for me.*

Robyn stepped between us, blocking me from his view. Her string was taut as she aimed it directly for the cloaked figure's heart. Samwell swung his sword in a circle at his side, and Gawayne angled himself better between me and the other attackers. The message the three of them sent back was clear.

Robyn's voice was ice as she straightened to her full height and spoke to the figures who had now drawn their long, curved blades. "It would be foolish for you to attack a Loxley inside of Sherwood. We are the keeper of the trees and protectors of all who live and travel under their branches. If you continue, you will meet your end inside this wood. Now is your chance to leave with your life."

The silent leader took one step forward, which was the only step he took before Robyn felled the companion to his right. The attacker fell to the ground in a heap. It was the only surprise we would get as the rest launched toward us.

Robyn drew another arrow, but they were too close now. She shoved the bow in my hands, drawing her sword. The sounds of metal clanging together split through my ears as her sword clashed against the assassin before us.

To my left and right, Samwell and Gawayne each fought a pair of attackers.

My mouth fell open as I took them in. Samwell was as silent and deadly as his foe. He dodged each slice of their curved blades, dancing between each assassin as if were some finely orchestrated waltz and not a deadly duel. Gawayne took on his two assassins, keeping his wide body low to the ground. Though he was stout, he moved in a blur, using the strength of his enormous arms to power his sword and push the attackers back.

Terrified by the ordeal around them, Samwell and Gawayne's horses burst by their masters, disappearing into the trees. Gold and Marengo made to do the same, but I grabbed their reins, digging in my heels in a desperate attempt to keep them.

We needed to flee.

Gold's whinny pierced through the air as I pulled on her reins. I turned in horror to see Robyn's attacker slice through the air. The edge of his curved blade grazed against Robyn's chest as she rolled to the side.

"Robyn!" I screamed for her as she leapt to her feet, narrowly avoiding another slice of the assassin's blade. She rolled again across the forest floor. One hand clutched her chest as she twirled her sword in the air.

Panic set in as our enemies pushed us closer. Samwell had taken one assassin down with one of his throwing knives. The attacker now lay with a blade sticking out of his throat. Only a few steps in front of me I knew Gawayne was beginning to tire. He thrust toward the assassins with loud, angry grunts.

Distracted by the attacker on his left, Gawayne missed it when the second one slipped past him.

Time seemed to stand still as I released the horse's reins. To my amazement, they did not flee as I faced off with the silent assassin now approaching me in the dark.

A strange calm fell over me as I stared at the dark mask gathering closer. We had taken three of their men down. We were evenly matched now. I felt the grin spread across my cheeks.

"The Silent Seven. I've read about you..." I moved back and forth, keeping as much distance between myself and the curved blade shimmering against the moonlight. At some point, I had dropped the blade Robyn had given me. The sounds of my friends dueling still filled the air around me, but I focused on the enemy before me. "I thought you were supposed to be silent, even when dealt a killing blow. Then why is it when I killed your comrade he screamed so loud?"

The assassin's eyes flashed with hatred and fury as he lunged for me. I dove through Gold's legs, skidding across the grass to the other side. Robyn's mare panicked--as I expected she would—forcing the assassin to dodge the horse's flailing legs.

My boots slipped on the damp grass as I launched myself toward the trees in the distance. A voice called out behind me, but I couldn't make out the words over the sound of my own breathing and my heart pounding painfully in my ears.

Something hit my back hard, knocking me forward onto the ground and forcing the breath from my chest. I reached my hands out to absorb the impact. My head bounced on the ground. A weight pressed me against the grass.

Instinct took over as I bucked the assassin off me, rolling away from him again. He was on me in a heartbeat, pinning my shoulders to the ground with his knees. I froze as his blade pressed against my throat.

His deadly gaze stared down at me, and I knew they would be the last thing I ever saw. Above me the assassin jerked. I closed my eyes and waited for death to take me.

When I opened my eyes, an arrow was sticking out of the assassin's chest. He grabbed at the shaft helplessly, before falling to the side.

Robyn stood only a few steps away. I watched as she briefly lowered her bow. Blood dripped from her torn tunic onto the ground. Behind her, Samwell and Gawayne had pushed our attackers back into the tree line.

"Get her out of here, now!" Robyn's command filled the clearing as she turned, firing more arrows into the night. Samwell stuck his fingers between his lips. The whistle spread as Gawayne and Samwell headed for me.

There was a flash of white as Gold appeared from the tree line.

Marengo stamped her feet angrily as she too came to our aid.

I pulled myself into my horse's saddle. Samwell winced, releasing a cry of agony as Gawayne helped him onto Marengo as well. It wasn't until then I realized a blood stain was spreading across the green of his tunic.

"Hold on, Sam." Gawayne's voice was thick with emotion as he mounted Gold.

"Put pressure against the wound!" I urged Sam, trying my best to turn in the saddle.

"Go!" Robyn ran toward us as the assassins ran in behind her.

New panic filled me as she turned to face them alone. Gawayne's fiery hair gave him a fierce look in the moonlight, but his eyes were sad as he glanced across at Samwell. The two seemed to share some silent understanding. New terror washed over me.

"Gawayne. We can't just leave her!" Tears threatened to spill as I screamed. My mind struggled against what was happening. I pulled on the reins, trying to turn Marengo around.

I had to do something.

Gawayne spun Gold around, and for a moment I thought he meant to ride back and get Robyn like we had for him. Instead, he smacked Marengo, sending her running into the trees. Samwell took the reins from my hands as I struggled against the tight hold he now had on me.

"We can't leave her! Turn around! Turn around!"

I tried to wrestle the reins from him, but Samwell's grip was strong. His chest was broad and solid, even as I felt the warmth of his blood seeping through my shirt. Tears poured down my face as both horses ran through the wood.

I called Robyn's name into the night until my voice was hoarse.

We passed the tents in silence as a sea of faces looked on with worried glances. Some of them I recognized immediately, others I did not. *Had it truly only been yesterday I had tended to so many of them?*

The horses were nearly spent as we ambled into the gates. News of our weary and bloody states must have made it to the castle. A host of royal guards met us at the city gates. Their green and gold uniforms shined from the light of the torches. Somewhere in my mind, I registered Asher's familiar face at the front of the crowd.

My body felt numb, as foreign hands helped me dismount, but I knew it wouldn't be long before the pain of tonight set in.

Behind me, Samwell cried out as someone helped him down too. Something snapped inside of me. "Kira! Someone get Kira!"

My assistant appeared out of the darkness. To my surprise, her hair was pulled back in a tight bun. Her face was stone as she looked Samwell over. "Bring him into the infirmary." Relief filled me momentarily. Between her and Duchess Elsie they would make sure Samwell was taken care of.

Someone's hand wrapped around mine, but I barely registered the touch. My feet were stones as Asher guided me toward the castle doors. Voices filled the air around me. All I could think about was Robyn's face and the sight of her blood hitting the ground.

Three against one, and we had left her to die alone.

Gawayne's deep voice echoed through the courtyard, startling me from my stupor.

"Bring me a new horse, damn it! I am going back NOW!" I turned to see Gawayne marching past the guards, back toward the gate.

"Asher." I stopped short, gripping the prince's hands tight in my own. My throat was raw, and fresh tears poured down my cheeks. "She's still out there. Please. You have to find her."

Asher's face was solemn as he looked me over. He gave the order, and two dozen guards followed Gawayne back out into Sherwood.

More voices told me to go and rest, but something else urged me on. A sea of strange faces filled the courtyard. Some of them were members of the guard I recognized, others were servants or courtiers who had shown up for the arrival of Princess Madawi. I forced their confused stares from my thoughts, focusing only on my slow steps.

I walked to the edge of the wall and looked up at the steep staircase. Each step was a mountain, but I finally reached the top.

Three against one. I pushed the thought away. The image of her blood spilling to the ground floated through my mind, but I pushed it away too.

Spread before me, it seemed every house in the city still burned candles. In the distance, the lights from the tents continued to shine as well. I prayed they would stay lit all night. Let them be a beacon bringing Robyn back to me.

She had to come back. Robyn would come back…and I would wait on this wall until she did.

Robyn

There was a sharp pain across my chest as I woke. I struggled to open my eyes, though the light around me was dim. For a second, I wondered if I had fallen asleep in the forest. I breathed in the air, and the smell of lavender wafted over me.

Memories seemed to tip-toe back across my mind. *Marian was on her horse. She was screaming my name. The woods had gone dark, and three assassins were before me. I'd run out of arrows.*

The hilt of my sword was warm in my hand as I stepped back into the trees. I would let them come find me in the woods and see which one of us was truly the assassin.

More images of blades clashing rang through my head. *I remembered the feel of blood on my shirt. I'd taken two assassins down, but there was still one more. My head spun with blood loss, and I had to do something to stop the bleeding.*

Again, I struggled to open my eyes. The pain was bearable, but my eyes stung at the onslaught of the light. A stone ceiling spread over me. The soft feel of pillows surrounded me, and I realized I was in a bed. To my left was a familiar desk.

I was in Marian's bed.

Something heavy held down my right hand, and for a moment my heart skipped, fearing I was bound.

I struggled to focus. *That didn't make any sense. Why would someone tie me to the bed?* I wiggled my fingers, turning my head to look. Whatever held me down was warm against my skin. The smell of lavender hit me again.

Marian's head rested on my hand. Her eyes were closed—as if she had fallen asleep at my bedside.

New pain hit me as my body fully awakened. The pain in my shoulder began to throb, and the cut across my chest ached. I looked down, pulling the thin sheets off. A breeze swept over my skin, and I realized I was definitely not wearing a shirt. I resisted the urge to consider who might have been the one to remove it. My bladder ached in protest at the movement.

Something sticky and green was placed over the wound on my breastbone. I touched it gingerly. The wound was no longer bleeding, but it would take some time to heal.

Marian jerked awake. Her head whipped to the door, and then back toward me.

She blinked a few times--as if struggling to understand. Her face flushed as she looked me over, and I quickly covered myself.

Marian cleared her throat, running a hand down her long hair.

"You had to come in here. Samwell is using the only bed in the infirmary. I" —Marian's blush deepened— "I had to remove your tunic to sew your wound. I put a tincture on it to stave off infection, but the one you made was good too." She smiled weakly at me.

I suddenly remembered stumbling through the forest. I had found a creek, and I knew I needed to look for a white flower with a red center.

"It took them almost an entire day to find you. Gawayne said you were in a cave." Marian leaned over, grabbing a cup of water from the desk and bringing it toward me as she continued. "You've been out for nearly two days. I didn't think you'd want anyone to see you, and I needed to be able to watch you, so I made them bring you to my room. But I also had to steal your sheets and your blankets since I had that incident with mine. I didn't think you would care though."

Marian's crazed speech continued as she paced the room. For the first time since I opened my eyes, I realized she was still in the clothes she had worn when we left the castle. Her white corset had been stained with blood. Her pants were not much better. The only part of her skin not covered in dirt was her hands. Dark bags blemished the skin around her beautiful, blue eyes, and her hair stuck out all around her head.

It had been almost two days since I'd been brought to the castle, and almost a full day passed before they had found me. My heart swelled a little as Marian rushed back to the bed, forcing me to drink another cup of water.

"I'm okay now," I whispered. "Did you find the knife?" My throat was dry, but I pushed through it.

Marian turned toward me. Her sapphire eyes glittered with unshed tears. Her nostrils flared as she forced out a breath I could hear all the way across the room. She nodded, gesturing to the bedside table where the small knife I had given her lay.

Then she turned around, disappearing out the door without another word.

I struggled to understand what had happened.

Why had she left so abruptly?

The first thing I did when my mind stopped reeling was relieve my bladder in the nearest chamber pot. Internally I took stock of my injuries. The truth was it could have been worse, but not much worse.

I found a tunic and breeches folded neatly on a chair nearby. Every muscle in my body ached as I painstakingly slid the clothes on.

When I was finally presentable, I stumbled to the door. Every pinch of my stitches was torture, but I finally reached the other side of the room as Gawayne rushed in.

"I knew you must be awake." I winced as Gawayne slapped me roughly on the shoulder. His large nose scrunched when he realized his mistake. "Sorry..."

I forced a smile for my friend.

I tried not to, but I quickly realized I would have to lean on him to stay upright. We walked slowly into the corridor. "That's the first time Marian has left this room since you arrived." Gawayne stared down the hall, and I could hear the catch in his voice. "She's been sending notes back and forth to Kira. Samwell is awake, and apparently not happy to be confined to the infirmary while he heals." Gawayne's laughter did not reach his eyes.

I didn't reply, though I was struggling with my own emotions. A shiver went down my spine. The truth was I had not expected to leave the forest alive, and if not for all my friends—Marian included—I would not have.

Gawayne seemed to read my mind, clearing his throat as we made our way down one step at a time.

The infirmary was in the wing of the castle closest to the barracks, but I had never noticed the distance as much as I did then. It took what felt like hours for us to arrive at Samwell's bedside.

"Ah, hell. If she can be up and about, I'm leaving!" Samwell threw back his blanket as we approached. The fabric floated to the floor, revealing Samwell's naked body. A large gash spread horizontally across his abdomen. It too seemed to be stitched closed.

I did not react. In the years of training and living with these two, I had seen Samwell's manhood more times than I cared to. Though Gawayne was suddenly studying the ceiling above us intensely.

"Marian said you could leave, but I have to put this on your wound first." Kira's firm hand pressed against Samwell's shoulder. She did not appear to react to his blatant display either. Samwell frowned but allowed Kira to cover his lower half again.

We watched as she rubbed the same sticky substance across Samwell's flat stomach. He did not wait for a single second once Kira had finished. Gawayne tossed a pair of breeches and a tunic toward the bed.

Unable to stand any longer, I sat at the end of his cot. Kira eyed me suspiciously, but I ignored it.

The only sign of Samwell's discomfort was how slowly he placed each arm in his sleeve. When he moved to pull up the breeches, he wobbled a little, but Gawayne was there to catch him.

Samwell sat back on the cot with a sigh, and the three of us stared at one another. I knew I must look as bad as my friends did—if not worse. Collectively, we breathed a sigh of relief.

Gawayne looked down on me and Samwell. He was the first to speak as the reality of the situation truly dawned on us all. "It's a good thing you assholes are hard to kill."

The sound of our laughter filled the infirmary. Samwell and I both clutched at our wounds, but that only forced us to laugh even harder.

Kira's brows furrowed together as our laughter died down. She crossed her arms over her chest, clearly disapproving of our antics. "If you fools are all done, make yourselves presentable before you leave the infirmary. Princess Madawi arrives this afternoon."

I tried my best to stay upright in the saddle as Gold and I stretched our ranks along the edge of the street.

Hundreds of people lined the docks of Colch Harbor. Their buzz filled my ears as one person after another tried to push past the guard for a better view.

Anxiety filled me as Prince Asher and the royal procession ambled down the dock. Even from here I could see their adornments glittering in the sun. This afternoon as we left the castle, Prince Asher had emerged as expected--in full regalia dripping with jewels. His crown glittered atop his head, and his green tunic was tight against his chest. Every courtier around him was also dressed in their finery.

A small tent had been erected on the dock. Its thick legs had been sunk deep into the sand on either side of the wooden planks. The nobles would rest under the tent until the ship arrived.

The sun beat down on everyone else. I could feel the sweat dripping down my spine and pooling under my breasts. I had not been able to wrap them as I usually did, and the thought made me uncomfortable and exposed. Gawayne sat atop his mount beside me, beads of sweat dripping down his brow as well. He shifted uneasily in his saddle. The restlessness continued to grow around us.

I might hate the prince, but we could not allow a crowd to overtake the harbor. Hundreds of lives might be lost if there was a sudden rush or brawl from the crowd. I continued turning Gold, trying desperately to keep an eye on the growing crowd. Every movement was torture, and I could feel my energy draining with each passing moment.

Worry filled me for a moment, thinking of Samwell and his injuries. I had sent him to stay close to the nobility. It seemed my worries were for naught. I watched him as he leaned toward a familiar redhead in a white gown.

I turned to scan the crowd again when a low chuckle came from behind me. Gawayne coughed, moving his mount away from Gold.

"Shit. You're in for it now."

Confused, I spun Gold around once more. Marian was dressed in a thin, white gown that barely reached her knees, and her blond hair was braided down her back. The silk wrap in her hair had been replaced since our excursions. Marian looked completely different from the disheveled woman who had woken at my bedside this morning.

Gawayne continued to move away, suddenly interested in the designs on his saddle as Marian stomped her way up the beach.

"It's not like I expected you to stay in bed all day, but by gods — what do you think you are doing?" Even Gold hung her head low as Marian scolded me.

"I'm doing my duty as a Captain in the king's Army."

"Your *duty* won't matter much if you fall off that horse, rip open your stitches, and die!"

"I told her that…" Gawayne whispered. Marian shot him a deadly look.

"But did you stop her? Did you even try at all to stop her or Samwell from coming down here?"

Gawayne's face turned red. All around us, the men continued to snicker. It was my turn to shoot daggers. Frustration grew inside me.

I will not be embarrassed in front of my men.

"Lady Marian, while I appreciate your concern — "

I immediately realized my mistake, as Marian's face turned as red as a ruby.

"You *appreciate my concern?* When? When did you appreciate that I spent nearly an entire day atop the wall waiting for them to bring back your lifeless body? Did you appreciate my concern when I spent two more days keeping you *alive?* Don't appreciate my concern, Robyn. Just stop being a fucking idiot."

Once again Marian turned around, storming back down the beach. Her slew of swear words continued as she left in a whirlwind of sand back toward the royal tent.

My mouth hung open, but I had no words. Gawayne snapped at the men to remain vigilant, and I mulled over what Marian had said.

"She was up there when I left to get you, and she was at the gate when I brought you back." Gawayne's voice was thick with emotion, but he would not meet my eye.

"Perhaps we all owe her much more than we ever realized." I reached out, patting Gold's long neck. The weight of the last few days truly fell over me.

The sun was beginning to set before the ship from Quados appeared on the horizon. Its white sails pushed the vessel right to the edge of the dock.

First down the gangplank were the royal guards. I expected a series of adoring attendants, but only the princess and another woman arrived to greet the prince. Prince Asher bowed low, bringing her hand to his lips.

After a lot of gesturing, which I assumed was introductions, Samwell finally gave me the signal that we would return to the castle. The men moved slowly into position, and the people of Colch began to disperse.

My entire body protested as Gold moved along the line. Up ahead, the royal caravan traveled up the hill. Marian passed me on her horse. I tried to ignore the feeling in my stomach when she did not look my way.

Chapter 17

Marian

It seemed Princess Madawi and her small caravan had arrived just in time. Prince Asher had urged everyone to disperse the moment we arrived at the castle. He would dine privately with Princess Madawi. I barely remembered the long walk to my chamber last night. I had fallen asleep the moment my head hit the pillow.

The morning after her arrival, I woke to the sound of rain battering against my window.

I rolled over in the bed, frustrated with today already, and buried my face in the soft down of my pillow. Rain meant I would be trapped in the castle today.

I stayed that way for a while, before forcing myself from bed and ambling toward the window. The sun was faint in the sky as I peered through the water droplets onto the garden below. My body ached with sleep as I rolled out of bed.

A soft knock tapped against my door, and seconds later Kira walked in with a tray full of food. My stomach growled in response.

Kira's smile was sweet as she brought the tray to the bed. Guilt prickled at my skin, and I shifted uneasily on the bed. I had spent hardly any time with the woman who was supposed to be my assistant.

"Captain Loxley wanted to make sure that you ate dinner when you awoke."

My brain was still filled with the fog of sleep, and my brows pulled together in confusion.

"Dinner? Is it not morning?"

I looked out the window again and realized the light had gone completely. Night had fallen in just the few minutes I had been awake.

"You slept for nearly an entire day, Lady Marian. Though, Samwell and Captain Loxley did not fare much better. They slept well into the afternoon."

A kind of relief fell over me, even as I remembered Robyn and Samwell's absolute stupidity. The fact that they thought they were well enough to ride was beyond reasoning.

I grabbed a piece of fruit from the tray, relishing the sweet taste in my mouth. Kira stood beside the bed as if waiting for me to speak or dismiss her. A few droplets of red juices fell to my white bedsheets, and the image of Samwell's bloody shirt immediately came to mind.

"Kira. I want to apologize for not telling you how much I appreciate that you were here. If you had not taken such excellent care of Samwell, we might have lost him." I shivered at the thought. "I have undervalued you as an assistant, and for that, I'm deeply sorry."

Kira's smile widened. We stared at each other for a few moments before I realized I had never asked her about the assignment I had given her just before we left for the village.

"How are the evening classes with Duchess Elsie?"

"The duchess is patient. She has asked all the ladies to attend her, so they might take knowledge back to their people. The ladies are...less patient."

Kira released a long sigh, and I knew exactly why.

"I'm sure they're just a joy to be around."

"The only one with brains enough to even keep the information is Lady Rochelle. She seems eager to learn."

I was surprised by that. Lady Rochelle had seemed interested in nothing but Prince Asher since her arrival. I chastised myself again for not making more of an effort to combat my assumptions about someone I truly knew very little about.

"Perhaps you can join us?" Kira shifted uneasily, and I knew it was a difficult thing for her to ask. This class had become her charge, and she was not easily ready to release control, even to me.

"I would be honored to sit in on your class and hear you speak."

An idea occurred to me then, and I remembered back to the village. I had learned a lot about the herbs and plants in Sherwood in just a few hours.

"Perhaps we could convince some of the healers aboard the trading vessels to visit the castle. Perhaps there are remedies from foreign lands we've yet to learn."

Kira was thoughtful for a moment before she nodded in agreement.

"Perhaps you could come with me and help me persuade them to visit the castle?"

"I would love to do so."

Thunder sounded outside, rattling the window behind me. Kira and I both jumped in response. I nearly toppled the tray of food beside me. Our eyes met. I was sure mine were as big as saucers as my heart pounded.

"I feel we should wait out the rains though," I whispered, turning to look at the darkness outside. Another clap of thunder filled the room, but this time Kira and I burst into laughter.

Once our laughter subsided, I thanked Kira for the food again and we made a plan to head for the docks in the morning if the storms had passed.

Although I had slept most of the day, my body reminded me just how much sleep I had lost over the last few days.

I ate the remaining fruit and crackers on my plate, but my mind urged me to do *something* productive today. It felt slothful to spend an entire day in bed.

I wandered the castle for a bit. Almost everyone had retired. The only faces I passed were servants shuffling from room to room. I smiled at them, recognizing a few immediately.

My feet were heavy, and I knew they would not carry me much farther. I stopped in the corridor for a moment, trying to consider where I should go. Though many in the castle were asleep, I was in no mood for polite company.

Nowhere in the castle was safe from the demands of court, except perhaps the soldiers' mess hall. There were only a few places in the city I had found the solitude I longed for. I thought back to the hours I had spent in the Colch library. It was certainly closed by now, and even if it weren't, the rain would certainly prevent me.

A thought occurred to me, and I suddenly felt renewed. Duchess Elsie had said there was a small library in the castle. In all the turmoil since my arrival, I had yet to visit it.

It took me nearly ten minutes to find my way to the royal wing. I wandered the corridors, afraid to open the wrong one or knock and disturb someone's private chamber. Finally, I rounded a corner at the very back of the castle and arrived at a set of double doors. An artist had painted a beautiful set of books on the front of the doors, and I knew I had found what I was looking for.

The room was surprisingly bright as I entered. Lanterns and candles had been lit all around the room. Several comfortable-looking couches had been strategically placed around the room. Large, thick pillows were also spread along the ground. I breathed in the smell of the books as I walked closer to one of the shelves.

The sound of pages shuffling nearby startled me from my wonderment, and I turned around to find an unfamiliar face staring back at me.

In the corner, sitting rigid and stiff was a woman with short, black hair. Her cold gaze seemed to assess me, and her hand rested on the hilt of the blade strapped to her leg. Five gold rings pierced her left ear, though the rest of her seemed to be free of any other adornment.

I jumped as another face appeared from behind the couch facing away from me. This face I recognized immediately.

Princess Madawi's bewildered face peeked up at me. Her long, black hair was free of its braids and jewels. She seemed to hesitate as she looked over at me. Neither of us seemed certain how to proceed.

Finally remembering my manners, I bowed low to the princess. Madawi stood abruptly, straightening her long gown. She was the first to speak as she nodded in my direction.

"Forgive me. I did not hear you come in, Lady Marian." I was surprised she had remembered my name. We had only met briefly along the docks. "It seems I got a little…lost in my book."

"That is why you are not allowed to read in public anymore." Malawi's guard whispered from the corner.

"It was not that bad, Joppa."

"You almost got trampled by a horse."

"A very small horse."

I smiled at their banter, watching as the princess visibly relaxed.

"I too have gotten lost in a book before, Princess Madawi. It happens to the best of us."

Madawi's smile grew, and I couldn't help but laugh as she gestured from me to Joppa—as if saying 'See, I'm not the only one'.

"If you prefer to read alone, I can leave, Your Highness." I could see now that the princess had probably chosen this hour of night specifically because she longed for solitude. It occurred to me that she probably did not receive the chance to relax alone very often.

"Nonsense! Find yourself something and join me!" I knew she was most likely just being polite, but I found myself wanting to join her regardless.

I walked along the bookshelves for a moment, scanning their spines for a title that interested me. Finally, I settled on a book containing folklore from across the kingdoms. Pulling the tome from its shelf, I was shocked by its weight.

Madawi had moved to the edge of the couch. Several pillows were propped behind her, and her long legs were pulled close. A stunning blanket with a swirl of gold and red designs sewn through it had been draped over her feet. The book she was reading rested against the tops of her thighs.

Several large, red pillows rested against the other end. I moved them into a comfortable position as I nestled in.

We read in silence together for a while. I was immediately entranced by the stories of magic, sorcery, and superstition in the tales. After a while, I looked up from my page to find Madawi's emerald eyes staring at me curiously.

I looked at her a moment before continuing.

"I need to ask you a question."

I closed my book, using my thumb to hold my place as I waited for her to continue.

"Are there giants in your mountains?"

I cocked my head, trying to process her words. "Pardon?"

Madawi closed her book, and I heard Joppa chuckle. "My grandmother used to tell us stories about the Impassable Mountains. She said they were named that because the giants in the mountains never allow travelers to live once they find them."

I resisted the urge to laugh as Madawi leaned toward me eagerly.

"I have not been to those mountains, but I don't believe so."

The princess seemed to deflate a little, sitting back against the edge of the couch with a frown.

"Can I ask you a question?" I thought back to a comment I had heard one of the other ladies make on the way back from the docks. Madawi's watched me for a moment, and then she nodded. "Does everyone in Quados sleep with a pet snake in their bed?"

Madawi and Joppa both broke out in laughter.

"I hate snakes." Joppa laughed from the corner of the room.

"Me too," Madawi added. "Though my younger sister is quite fond."

The air had changed in the room, as though our questions had somehow opened a door between us. Once again, the princess visibly relaxed, and that put me at ease too.

"Are you looking forward to your trip to the capital?" I asked the princess. "I haven't done much traveling, but I hope to someday."

"I enjoy traveling, though I miss my people and my family greatly." Madawi's face fell. She studied the soft fabric of the blanket on her lap.

"My mother gave me this blanket. These are the colors of our people." Madawi held the fabric higher in the air, and I could see now the deep crimson and gold woven into it.

"It's beautiful." I adjusted in my seat, unsure how to respond to such a heartfelt moment.

"Do you miss your mother or is she in this city too?"

My heart fell at Madawi's words. It had been a long time since I discussed my mother with anyone.

"She is no longer living. She died shortly after childbirth. I was raised at court as a ward of the king."

"I am sorry, Lady Marian." Madawi's hand reached out, squeezing mine tight. I smiled weakly in response.

"I expect you will get to meet the king and queen soon when we leave for the capital next week." I tried to change to subject to something lighter.

"Yes. I am...excited to meet the queen and king. Prince Asher speaks highly of them."

"And himself..." Joppa murmured from the corner.

I bit my tongue—not wanting to insult the princess's suitor.

Madawi brushed her long hair back from her face. Then, she leaned toward me, lowering her voice. "I have never met someone who has talked so much about themselves before. You would think he must lay his manhood out on the table every day and force his servants to measure it—just to make sure it was as long as the day before."

"Princess!" Joppa's incredulous voice sounded from across the room.

Again, we all broke out into laughter.

We were still laughing minutes later when the double doors of the library opened, and Robyn stepped through.

Startled by the sudden disruption, we all turned toward the door.

Robyn's gaze immediately followed the sound of our laughter and landed on Madawi's hand still in mine. Robyn's beautiful, golden eyes grew round, and for just a second her mouth was agape.

I pulled my hand back immediately as a warm flush grew across my cheeks.

"Captain Loxley. To what do we owe this honor?"

Robyn's back straightened, and she walked forward with a new purpose.

"I came to see if Lady Marian had received her supper. However, she is clearly without need of aid. I apologize for disturbing you both."

Just like that, her brave facade was gone, and Robyn hurried from the room.

Madawi and I looked at one another again. The princess cocked a brow at me. I knew she was asking a question I wasn't prepared to answer

Robyn

I walked back down the long corridor, trying to shake the image of Marian and the princess from my mind. A furious, unsettled feeling crept through my stomach as I seethed.

I reminded myself that Marian was free to consort with whomever she wanted, but it did nothing to fix the feeling settling over me.

My sword rocked in its sheath at my side, and I had to fight the urge to pull it out and stab something. I made my way to the main entrance of the castle, suddenly eager to get out of its oppressive stone walls.

The main entrance to the duke's castle was empty except for the flicker of candlelight reaching from the sconces on the walls. The guards on each side of the double doors nodded at me. The one on the left opened the door, allowing me to pass.

I walked into the courtyard, surprised to find a group of riders dismounting. The whole lot was soaked. Their cloaks hung limply at their sides, and their horses looked none better. I immediately recognized the colors on the bridles. The white and gold banners waved in the breeze. At the front of the group was a black stallion. Gold trim lined his bridle as well. Each droplet of rain glinted in the low light of the courtyard like stars.

A gray-haired man looked down on me from the stallion's back. His nostrils flared almost as wide as the horse's. There was no smile as he looked down at me. A chill crawled down my back and all the way to the ground.

"I wasn't expecting you, Father." I tried to keep my voice steady.

"After the sudden lapse in your correspondence, you should have. I heard you were injured, though clearly you still have both hands and are therefore still capable of writing a letter."

My father's men bristled. Behind him, Sir Johnathan dismounted from his horse as well. He did not speak as he stepped over to stand behind my father.

"I only just woke this morn. I fully intended on sending you a letter tomorrow."

Father pursed his lips together in a way that told me he did not believe my words. In truth, I had meant to explain everything that had occurred between myself and Asher before my impromptu trip with Marian but had been avoiding the inevitable thrashing my father would surely rain down upon me.

The rest of the men continued to dismount. Their swords swung at their sides as they ambled toward the stables. Sir Johnathan took the reins of father's stallion without a word. His eyes darted between the Baron of Loxley and me. I knew by the look of concern on his brow as he walked away exactly what I was in for.

A few moments passed until it was only the two of us in the dark courtyard. Father's men were barely out of sight before his gruff hand grabbed at the shoulder of my tunic, pulling me into a far corner of the courtyard. I did not resist as we blended into the darkness.

This would not be a conversation we wanted others to overhear.

"What the fuck were you thinking?" Father's voice was barely above a whisper, but he still managed to send a feeling of panic down my spine. Like the time when I was six and I had been caught swimming nude with Gawayne and Samwell, I knew I was in a whole different mess of trouble.

"You have jeopardized everything we have been working for. You threatened the prince, and showed an outsider one of our villages—"

"Lady Mar—"

"I don't want to hear it." I felt the sting of father's hand before my mind registered what had happened. As my head twisted around, pain ricocheted through my center. My sensitive ribs protested at the sudden movement. It was by sheer force of will I stayed upright.

Father stepped closer to me and the pain across my cheek reminded me that I was not simply speaking with the man who was married to my mother. This was the Baron of Loxley, head of the oldest families in all of Notting. He had led thousands of men to battle and taken countless lives. He was trying to overthrow the king.

His cold eyes leered down at me as he fumed. Thunder shook through me as I listened to his words. "I don't give a damn who you bed, but you will not endanger us again by bringing your flirtations into the homes of people who depend on us—who depend on *you*. Two of our most-trusted men have disappeared this week alone. That messenger I sent to you? This morning we found him tied to a tree with his throat slashed."

My breath caught in my throat. The young messenger's face flashed through my mind. Whoever had grabbed him had clearly believed he carried sensitive information—and they had been correct. They had just been too late to retrieve it.

Father rubbed at his temple as he lowered his head with a sigh.

"What's done is done, but more men will die, Robyn. Their blood is on your hands."

My hands shook at my sides, and I fought the bile threatening to spew from my mouth. I cleared my throat, fighting back the tears that threatened to fall. I blinked a few times as I followed after my father toward the grand entrance of the duke's castle.

I studied the cobblestones as we walked. The rain continued to pour around us and I thought back to everything that had happened in such a short amount of time. Helping Marian had been the right thing to do, but if I had simply allowed Asher to wake alone in his rooms, he may not even have remembered the events at all.

Still, despite the look of disappointment on Father's face and the knowledge that I had most likely cost three men their lives, I couldn't bring myself to regret threatening the prince away from Marian.

The only thing I could hope for was to bring down the royal family before even more lives were lost.

I stared at Father's wet hair as we approached the front steps. The two guards at each door did not nod this time.

Daughter or not, captain or not, I had let him and our men down.

Father muttered something ahead of me, and I jerked to attention as we entered the front hall. Standing in the entrance, with the glow of firelight glinting off her golden hair, was Marian.

She nodded toward my father, but her sapphire eyes met mine and I watched as horror spread across her face.

I had stepped into the light of the hall. No doubt the side of my face where father had struck me was still red and swollen. I would not be at all surprised if it bruised. Despite the rain, the shoulder of my tunic was still ruffled from where father had dragged me.

"Robyn—" Marian's voice was a whisper.

"Lady Marian, I don't believe you have met Sir Sebastion, Baron of Loxley."

"Lady Marian, how nice to meet you. It is quite a late hour to be wandering the halls." Father's tone was reproachful, even as he leaned to kiss Marian's hand. It was clear why he thought she might be up so late.

He knew she was looking for me.

Marian finally looked at me again, and I could see the same, stubborn look growing across her brow that she had given the man in the camps only days before. She understood exactly what had occurred between my father and me.

"It is quite late, Baron. Perhaps we should all get to bed so we can have more level-heads in the morning." Marian's dismissal was clear, and I felt my jaw fall open. I had never heard someone speak to Father in such a manner.

Father paused for a moment before straightening his shoulders and rising to his full height before us.

"It is late, Lady Marian. Perhaps we should all retire to our *own* rooms." Father stiffened. His mouth drew into a hard line as he looked back at me before disappearing down the hall.

Marian and I stood in the corridor. The silence hung between us.

Unable to bear the weight of the guilt and the shame weighing down on me, I began the trek toward my room.

Marian was quick to catch up to me. Her hurried footsteps followed me, though I walked faster to avoid her. Each step was still a chore as I turned down a new corridor.

"Robyn. What was that?" Why…why would your father…"

"Why would my father 'what,' Marian? Why would my father be furious with me? Why would he ride all night with his men, in a storm, from the gods-only-know-where to see his daughter? Probably because his daughter is a proper failure as a captain."

"You're not—"

"I am. The prince nearly died on the road here. We all nearly died. I have almost entirely ostracized myself from court by directly disobeying the duke's orders. I took Gawayne and Samwell into

Sherwood and almost got them killed. I took *you* into Sherwood even though I am sworn to protect its people, and then I almost got you and myself killed."

"Robyn. You helped me save lives. The people in the camps need care. The people of Hazo needed care."

"They didn't need *you!* They didn't need someone who could give their location to our enemies. They didn't need the crown's lapdog to know their secrets!"

Marian's eyes grew wide at my words, and I watched her take a step back from me. She wore the same look I had worn only minutes before. She looked as though she had been slapped.

I knew I had gone too far, but Father's words still rang in my ears, and I thought again at the lives I had endangered by bringing Marian into Sherwood. I thought of the young man who had ended up tied to a tree with his blood pooling to the ground. It was too much.

Just like my father had done, I straightened my shoulders and became the person I was always meant to be. I was just another soldier in my father's army. I was another enemy of the crown, and Marian was everything the crown represented.

"We are finished, Lady Marian. I am thankful for your services and aid these last few days. However, I see no reason for us to continue acting as though we are friends or anything more."

Marian's delicate chin quivered a little, but she said nothing as I turned and walked down the corridor.

Each step was a chore. My ribs ached and I found it hard to catch my breath. I had woken this morning physically exhausted, and ended the evening emotionally beaten.

I closed the door to my room. When I lay in bed, the smell of lavender drifted over me. Marian and I had spent hardly any time together at all today, but her sent clung to me like the flowers in the forest in springtime. She had embedded herself into me, outlined her name on my skin with every careful stitch. All the aches in my body were nothing compared to the pain in my chest as I remembered the way her chin had quivered tonight.

I thought of the wounded look on her face, and I finally allowed myself to weep.

Marian

I woke early in the morning to a pounding on my door. I meandered from my bed, groaning at the feel of the chilly floor on my bare feet. The gentle, but insistent, knocks continued and I wondered if I waited long enough might the person behind the door go away. The pounding grew more insistent, and I knew my hopes were lost.

A bright-eyed Kira was standing outside my door. The shy maid, Lilliana, who had been assigned to us both, stood next to her. A beautiful, white gown was draped over her arms. At the look of the two of them, I knew immediately that skipping out on dining with the members of Court was no longer an option.

Kira was already dressed in a beautiful, gray gown marking her as an acolyte.

"Princess Madawi requests your presence at breakfast."

My attitude immediately improved as I registered Kira's words. Perhaps attending meals with the rest of Court would be a bit more bearable with my new friend present.

"I should love to dine with the princess." I took the soft cloth as Lilliana passed it over to me. The dress was light and airy. It was perfect for the hot, humid weather.

Both women stepped into my room as I moved toward the bed to lay the dress out. Kira and I were no strangers to nudity, and she did not balk as I stripped into my undergarments.

Lilliana's adept hands worked along the strings at the back of the gown. I adjusted my breasts as the top grew tighter.

When Lilliana had finished with the silk strings, I turned to look in the long mirror across from my bed.

The white dress was surprisingly sheer, tucking tight against my curves and revealing a bit more in the bodice than I typically preferred.

Kira didn't hesitate to begin plaiting my hair. She wrapped my long, silk scarf through my locks. I squeezed her hand as she tied off the leather wrap at the end. I was truly thankful that she and I had grown accustomed to each other in such a short period of time.

Kira's fiery-red hair shone brightly in the mirror as our eyes met. She returned my smile, and I knew she felt the same.

I thanked Lilliana for her help as Kira and I made our way out my door.

"I was. . . returning from the barracks early this morning. . . " —I give Kira a knowing smile, sure I knew exactly why she was walking back from the barracks in the early morn — ". . . when I spotted Captain Loxley firing an entire quiver full of arrows into a field dummy."

I said nothing as we walked down the corridor, but Kira continued on.

"She seemed determined to annihilate whomever the dummy represented. The head of her target had been hit with more than a dozen arrows at least—almost like she had been out there for hours."

Anger rose inside me as I remembered Robyn's words from last night.

"I think I should like a turn relieving my frustrations on a field dummy."

Kira raised a brow at me, but I said nothing as we entered the great hall.

The guards on either side of the doorway opened the doors wide. I found myself barely able to pay attention as I seethed. We entered the hall where a long table had been erected. My fury continued to grow as I realized, despite her malicious words last night, part of me hoped that Robyn would be present.

Kira left me, heading toward Samwell seated along the middle of the table. His smile was broad as he watched her approach. I ignored the jealous feeling growing in my stomach as I watched him pull out a chair for her to sit.

Hesitation filled me for a moment. I was unsure where to place myself at the long table. Prince Asher sat to the right of the duke. On the duke's left sat Robyn's father. The duchess and her daughter were across from Princess Madawi. I watched Duchess Elsie gesture to something green on her daughter's plate and I couldn't help but smile as the little girl made a face that looked like she might retch.

There was only a second of hesitation though before Princess Madawi's bodyguard appeared like a phantom beside me. I startled a bit as the woman suddenly loomed over me. Last night in the library I had not truly realized just how towering she truly was.

All traces of humor had also gone from her face. Before me stood the woman dedicated to saving the princess' life, and I found myself a bit intimated as she stared me down.

"Princess Madawi requests you dine next to her."

I nodded and followed Joppa as she walked to the other side of the table.

I curtsied to Asher, Duke Inglis, and the Baron as I neared. Each man looked up at me in greeting, but it was Asher's mouth that fell open as he stared at the depth of my bodice. I resisted the urge to cover myself under his lustful stare.

Ahead of me, Joppa coughed politely. She stared at me with cold curiosity as her eyes passed between the prince and me.

Unlike her guard, Madawi's greeting was warm and inviting as I approached.

"Thank the gods. I was about to lose my mind. . . " Madawi's voice whispered in my ear as I took a place at her side. "Do you not sometimes wish you were still young enough to go by unnoticed? My younger sister brings a book with her to nearly every meal, but apparently, if I were to do so that would be *rude.*"

I laughed under my breath as she rolled her eyes. Before I could respond, a servant appeared to my left and began shoveling food on my plate. I watched the young man attempt to place some foul-smelling sprout on my plate, but I quickly declined.

"See! Even Lady Marian doesn't want sprouts, and she is a healer!"

Eva's voice carried across the room, and suddenly I found that all eyes were on me. The servant next to me paused, and we were both caught with indecision. I motioned for him to leave a sprout on my plate.

Eva stared at me from her seat, and I begrudgingly placed the sprout in my mouth. It took all of my willpower not to spit it back out onto the table. There was an eruption of laughter around me as I finally managed to swallow the disgusting thing.

At the end of the table, Prince Asher's voice bellowed above all the others. The laughter quickly died as he stood.

"On that note, the duke I have made a decision. It has been far too long since his men and mine have dined on some real meat. Today we will set out into Sherwood with our best trackers, and we shan't come back until there is enough boar or stag to feed everyone at the castle!"

"What a brilliant idea."

"The prince is such an excellent hunter."

On the other side of me, a soft voice whispered something I was certain I was not meant to hear.

"Some in Notting have nothing in their bellies, let alone meat."

I turned, surprised to see Lady Rochelle staring at her untouched plate. She looked up at me, and I knew she instantly regretted her treasonous words.

Something passed between us, and realization struck me. The people of the Western River must be desperate if Duke Griffiths was suddenly willing to force his daughter into a marriage she may not want.

Rochelle looked at me for only a second, but I could see that she knew I had put the pieces together.

Our attention was drawn back to the end of the table as Prince Asher's entourage called for him. Several ladies, including Lady Rochelle, raised their glasses toward him, clutching at their breasts with their free hand and wishing all who attended safe hunting.

Once the noise had quieted, it was the baron of Loxley who whispered across the table.

"There have been reports of more bandits, Prince Asher. Perhaps a fishing expedition would be better advised."

A dark looked passed over Prince Asher, and it was one I immediately recognized from my former friend. He was not used to anyone arguing with him.

"Surely, with such fine men at our side, there will be no danger. Unless you can think of some other reason it would be unsafe to enter Sherwood?"

Asher's tone was lethal as he arched a brow at Sebastion. Something I didn't quite understand seemed to pass between them.

Why would Asher think that the baron was trying to keep him out of Sherwood?

"Of course not. Your Highness is always welcome amongst our trees."

Prince Asher's hands slammed down onto the table, rattling the glassware.

A new hush fell over the table at the baron's treasonous words and the prince's reaction. From my periphery, I watched several soldiers along the table tense. I whipped my head toward Samwell, who seemed to be holding his fork tightly in his hand. Kira's hand gripped his wrist, and I knew it was a silent warning between them. I knew without asking whose side Samwell would take.

Prince Asher once again rose from his seat as he leered down at the baron.

"Make no mistake, Sebastion. Sherwood belongs to the crown, and I shall do as I see fit."

The Baron of Loxley did not even look up from his dish as the prince spoke. He continued cutting up some of the fruit still remaining on his plate.

"Of course, Your Highness."

The tension in the air was palpable as we continued the meal in silence.

After breakfast, I had returned to my room to don my white pants

once more. They would be much more suitable for riding. I couldn't be sure of how far we would travel or if I might be needed during the hunt if someone were to be injured.

I grabbed some supplies, shoving them deep into my pack. The long, wooden box from Robyn sat on my bed. I could not bring myself to carry it just yet. Not while I carried so much fury for its giver.

The hunting party was quickly arranged, and nearly all Court members were present in the courtyard before the sun was at its peak.

Duchess Elsie had quickly decided that a hunt was no place for ladies, but instead, we would ride out the gates and lunch in a clearing nearby. I said nothing as we waited in the courtyard. I had become friends with Captain Sagar, so Asher was insulting more than just the stubborn and pig-headed captain in the king's guard.

Marengo and I waited with the others. Kira rode on a gray mare right beside us, and I watched as she inspected the saddlebags. She too had brought a pack filled with supplies. All around us, the ladies tittered over the oppressive heat, and this time I was inclined to agree.

Sweat had begun to drip down my brow by the time Princess Madawi and her small entourage arrived. Madawi's face was flushed and her arms crossed tight against her chest as she neared. A black mare walked behind Madawi, but the princess ignored its presence entirely. Joppa rode a gray steed, pulling Madawi's horse as they followed. The princess repeatedly ignored her bodyguard's attempts to pass over the leather straps.

She smiled at the duchess, but the sour look still remained on her delicate features.

"What is the matter, Your Highness?" I looked again between Madawi and her stern guard.

Madawi's nose crinkled as she looked back toward the mare.

"I am. . . unfamiliar with these animals. I much prefer the animals of Quados."

I nodded in understanding, suddenly remembering one of the stories Madawi had told me last night about the hump-backed animals her people often rode through the sand.

All around us, members of Court whispered. Even Prince Asher looked impatient as he waited with the duke nearby.

The flush on Madawi's cheeks deepened and she pulled at her long hair anxiously. Asher walked over to us, bowing low before helping Madawi mount. Almost immediately, the horse began to prance nervously.

"Princess, perhaps you should ride with me? I can provide you something safe to ride on." Asher's words were barely a whisper, but it was hard not to miss the innuendo.

To her credit, Madawi smiled sweetly at her soon-to-be betrothed, but I could see her surprise at Asher's words. From the corner of my eye, I watched Joppa's nostrils flare.

Behind us, Kira moved her mare away from the nervous animal. I watched as she moved to the other side of the large wagon horses holding the supplies for our short excursion. The long ropes holding the packs tight against the horses' backs gave me an instant idea.

"Your Highness" —I struggled to raise my voice above the commotion-- "I fear that my mare will be unable to contain her excitement around all these other horses. Perhaps, if you rode next to me, and Marengo was allowed to lead your horse, she might calm. If it is not too much of a burden?"

Asher's head whipped toward me, but I did my best to ignore him. Madawi's eyes shone with sudden understanding.

"Prince Asher, I truly fear allowing your Royal Healer to get injured on the way to a hunt where she will surely be needed. Perhaps I should help her to keep both horses calm."

Prince Asher looked furious as he eyed us both. His mouth grew into a thin line, but he could not very well call the princess a liar and insult her.

"On the way back, then. Marengo will surely be too tired from our journey to cause such problems."

Princess Madawi nodded, and just like that we were off toward the city gates.

A while later, after passing through the sea of tents once more, we arrived at the edge of Sherwood. Madawi thanked me quietly once the bustle of the city drowned us in its noise.

As we neared the top of the hill from which we had arrived only weeks before, I couldn't help but look around at all the faces in our caravan.

I was just about to give up my search as a familiar voice called out from the front.

"We have tracked a pack of boars near the edge of the forest. Whenever you are ready, Your Highness, we can lead you to them."

Robyn's words last night rang through my mind, and I had no doubt that the boars had been driven to the edge of the forest to keep the prince far away from the secrets hidden in Sherwood.

It was several more minutes before the ladies had unpacked all their supplies for the day. The duchess had two large tents erected where the ladies would "wait patiently for the men's triumphant return."

Prince Asher continued to delay, even as the other men returned to their mounts. It was clear to all that the prince was failing to hide his nervousness.

Finally, they were ready to depart.

Robyn and I had done a fantastic job of ignoring each other's presence, and it didn't take long for Madawi's keen insight to notice something was off.

"Marian, perhaps Captain Loxley should take some of your supplies with her. Just in case there is a sudden injury."

I seethed at Madawi. I knew exactly why she was suggesting such a thing. She was trying to force us to interact.

"I will happily give some supplies to one of the king's guards. However, Captain Loxley seems barely able to stay atop her horse. It would be wise of her to wait with us, and continue to recover from her injuries."

I let my gaze settle over Robyn. Her back was stiff in the saddle, as were her movements.

She should not be riding off into a hunt where she might get further injured.

A curious look crossed over Robyn's face as she stared down at me. Her face fell, and I could have sworn it was something like guilt written on her features.

"Thank you for your concern, Lady Marian. I will be fine. However, it may be wise to take some supplies with us."

I handed over my pack, and once again I noticed the look of hurt settle over her. She had certainly noticed what I was not carrying today.

Without another word, Robyn followed after the rest of the hunting party. I watched her disappear into the trees once more and my heart ached in response.

"I'm sure she will be fine. . . " I jumped when Joppa's deep tenor resounded next to me.

"I'm sure they all will be," I replied to the strange guard, before turning my back to the forest.

Madawi had already been swept up by the duchess and I felt a sense of awkwardness overcome me. Although I had enjoyed Duchess Elsie's company during my tour of the market and the city library, we had not exchanged more than a few words since.

A young hostler had taken Marengo and the other horses away to graze in a nearby field, and I found myself suddenly alone.

"It will be grand!" Duchess Elsie's voice drowned out the murmur of the women. "The duke has been looking forward to this ball for *ages.*"

I walked toward the small table where food had been placed for the ladies. Though none of the others seemed interested, I began to grab bits of fruit and piled them onto my plate.

"I am looking forward to it. Though, I am unaccustomed to Notting's dance styles." Madawi's voice was polite, but I recognized her tone immediately. No doubt my friend was feigning an inability to dance to excuse herself from the party earlier and slip off to the library.

"The prince will insist everyone dances." It was Lady Rochelle who spoke now.

I paused in the midst of popping a grape into my mouth. Lady Rochelle's words were clearly a challenge toward Madawi—an unclever attempt to get the princess to embarrass herself before the members of Court. The tent grew quiet as the other women halted their conversations to better listen in.

"Well, if everyone must dance then surely, Lady Rochelle, you would not mind showing off your skills. I'm sure I could learn much from you at the ball."

A smug looked crossed Rochelle's face, and I knew immediately that Madawi had fallen into her trap.

"Of course, Your Highness, I would be delighted to start off the ball by demonstrating some of Notting's most beautiful and elegant dances."

I had no doubt in my mind that Rochelle had planned her words carefully to be able to ask for exactly that. She would show to all the men at Court she was not merely Asher's castaway.

There was a small clamor as I bumped against the table, spilling several of my grapes to the ground. They spilled across the grass and landed precisely at the duchess' feet. My face warmed as I suddenly realized that all eyes in the tent were on me.

I searched for something to say as panic threatened to overcome me. I began hastily grabbing up the grapes, whispering my apologies. I searched for the hidden fruit as I became acutely aware of exactly how idiotic I must look.

Suddenly, a warm, brown hand rested against mine, and I looked up to see Madawi's smiling face.

"Lady Marian has reminded me of exactly how famished I am. Shall we eat before this fretful wind knocks all of our food to the ground?"

There was a murmur of agreement as ladies stood from their pillows and began to amble toward the tables of food.

Madawi's warm arm hooked around mine and she led me toward her cushions. I breathed a sigh of relief once I was seated next to my friend.

"If all these little birds with their noses poking the sky are any indication, this ball may be the most boring event I have ever attended. . . "

I smiled at my friend, thankful for my rescue.

"By the way, I have the perfect thing for you to wear." I felt my heart sink at Madawi's words. I had been hoping to avoid the ball altogether and had been planning to make an excuse about seeing a patient in the city.

It seemed I would be forced to go. I could only hope that it would be as boring as the princess expected. My days had already been far too adventurous.

Robyn

"The King has lost his mind."

Father spilled his fury to the forest. Even though he should be safe among our men, the treasonous words sent a tremor through everyone present.

Sensing my discomfort, Gold shifted uneasily. I ran my hand across her sweat-filled mane, trying to ease her.

The men were silent. No one spoke as my father fumed atop his horse.

"His people starve in the streets. His soldiers starve in their tents, and still, he hosts another party!" The Baron of Loxley raked his hands through his hair once again.

"Something must be done." The solemn words of my father's second, Sir Johnathan, brought a series of nods. I watched as Father's gaze trailed across each face. Each beard was unkempt, each cloak threadbare across heavy shoulders. Lines spread beneath every pair of weary eyes. These were the captains of my father's private army, and they had seen enough desolation throughout Notting to last a lifetime.

"It's time to send a message to the other nobility. It's time for the Court to take a stand." I could hardly believe the words as they slipped past my lips. My heart thumped wildly in my chest. A sour feeling sat in my stomach.

There were members of the Court who wouldn't take a stand. Members who had no family left to back them if they risked it all.

Members like Marian.

"And what of those who won't?" Father's face was filled with questions as I urged my horse toward the center of the circle.

Perhaps the king is not the only one to whom father has sent his spies. . .

I locked eyes with him as I approached.

"Then they shall find life in the capital, especially getting supplies to the castle, much more difficult."

A murmur of approval went through the small crowd of men as a smile spread across father's face. I had not yet earned his forgiveness, but he was listening to my advice nonetheless.

My breath caught in my throat as I approached, guiding my horse beside his. He waited for me to continue.

I scanned the faces around me. No one in my father's service doubted the will and determination of women. When my mother was alive, she had seen us through every harsh winter. She had cared for the sick, managed my father's estate, and fought alongside his soldiers when the desert people attacked. I thought of her as I continued.

"The fields to the north are dying. Only the villages along Sherwood are still thriving. The northern nobility are depending on those supplies. They must run the supplies through the twin rivers or along the hills of the Great Valley. It's time to make it harder to supply their land. It is time to force their hand with the cries of their people."

Father's eyes were cold as he looked at the men around him. The hairs along my neck and arms stood on end. "Soon, the Court must decide and then either King Ruelle will step down willingly or he will be taken down forcefully."

Father's fury had stirred something in all of us as we trickled back toward the castle. Jonathan and the other men would spend the evening in the city making their plans, while we would continue gathering information inside at the banquet.

The duke was known as someone who spared no expense, especially when it came to his wine. There would be plenty of loose lips tonight.

As we entered the main corridor, Gawayne and Samwell nodded to me as they left for their chambers. They were already late for tonight's festivities. The corridors were quiet as I wound through the castle.

I replayed it all in my head. I had meant every word. It was time that sides were chosen and real steps were taken.

My heart quickened again at the thought as my head spun at the reality of what was coming. There was no going back now. The rebellion would succeed, or Notting would fall to anarchy.

Different dread filled me as music floated through the air. The castle was stirring with energy as the throng of nobility spilled in and out of the grand hall. Unwilling to face the sea of judgment, I headed toward the gardens.

Music followed me out the glass doors as I walked along the hedges. Vibrant pinks and oranges of the strange, tropical flowers grew along the walls. Their sweet aroma wrapped around me, settling the turmoil inside my mind.

A soft rustle of pages greeted me, and I was surprised to find Marian tucked away against the outer wall. A torch had been lit above her and an enormous tome, probably borrowed from the duke's library, rested in her lap.

"What are you doing out here?"

I watched Marian startle. The book she had been reading fell to the ground at her feet. Torchlight twinkled around her, making her hair glow as it lifted in the breeze. Memories of her hair billowing behind her as we raced away from the assassins sat in my mind. I remembered how she had stunned the men that night.

A thought itched at the back of my mind. *She had stunned me too.*

I ambled slowly toward her. Something stirred inside of me at the sight of her in the dress. A gold band held the thin pieces of fabric together at her shoulders. The long cut in the front was low, accentuating her breasts. Long swaths of black fabric pooled at her feet.

It certainly wasn't the style of our Court. The delicate, black satin was as priceless as gold. The tiny jewels glittered against the darkness. She had become a star made flesh.

The princess had truly given Marian a beloved piece and the angry, jealous feeling I had been resisting since the night I caught them holding hands rose in my gut again. The other events of that night played in my mind as well. I had no right to be jealous after the way I had treated her.

I resisted the urge to smile when I spotted the blade I had given her tucked against her leg.

"Leave me be, Robyn." Marian retrieved the book from its place on the ground, affording me a glance at the low dip of her dress. I could not help but consider what else might be hidden beneath the soft fabric.

"Shouldn't you be inside dancing?" My ribs still ached as I came to rest against the edge of a large, granite fountain in the center of the garden.

Perhaps an afternoon on horseback had been too much.

The corner of Marian's mouth twitched, and she jutted her chin forward. She had seen me wince.

"You are in no position to tell me what I should or shouldn't be doing, just as you have made it perfectly clear that I cannot tell you what you should or shouldn't do."

I knew I was in no position to argue. She had obviously been right. I should not have joined in on the hunt, but something in her furious stare kept me going.

"Why worry about me so much, Lady Marian?" I stretched my legs out in front of me, crossing my arms against the ache in my chest.

"You're right, Captain Loxley. Do as you wish. I'm just the one who has to put you back together each time you insist on acting like you're disposable." Marian raised her voice, drowning out the music around us.

I watched as she raked her fingers through her long hair before slamming the book closed. "You act like your life doesn't matter, and you can risk it as you see fit!"

"It doesn't, and I can."

A blur of red zoomed past my face. I dodged instinctively, watching the book skitter and bounce on the walkway behind me. I stood up from the fountain, heart pounding. My mouth fell open in absolute shock as Marian stood from her place on the bench.

"Did you just *throw* that enormous book at me?"

Marian crossed her arms over her chest as she stood defiantly before me. The black silk of her dress shimmered around her feet. "Yes, I did. Next time, I shall try harder not to miss."

"Why are you throwing books at me?" I laughed as I looked once more over my shoulder to where the book was splayed on the ground.

I didn't hear Marian close the distance between us, and when I turned around she was square with my chest.

Her lips had been painted a deep rouge and her eyes lined with kohl. I found myself instantly mesmerized as I looked down at her.

I could not fight the gentle lift of my lips as she jutted her chin outward. She placed a delicate finger against my chest and my body throbbed in response.

How could just a single touch ignite such a fire?

"Because, despite the fact that you push me away, and despite the fact that you hide behind this bravado where you pretend not to care about Court, or the prince, or me, I know the truth. I see the way you looked at me when I was with Madawi. I see the way you look at me when I'm with Asher—even though his attention makes my stomach turn. I see the way you look at me, Robyn, and you're an absolute idiot."

My heart stopped for a second as Marian brought her hands up, placing them on the sides of my face. Her soft hands pressed against my cheeks. My blood raced as she pulled me closer.

Her lips were velvet against mine as she stole my breath. This wasn't a soft or delicate kiss. There was a deep hunger in her touch as I opened my mouth, allowing her tongue to explore. My resistance melted away with her touch. Her tongue danced in my mouth as she deepened the kiss. Her fingers wrapped into my hair.

Warmth spread through me. I needed her in a way I had never experienced. I longed to lift that dress, to feel the soft curves of her body against mine. I reached out to wrap my hands around her waist, but just as quickly as the kiss had come, her lips left mine. One moment her mouth was there, and the next she was gone.

My breath came out in quick bursts as I gasped, stumbling back into reality. I turned toward the walkway, but Marian had already picked up her book.

The glass doors closed behind her, and with the click of the latch both her and the music had disappeared.

Marian

I knew Robyn might follow, and I tried in vain to convince myself not to care, but it was almost impossible not to turn around. The music drifted over me, and despite my earlier protests, I stepped back toward the Grand Hall.

All manner of men and women had joined the dance since I had left. Once Lady Rochelle's debut was over, I had longed to slip out as quietly as possible.

Madawi and Asher sat on a temporary dais. The sight of them together stopped me short. His hand rested on hers, and she seemed to smile at whatever he was whispering. For the first time, it really hit me. One day, they would not only marry, they would rule the kingdom together. It was hard not to picture the future as they looked down from their seats above us all.

A shiver went down my spine as I looked at my newest friend and the man who used to be my oldest friend. Madawi was much more adept at these events than she gave herself credit for. Even from a distance, her laughter seemed to carry. Whether she was comfortable next to the prince or not, no one would be able to tell.

As for Asher, the prince was once again well into his cups. Though he seemed to whisper something to his betrothed, every few seconds his gaze would linger just a little too long on the ladies gliding across the dance floor.

During Lady Rochelle's *glorious* display of all of Notting's finest dances earlier, I had found myself indulging in the wine that servants were readily handing out.

No doubt, that was what had caused my rather impromptu violence toward Robyn, and the rather spontaneous action that followed.

I grabbed another glass of wine from a silver tray being carried by a rather good-looking, male servant nearby. The man's long, blond hair was tied back away from his face and his brown eyes twinkled with hidden mischief as he nodded at me.

The cool wine slid down my throat as I drank the entire glass. Though the wine had obviously been chilled to combat the oppressive heat of the Grand Hall, it did not stop the unfamiliar burn of the alcohol.

It wasn't very often that I imbibed. As an apprentice, I had seen far too many widows crying over their drunkard husbands. Men with faces like yellow leather often arrived at the tower after too many nights at the local taverns. Usually, by the time they came to see Mistress Genevieve, it was already far, far too late.

Still, the image of Robyn atop her horse played through my mind as I picked up another glass from the tray. I knew I was drinking too fast, and I had left the ball earlier before any food was served.

Music played around me, and I felt the handsome servant step a little closer.

"I have been told that my duties here will be complete by midnight if the lady will be in need of help later in the evening. . . "

The servant's gaze was hooded as he whispered. The part of me that was drunk and lonely battled against the part of me that had been fixated on a pair of plump lips I had just tasted. I briefly considered the man's offer.

It had been such a long time since someone else had truly warmed my bed. . .

"Actually, I believe your shift will be extended to the morning." Robyn's voice was ice as she approached from behind. Next to her, Samwell's sly grin peeked at the corner of his mouth.

"Captain Loxley—"

"That will be all." It was Samwell who spoke now. The young man disappeared in a hurry. My jaw ached as I gritted my teeth. I took a deep breath as I faced Robyn and Samwell. Though I was fairly certain I would not have taken the young man up on his offer, it wasn't as if Robyn had made any offers of her own.

"Lady Marian, are you quite enjoying yourself?" Samwell's voice was filled with suppressed laughter as he raised the glass in his hand toward his mouth.

Next to him, Robyn's looked at the man with unleashed fury. She closed the distance between us quickly. I struggled to focus as she moved.

"You have made quite an impression on many tonight, Lady Marian. . . " Robyn angled herself so that she stood between me and the rest of the room. Kira had tied dozens of loose, white ribbons all throughout my hair earlier that night. I felt my breath catch in my throat as she brushed one of them away from my exposed collarbone. As it had been in the garden, I felt her gaze dip down the center of my dress.

A shiver ran down my spine and I felt myself step closer to her. It was suddenly impossible to stop staring at her mouth, and the drunken voice in my head urged me to taste her lips once again.

Like an invisible tether had been snapped between us, Robyn jumped back as I moved closer. My vision suddenly came into focus, and I was once again doused with the sobering reality that I was unwanted.

Fine.

I felt something inside of me snap too. I hadn't imagined her hooded looks. I hadn't imagined this heat between us. I had tired of playing these incessant games. I swallowed the rest of my wine as I turned my back to Robyn--setting my sights on another.

"Samwell. Would you care to dance?"

Samwell's eyes grew big and round. He looked panicked between me and Robyn. I snatched the glass of wine from his hand as well, downing the rest and handing the glass roughly to Robyn. I did not wait for a reply as I grabbed his hand and walked toward the center of the room.

Ever the charmer, it became quickly apparent why Samwell had achieved his reputation with women. Without missing a beat, my handsome partner fell in step with the music. His hand fell to the soft silk along my waist, guiding me across the dance floor with the other.

Samwell's firm body pressed against my hips as he pulled us closer.

"She was right, you do make quite an impression."

My mind was spinning as the tempo increased and Samwell and I moved faster. In a move I hadn't expected, he dipped me back into his long arms. My head continued to spin as suddenly everyone was watching from the ceiling.

"I know she can be difficult, but you have no idea what she would risk," Samwell whispered against my neck. I leaned my head upward, arching a brow at my dance partner.

Gentle, but quick, Samwell righted me and we were off again. As we turned left and right, I felt his firm hands guiding me from one position to another. He seemed to lift my body with ease, and I marveled at his skill.

We danced like that for several minutes. The music seemed to flow through us as we made our course around the room.

"She went to the prince that next morning and held a knife to his throat. She made it quite clear what would happen if he behaved like that around you, or any woman, again."

The reality of Samwell's words settled over me as the music came to a stop. I watched in a haze as he leaned over to kiss the top of my hand. There was a startling sincerity in his gaze. When our eyes met, I knew he had spoken the truth.

Robyn had placed her own life before mine—just as she had been doing since we left the
capital.

I turned back to where I had left her, but Robyn was already gone.

Over the next few days, I hurried back and forth to the markets to gather as many supplies as I could. Kira joined me every day. Despite my dance with Samwell, she was eager to help.

"I knew what you were doing. . . " —Kira told me the next morning with a wink-- "It's about time Captain Loxley stopped acting foolish and decided what she wanted. Besides, I made Samwell make it up to me after the ball. We danced together *several times* in my chambers last night."

I couldn't hold back my laughter at Kira's blunt words. I had come to admire her unique ways. Kira seemed unabashed in her desires. It was not uncommon to hear her and Samwell's exploits at night if you wandered too close to their chamber door. Even Captain Danyeil had been rumored to have been spotted leaving their chambers in the early hours of the morning.

Finally, the supplies had been gathered. I had talked to every captain in every ship that made port at Colch. I counted the load of supplies that were to be sent to the capital. It wasn't as much as I had hoped, but there was nothing else to be done. Kira and I had been working to smuggle supplies into the camps as well. Every night Kira and I had taken as many supplies as we could carry out to the camps. Each night, Samwell had been assigned as our guard. The people had come to expect us, and it worried me to leave them behind now.

Between the camps outside of Colch, the hidden villages inside Sherwood, and the tournament in the Capital, the supplies were spread almost as thin as when I had arrived a the eastern markets.

Just as they had arrived, so did the caravan gather in the Duke's courtyard and prepare to leave. I sat atop Marengo as the mare paced anxiously in the crowd.

It seemed this time there would be a great many noblemen taking carriages back to the capital. Though the guards around us remained alert, I was sure it was a relief to many. With the addition of the princess and her guards, as well as the extra nobility that had arrived to greet her, the caravan was vast. Carriages and their guards stretched well out of the courtyard and toward the city gates.

Madawi had invited me to attend her in the carriage, but I politely declined. Though a carriage would be more comfortable at times on the long journey, I wouldn't miss the chance to see the camps again. Nor would I miss any opportunity to assure them that I would not forget them when I left Colch.

Samwell and Gawayne appeared beside me. As before, Gawayne skillfully directed the large pull-horses through the crowd. The horses were pulling my last cart of supplies behind them.

Samwell's smile was full as he winked at me. Only seconds later, a group of ragged-looking men entered the courtyard.

The men and their horses stampeded around us. Each man spread himself out on the edges of the caravan. A banner-man rode to the front, carrying a green flag with golden trim. Three enormous trees had been embroidered on the flag.

It seemed the men of Loxley would be our guard for this journey.

Worry built in my stomach as I remembered the tense conversation at breakfast only a few days before. Had Prince Asher asked Baron Sebastion to lead the caravan to provide extra security since the princess would now be part of the company? I tried to count the number of men wearing the Loxley colors, but it was hard to keep track as the men got into formation. It seemed an excessive amount of men just to provide an escort—especially considering Duke Inglis had already offered two dozen of his men as additional security.

Was this an attempt to dissuade more attacks on the road or some sort of show of power between the Baron and the prince? Something in my gut told me I did not want to know the answer.

"My men have left out some rather crucial details of your journey." My heart leapt to my throat as the Baron of Loxley rode up to Marengo's side on a tall, black stallion. Robyn pulled up behind him. Her gaze was downcast as she rode Gold in silence.

"Why do you say that, my lord?"

"It seems none of them have prepared me with accurate descriptions of how beautiful you are, Lady Marian."

I struggled not to laugh aloud at the Baron's blatant attempts at flattery. One thing I had learned since the Baron's arrival was that he was the last person I wanted to know better.

I forced my face to remain passive so as not to show this powerful man my disgust. I had not spoken to him at all since his arrival, but I had seen enough servants run from his path to know the kind of man he truly was.

Images of Robyn's ruffled tunic and the red mark on her cheek flashed through my mind. I took a breath to steady the anger growing inside of me once again.

"Though, I should not have been surprised. . . " --Sebastion continued, oblivious to my antipathy toward him-- ". . . since your mother was a great beauty as well."

Marengo responded to my sudden discomfort with a tense whip of her head. Now, beside me, Robyn quickly steered Gold clear. I ran a hand down my horse's long neck as I gathered my rapid thoughts.

"I did not know you knew Lady Reay, Father." Robyn's words were filled with curiosity as she once again steered Gold closer.

"I was actually with her when she came to this country with the queen. King Ruelle and Queen Naomi were to be wed in the capital, and Lady Reay came to accompany."

My heart raced as I listened intently, suddenly desperate to hear more. No one had ever told me of my mother, except to express sympathies of her passing or when the queen reminded me of my yearly dues.

I tried to keep my voice level with great difficulty. "In what way do I resemble her?"

Lord Sebastion's face filled with softness as he looked me over. Unlike the gaze of most men, his did not make me squirm. There was no heated assessment. I didn't feel the sudden desire to don additional clothing. To my surprise, his gaze held sudden warmth, as if recalling a fond memory.

"When I met your mother she wore her hair in braids much like yours, but tighter against the skin. Sometimes the northern people would even braid strings or feathers into their long locks. They are a wild people, stealing land and crops from each other for centuries. But, you will never find better horsemen."

Sebastion shifted in his saddle, and this time he looked over Marengo.

"It's odd you would end up a healer, and so you would ride that white mare. It wasn't until your mother's people came to Notting that we bred them. Your mother had a white mare as well. Her people loved horse races, and in all the months I knew her she never lost."

My mouth fell open. I had never learned so much about my mother, and Lord Sebastion had no idea the gift he had given me. Tears welled in my eyes, and I fought to keep them at bay.

"Marian has a gift with horses as well." Robyn declared beside me. Once again I found myself struck.

Had she truly just complimented me?

"She helped Gold after that arrow sliced her." It was Robyn's turn to reach down and pat her horse lovingly.

"Ah, yes. We were all fortunate that more injuries were not sustained in that fight." Sebastion looked to Robyn, who nodded in agreement. There was no missing the condemnation in his words.

"It would have been far worse if not for Robyn's quick thinking. She rounded the men so quickly, and recognized the trap before anyone else." Robyn's head drew back quickly, and then she seemed to freeze for a moment atop her horse.

I realized that she wasn't someone who usually accepted or expected praise. A familiar pain filled my chest as I looked at the brave warrior who had nearly sacrificed herself for me.

"I have a feeling our journey back to the capital will be far less eventful." Gawayne's deep voice carried over the noise of the cart.

We all nodded in agreement. Even Baron Loxley. Most, if not all, of the assassins were dead deep in the heart of Sherwood. With the princess' guards, the ones added by the duke, and the men accompanying Robyn's father, it would take nothing short of an army to breach our defenses. Still, a shiver went down my spine, raising the hair along my neck and arms. I found myself looking at the road ahead, wondering what dangers might wait for us at home.

Robyn

In all of my memory, there had never been someone as unimpressed by Father's charm as Marian clearly was.

Though Marian was clearly desperate to learn more about her mother, she would not fall prey to Father's charms as other women had.

As the sun began to shine high overhead, the caravan finally began to move. Our pace was painstakingly slow as I moved Gold beside Marian's horse.

We passed through the Duke's outer gate, beginning the deep descent toward the city below. It took nearly an hour to get through the road leading to the city gates, and my anxiety grew with every passing moment. This caravan could not be more different than the one we had used to enter Colch. The clattering of hooves and the clunk of the carts filled the air around us. Though I was not the commanding officer of this caravan, and though we had far, far more men with us than before, I still fell ill at ease.

As we walked beneath the city gate, my fear only heightened. If one of the horses were to spook and cause a stampede, it could become more deadly than the most highly-trained assassin.

Scene after scene of the deadly possibilities played over in my mind. Marian had, of course, been correct that I wasn't fit to participate in the prince's hunt. As my back ached, I feared the rest of the journey.

I shifted atop Gold, straightening and stretching my stiff muscles when I felt a nudge along my leg. I turned to see Marian's sapphire eyes staring at me intently.

My heart pounded in response as looked toward her. We had barely spoken since the night of the ball, and I found myself remembering how stunning she had been in that long dress.

I had spent many long hours obliterating a field dummy that evening. Though I held no ill-will against Samwell now, I had certainly imagined his face on that dummy many times as I fired my arrows into it.

A small smile curled at the edge of Marian's mouth, and I wondered if she was reading thoughts.

Her long, blond hair was plaited down her back once more. The white ribbon caught in the gentle breeze, trailing across her arm between us as I looked down at the offering in her hand.

"For you," she whispered. I grabbed the tiny vial from her hand as confusion filled me. "It will help ease the discomfort of the long ride."

I looked at the glass in my hand, and for a moment I was truly stunned. It was a tiny thing, obviously meant for a single dose of whatever lay inside. Still, it nearly brought me to tears as I pondered the implications of such thoughtfulness. Despite my rudeness—despite everything between us over the last month, she had still remembered me in her preparations.

The sudden wave of emotions surprised me, and I drank the contents in one swig.

"Lady Marian, we are truly blessed to have you as Royal Healer." I handed the empty vial back to her, careful not to drop it as our horses bumped closer.

My heart swelled even more as a deep blush grew over her cheeks.

After a second too long of staring, I felt a sudden warmth across my cheeks as well. Suddenly, I found myself looking intently at the back of Gold's long mane.

It wasn't long before the atmosphere around the caravan changed once more, and I felt my long-honed instincts itching for me to pay attention. The guards around us went silent, and the air itself seemed to shift. We were free of the city gates, and what stood before us was astounding.

A sea of faces lined the roadway leading through the camps. Young and old, man and woman, and children of every age stood still. Their faces stared into the caravan.

In front of us, Prince Asher and Princess Madawi had pulled open the windows of the carriage the couple shared. I strained to see past their host of guards, but the glint of gold on the prince's hand was evident in the sunlight. For once, the prince was showing up for his people.

Something unsettling sat in my stomach, and I peered through the crowd as the caravan slowed. All around me, the faces of the men in the guard showed it too. Something was off about the way the people stood along the road. No one shouted. No one even acknowledged Prince Asher or the princess.

Instead, each face in the crowd seemed to search the caravan for something—or someone— else.

Beside me, something shifted in my periphery. I realized too late that it was Marian maneuvering her white mare behind Gold. Her Marengo's long mane seemed to glisten in the sunlight as she moved the horse toward the outer ring of guards.

Panic filled me, and I spun Gold around to follow.

As if they too were stunned, the guards allowed Marian to pass. I knew the moment the people had been waiting for had come as Marian emerged from the caravan.

Every face in the long line of people turned. I urged Gold closer behind her, and I could see the changes in every face as they recognized Marian. The murmur around us grew, shaking through the camps as thousands of people called to her.

As if on cue, a young girl just out of reach unrolled a long, white cloth. I watched as the breeze picked it up and the girl's smile widened. Next to her, an older gentleman unrolled his white cloth, and then another, and another and another. Until, all across the camp, and stretching far up the road, was a river of white ribbons.

The people in the camps had not lined up to see their prince--they had lined up to say goodbye to their healer.

Marian's brought her hands to her face, clearly feeling shocked as she turned again to look at me. I pulled Gold just behind Marengo. For a second, we marveled at the scene before us.

"They are on both sides of the road." A guard next to us remarked. "Perhaps you should ride at the front of the caravan, where you will be seen by all."

Marian looked at me, and I could see her indecision. She was trusting me with her safety--like she had on the road here and again in Sherwood. I would not let her down again.

"Samwell!" I called above the clamor, but my second was already close behind. His face was also full of amazement at the spectacle before us as he approached.

"We will give them what they want. . . " --I looked back at Marian— ". . . and what they want is clearly to see their healer."

Marian's chin quivered for a moment as she looked between Samwell and me. With a nod, she turned to face the road. Marengo took off at a trot toward the front.

The noise grew deafening as Marian traveled further up the road. Now that the citizens of Notting on all sides of the road could see her, there was no hesitation in their voices.

I watched her golden hair glide in the wind. The white coat of her horse and the soft, shimmer of her skin seemed to combine as she rode into the sunlight. Just as before, the people of Notting were stunned by

the glow of her beauty—and this time, so was I.

Marian, Samwell, and I arrived at the outpost well ahead of the rest of the caravan. Riding outside of the thundering herd of guards had afforded us plenty of space—even with Marian stopping to smile at every child she passed by.

It had been hours since we left the camps behind, but still, it seemed none of us knew what to say. We rode in silence until we neared the faint light of the outpost.

When we passed the first look-outs, their alarmed faces were no surprise to Samwell or myself. Samwell hurried to ride ahead. He would explain to the outpost commander that there was no need for alarm.

Beside me, Marian pulled on Marengo's reins abruptly. This time when I looked at her, her brows were knit tightly together and she chewed at her bottom lip. A tremble seemed to shake her as the reality of what had happened along the road settled over her again.

"Come with me," I whispered into the air between us. Pulling Gold's reins to my right, I urged the mare closer to Marian. As I grabbed at the reins in Marian's hand, I couldn't help but notice their tremble.

The trees of Sherwood stretched along our left, but this time I took Marian away from their comforting branches. We rode in silence for a few minutes as the incline steadily increased. To my surprise, neither she nor her horse seemed to resist as Gold and I led them higher and higher up the rocky terrain.

Time passed and night fell around us. The soft glow of the moonlight settled over us, and the sounds of the road had long faded away.

Finally, when I sensed we were near enough, I pulled Gold to a stop. Marengo pulled to a stop behind, and in seconds Marian and I had both dismounted.

Marian stared at the ground beneath her feet, and I knew the weight of her worry. She did not resist as I took her hand and we walked away from our horses and into the darkness.

The hard rocks beneath our feet threatened our every step, but Marian and I finally reached the edge of the cliff.

"This is not the highest point in Notting, but it is the highest point between the capital and the Impassible Mountains."

As if startling from her stupor, Marian seemed to awaken as she looked around us, and then gazed up at the sky. I watched the soft rise and fall of her chest as she took it all in.

Her slender neck stretched toward the heavens, and I found myself brushing her delicate skin with my fingertips. Her chin dropped back down until her gaze was again level with mine.

"That night you rode into the camp I think every man who laid his eyes on you fell in love." The words left my lips before I could stop them, but I could think of nothing truer to say.

Marian looked at me and I could see her doubt. Part of me knew it was doubt that I had put there. There were only so many chances you were given to show someone who you truly were before they believed it. There were only so many times you were allowed to fail them before they walked away forever.

As I looked at Marian in the starlight, part of me prayed to whatever gods that might be listening that she had not completely given up on me yet.

"I am afraid." Her voice was soft as her warm breath tickled against my skin.

I stepped closer to her and my fingers were once again lost in her long hair. Marian bit at her lip and I wondered briefly if she spoke of her fear of me, or of the display we had just taken part in.

"Prince Asher and the king and queen will not like what happened today—not when they have had so many problems throughout the kingdom."

I felt myself harden at her words, but I did my best to keep my tone in check as I thought back to all that the royal family had cost the people of Notting.

"They should worry. Today their people showed true devotion, and the royal family has no idea how powerful that can be."

"But what if they *do* know? What if they realize how misplaced the people's devotion is?"

Marian's head dropped to her chest as she sighed deeply. I felt the shudder of her breath as I stepped closer.

"I will not let harm come to you." I ran my thumb along her cheek, raising her face toward mine again.

"Even you cannot stop the Crown." Marian's brows pulled together once more. Guilt ate away at my stomach. I would do anything to keep her worries at bay.

"We shall see." I smiled at her as we stood in the starlight.

She had no idea what the Loxleys had been planning. She had no idea just how ready we were to begin.

"Can we stay here tonight? I don't think I can stand the gossips in the tents." Marian's laughter was forced now, but I knew she was right. There was no doubt what topics had been on everyone's minds, and whose name had been on everyone's lips.

"We will not be able to light a fire."

I still had not moved my hand from her neck, and her warm skin reached for mine.

"Then we shall have to move our bedrolls very, very close. . . for warmth, of course."

As I looked at her smile full of mischief, I knew there was no turning back.

Marian

The next few days were the busiest I had ever seen in the tower. True to her word, Genevieve met us at the gate dressed in a plain, gray dress—a clear sight to the acolytes and to the Court that the new Royal Healer had arrived.

Since then, there had not been a moment where we were not hurrying to finish preparations.

It was the second day in a row I had failed to leave the tower for even a moment. Kira and I had been working without pause to make sure each acolyte was prepared for their duties.

It was not until a messenger direct from Prince Asher summoned me to the tournament area, that I finally emerged from the Healer's Tower.

The morning was already hot, though the sun had only just peaked above the trees in the distance. I rode through the city on the back of Marengo, mentally running over the tasks still yet to be completed. As the people of the capital emerged from their homes, I reminded myself to double-check which acolyte I had assigned to help those in need.

Though most of our aid would be to injuries sustained in the tournament, I could not allow the people of the capital to suffer either. With the influx of people, the stores of food would be depleted well before harvest time.

Genevieve had shared such information with the king months ago, but it seemed just like the people in the camps outside of Colch, the royal family could not be bothered with something as trivial as whether or not the common people had enough to eat.

The field just outside the city gates had been prepped while we were away. Great, wooden stands had been erected to help spectators gain a better view of the events. As I urged Marengo closer to the field,

I watched the long, flowing banners representing each of the great houses of Notting, which been mounted along the length of the stands.

As we continued our approach, I was reminded of the scene outside of Colch just days before. When Robyn and I had finally returned to the caravan, it was hard to hide from the whispers. Even the guards had questions in their eyes as they watched me curiously.

Why had the citizens of Notting responded to me so strongly? How would the King respond, especially once he learned of the disdain the people held for Prince Asher?

In between finishing task after task, I had waited anxiously to be called to the throne room or questioned by the captain of the guards.

A sour feeling sat in my stomach as I looked down at the piece of parchment in my mind, instructing me to go to the royal tent. Above the stands, a temporary throne had been built, where the king and members of Court would watch and judge the events. I swallowed back my nervousness as I dismounted Marengo and climbed the steps to the platform above.

I reached the last step, but no one was waiting to greet me.

I looked out over the field beneath the stands. My stomach churned at the idea of the macabre scene that would soon grace the lush field before me. In only a few days' time, the field below would be stained with blood. Again, I was reminded of the true purpose of the tournament. It was one thing for the king to host a tournament where the participants would join freely—it was another to force the great families of Notting to compete for their share of bread.

"Hello, Lady Marian." Prince Asher's smooth voice startled me from my thoughts. I had not heard him approach.

I immediately realized why. For once, Asher was without his entourage. Alone, before me, was the man who had once been my friend. His smile was sweet as he approached, but it brought me none of the comforts it had in childhood. There had been too many late nights and too many hooded glances to ever go back to what once had been.

"How go the preparations? It is said that you or your assistants have hardly left the tower since our arrival."

His words sent a chill down my spine. *Had he been watching me?*

"The preparations have gone well, Your Highness. We will be ready in time for the tournament."

Asher circled me once more. His blue eyes seemed to search my face for answers to questions he had yet to speak. I resisted the urge to bristle beneath his stare, or to reach for the dagger tucked tight against my thigh.

"Things are changing in Notting." Prince Asher looked out over the field before us now. I turned to watch as he leaned against the railing separating spectators from the steep fall below. "It is good that you have finally become Royal Healer and can now stay so close." His lustful stare traveled over me again, and this time I couldn't help but shudder. "This tournament will undoubtedly present opportunities for marriage proposals, trade agreements, and other alliances to form." Asher ran his long fingers through his hair, and I waited for him to continue. "Though I will be promised to another soon, I hope you and I can still remain close."

Asher closed the distance between us before I could respond. My heart hammered wildly in my chest as he took my hand. His grip was tight as he held on.

"I would hate to see you lose your place in Court for choosing the wrong match. I have informed Mother that without a father to choose a suitable match for you, I shall take over the duty."

My heart dropped into my stomach as he continued. Asher's voice was ice as he brought his free hand to graze my cheek.

"Should I feel that you are choosing unwisely, I will be forced to find you an appropriate suitor. Perhaps someone like Captain Sampson. That way you can still be close to the capital."

Asher's threat was clear as he cocked his head. I was not to be anyone's but his—including Robyn's. He would marry me off to someone old enough to be my grandfather if he had to. Asher would find a way to keep me from escaping.

His mouth was only inches from mine, and I fought back the urge to vomit. I leaned back from Asher, acting sheerly out of instinct. A burst of sharp, disjointed laughter rose from him.

"That is what I thought." He sneered as his grip threatened to break the brittle bones in my fingers.

"Asher. You're hurting me!" I struggled to wrestle my hand free. Instinct finally kicked in as I remember a trick I had learned during my brief trainings with Danyeil and Robyn. I turned my hand in toward my thumb, forcing him to release his grip.

Something seemed to click as I stepped back from the prince. A look passed over him, and the calm demeanor from moments before returned.

"Mother says you are to attend the royal tent during the tournament—in case one of the ladies suffers from the heat or needs attention. Prepare your acolytes accordingly. I shall see you then."

With that, Asher was gone, leaving me alone with the dreadful reality that my life had just become.

I had taken my time returning Marengo to her stall. Though the hostlers offered, I needed time to process everything that had just occurred. There seemed no better way to do that than by brushing down the beautiful, white mare.

Asher's words were sitting heavy on my mind as the day continued. The doors of the barn had been opened to allow the gentle breeze to push through. As always, I plaited her long mane to match my long strands. It made me feel even more connected to the horse— and she certainly didn't seem to mind. When nothing else was left to be done for Marengo, I finally turned to go.

A hard shove against my shoulder brought me to an abrupt stop. I turned, surprised to find Gold's soft muzzle reaching from her stall.

"Oh, well if you insist." I reached up, rubbing my hand along her soft neck. I entered Gold's stall as the horse continued to swat its long tail at me. She was obviously impatient for me to begin.

"I have never seen two mares behave so oddly," Lee's gentle voice came from just outside the stall. "This one nearly kicked down the door of its last stall. She won't allow anyone to remove her or take her to the pasture without Marengo here by her side."

"I thought she hated the city?" I brushed gently along the grain of Gold's coat, thinking back to the day we had left for Colch.

"It seems she can adjust to her time here if this one is by her side. . . "

The old man's gentle laughter brought a smile to my face and I felt my cheeks flush. I looked over Gold's beautiful coat, trying not to let myself remember her owner I was so desperate to see. Though she had not left my side during the ride back to the capital, Robyn and I hadn't seen each other since we arrived at the city.

As if summoned by my thoughts, Robyn appeared at Gold's stall door just as I finished braiding the horse's long mane.

"Never in my life did I think I would be jealous of a horse."

I startled at her sudden words, though I couldn't help the smile that grew on its own.

"She does look quite beautiful," I remarked as I tied off the horse's hair with a leather strap.

"She does." I turned to see Robyn staring at me intensely, and my breath quickened in response. "Are you hungry?"

"I am, but I fear I have been hiding out in here for far too long already. Kira must be panicking and wondering where I have been."

Robyn's face fell a little, and an ache grew in my chest.

"Dinner tonight? You could meet me outside of my chambers?"

A small smile rose at the corner of Robyn's mouth as she nodded.

We walked back to the Healer's Tower in comfortable silence, and I thought about that small smile for the rest of the day.

Unfortunately, I had been unable to keep my word to Robyn. I had sent a messenger with a note, but guilt still ate at me all through the evening. It wasn't until well after midnight that I was finally able to step away from the day's chores.

My feet were weary and my bones felt heavy when I finally made it to my chamber door.

To my surprise, a long pair of legs jutted out from the wall as I approached. My heart skipped a beat as memories of the nights Asher had appeared at my door flooded my mind.

Perhaps he had more to say about this morning. . .

I felt hesitant as I moved forward—inwardly debating whether I should return to a more public place like the workroom.

I breathed a sigh of relief when I noticed the shadow had lush, feminine curves and held a tray filled with food.

"I cannot believe you came so late."

"Why? Were you expecting someone else at your door this late at night?" Robyn's laugh carried through the corridor, but I noticed how it had not reached her eyes. I knew she sensed my fear.

"Everyone who comes to my door this late at night, early in the morning--whatever you call it is most definitely unwelcome."

"Well, the tournament starts tomorrow. I'm sure plenty of contestants will be looking to impress the beautiful Royal Healer."

"Including you?" The words left my lips before I could stop them. Robyn stepped closer to me now, and I felt myself step back against the door. Robyn placed the tray of food on a small table nearby.

"It seems I will not be allowed to compete. I shall merely have to watch." She leaned closer to me, and I watched the rise and fall of her chest while my heart pounded in response. "Prince Asher, it seems, has been busy. I heard he summoned you to the field."

I nodded. "He had much to say about my return to the capital and my position becoming official." Though I didn't understand it, I did not want to tell Robyn what Asher had told me this morning. He was the prince and there was nothing to be done about it.

"It seems I shall have plenty of time to watch. Prince Asher has informed me that Queen Naomi has declared that I am to attend the ladies of Court should one of them fall faint at the heat or the dreadful sight of blood."

I could not keep the disdain from my voice as I spoke—but it was not as if I could ignore a direct order from the queen. Just, as it seemed, I could not escape the prince's reach.

"That seems a waste of both your time and skills." Robyn's voice softened as her eyes raked over me. Unlike this morning with the prince, I welcomed the heat behind her stare.

"I could say the same for you being on the sidelines. They are probably too afraid to be bested by a woman." This time, I meant the words that came out. Robyn's mouth perked a little at the side, and my hand found its way to her cheek as if moving on its own.

Robyn's soft hand grazed my skin as she stepped closer to me, wrapping a loose strand of my hair around my ear. Her breath was fire against my skin as she whispered. "If I were to compete, I would beat them all, and I would do it in your name."

My breath came in quick bursts as Robyn's rough lips pressed against mine. Her hands fell against my hips, pressing my back roughly against the door frame. Her tongue invaded my mouth, dancing with mine until I was weak.

Her hands left my hips, wrapping around until they settled on the thick fabric along my behind. I released a soft moan at her touch—and just like that Robyn stopped.

"Come inside with me," I whispered against her mouth. One of my hands had found its way across the back of her neck, while the other was up, underneath her shirt.

"Tomorrow and the days after will be a trying day for us all." Robyn's breathing was uneven, and again I found myself pressing my lips against hers.

"It may be some time before I can get away. You could come inside now though." I bit playfully at Robyn's soft lower lip, pulling it gently between my teeth. This time, the moan came from deep within her.

"There is nothing more that I would love than to be beside you tonight, and that time will surely come. But there are only a few hours until sunrise, and the first time I get you to myself, we are not leaving that bed for *days.*"

Robyn's promise left me speechless as the space between my legs throbbed in response.

She kissed me briefly before leaning down and retrieving the tray of food from the table. "Eat that." She nodded to the tray of food as she stepped back and disappeared down the corridor.

She was gone before I could collect my thoughts or still my breathing.

Despite the absolute fatigue and exhaustion that had fallen over me only minutes before, when I lay in my bed that night I could do nothing but stare at the ceiling and remember the taste of her lips on mine.

Chapter 24

Robyn

The morning was crisp and cool, and my hot breath mingled with the air as the grass crunched beneath my feet. Frost had come early this year, and the reality that it brought was terrifying. The people of Notting could not afford to lose any more of their crops.

We had been stealing what we could from the castles. Our men were spread thin across Notting, taking gold from the noble families and using it to buy food from traders and merchants. It wasn't enough.

My bow was heavy in my hand as I strained to pull the cord tight around the ends. Although I preferred the solitude of the range in castle Loxley, this would have to suffice for now. The Queen's range was far from the hustle of the inner castle, tucked tight against the thick, green walls of the gardens. With the tournament beginning today, and the unrest that seemed to permeate throughout everyone in the castle, there was nowhere else to go.

The quiver settled between my shoulder blades as I took my stance before the target in the distance. Lowering my weapon, my frustration grew. The yellow and red circles taunted me. The target needed to be moved back several feet. I was desperate for the extra challenge today. I did not need my mind to wander back to the events of the last few weeks.

Images of Marian at the stables the morning before filled my head. The former Palace Healer had gifted Marian a new pair of white breeches—a spare to the ones she had left with only weeks before. It had been so difficult to ignore the way the leather wrapped tight against her curves as we made our way back toward the tower.

I shook my shoulders loose, trying to rid myself of the memory and the desire it brought forth.

Though there would be wrestling, sword fighting, and hand-to-hand combat, everyone in Notting knew that Queen Naomi favored mounted archery. A special course had been designed for this event, tucked away on the edge of Sherwood. Queen Naomi had overseen the course herself, and no one was to see it until the day of the event.

My frustration grew again as I realized I would most likely never see the course. Prince Asher's declaration that only men could compete came only minutes after I had signed the parchment with my intent.

The morning sun spread across the sky as I refocused. Streaks of the red dawn had appeared, and I tried to ignore the feeling of foreboding that accompanied it. I pushed my hair from my eyes again. It had grown far too long for my liking.

Steadying my breathing, I brought the bow up once more, knocking the arrow into place. The sound of footsteps and crunching leaves came from behind me, startling me from my heavy thoughts. Several voices carried over the morning air. I lowered the bow again, turning to face the royal party.

The king and queen emerged first from the large gate dividing the gardens and the range. The king's airy tunic was golden. It was gaudy, lined with thick, braided, green ropes along the seams.

Queen Naomi walked beside him. She too was dressed in the colors of the Court. She was also bejeweled—although her finery seemed to pale in comparison to her husband. A simple, elegant ruby was nestled against her thin throat. It instantly reminded me of blood.

"Your father says you are the most skilled archer in all of Notting." King Ruelle's grating voice called from the back of the range as they approached.

"He says that because I am."

I bowed low to the royal family. Though I had spent much more time with Prince Asher than I preferred, it was the first time I had been this close to the king or queen in years.

Behind them, the hoard of nobility following the royal family all tittered at my reply. But, behind Asher, a familiar, blond braid appeared.

My heart instantly responded as Marian smiled. My stomach did flips in response as I winked at her. To my surprise, her smile seemed more guarded today than it had last night. She turned toward the older man at her side as he seemed to whisper something in her ear, and I immediately recognized the commander of the king's guard, Lord Sampson.

Something grew in my gut as I looked at the way he stood too close to Marian. He seemed to hover over her and focus on her as he whispered. I realized with a shudder that his posture reminded me of a lover trying to share secrets in a crowd.

I watched Marian lean away from the man. Her back was rigid and her smile was polite. Whatever had happened, she was clearly uncomfortable.

Prince Asher's voice pulled me from my thoughts. He had ignored my words, turning instead to Princess Madawi. "It is too bad Loxley doesn't have any true contestants to fight for them. I hear their people could use the provisions."

Anger rippled through me at the insinuation. If the prince were anyone else he would have found himself struggling to speak through the pounding I would be giving him right now. However, he wasn't any other man and I struggled to keep my temper in check.

I took a breath to steady my voice.

"My people do just fine."

"My people." Asher's voice was lethal as he approached me. Images of the prince's terrified face the morning I had threatened him played through my mind. By the look of pure loathing on his face, I knew Asher was thinking the same thing.

That morning I had held his life in my hands, but while we were at the capital, he was in a position of power. He might not order my death, but that did not mean he would make my life any easier. As I glanced quickly at Marian, I realized it seemed the prince was determined not to make hers any easier either.

"Do you intend to compete in your mother's competition, Prince Asher?" Madawi spoke with calm, but calculated curiosity.

"Of course—though it seems my wise mother will not allow even her son to see the course." Prince Asher smiled at his mother, who playfully rolled her eyes at her son.

"It must be fair." The Queen smiled as she squeezed her son's hand lovingly.

"The Queen's event is a reflection of her skills with a bow." King Ruelle remarked.

The nobility around us immediately responded by drowning Queen Naomi in compliments. Then, almost inaudibly, a voice rose above the crowd.

"I have heard of your mother's skills, Prince Asher. I just don't see why you would insult her though."

Princess Madawi seemed to look between the prince and the queen. It took my mind a second to wrap around her words.

"Whatever do you mean, my sweet?" Prince Asher turned to look at the woman who would soon be his betrothed.

"Well, it was my desire to honor your mother by having Joppa compete in the competition, but she was told that women would not be allowed to compete—and now I'm afraid I will be unable to glorify someone who will soon be my family."

Madawi's chin seemed to quiver a bit as the princess placed one of her delicate hands on the prince's arm. I watched Asher calculate her words for a second. The courtiers around us suddenly sounded their sympathies.

"We *must* honor the queen." Marian's soft voice agreed from the crowd.

All around me, everyone present seemed to wait in anticipation for the prince to respond.

Prince Asher cleared his throat, looking nervously between his mother and father. Neither the king nor queen spoke a word. Though, I watched Queen Naomi inwardly seethe. Her lips pursed together as she stared daggers at Princess Madawi.

"It seems you are right." Prince Asher smiled as he took the princess's hand. "We shall have to honor the queen."

I struggled to keep my jaw from dropping open.

Suddenly, the women of Court were eager to step forward and learn archery—all in the name of honoring the queen. I spent the better part of the morning teaching the spoiled nobility how to hold and draw a bow.

By mid-morning three of the bows from the barracks were broken, despite my constant reminders not to draw the string back without an arrow. The king and queen had long disappeared back into the castle, but still, the ladies persisted.

It was well into the afternoon before the crowd finally dispersed and only Princess Madawi, her guard Joppa, Lady Rochelle, and Marian. Lord Sampson had finally slithered away once the royal family returned to the castle—but not before leaving a lingering kiss on the back of Marian's hand.

I had to resist the urge to laugh as Marian fumbled with her bow.

"How many arrows does it take you to take someone down?" Lady Rochelle's voice was sweet as honey, but the question brought everyone present to a pause.

Princess Madawi's leaned away from the other woman as her over-protective guard stepped just a little closer. Marian's jaw had fallen open. We all sat in stunned silence for a moment.

As if suddenly realizing what she had said, Rochelle's face paled a bit as she lowered the bow awkwardly.

"Well, I was just curious."

All at once, everyone in the range burst into laughter. Rochelle's face flushed with embarrassment, but she quickly joined in the laughter.

When we had all caught our breath, I approached her once more. This time, I pulled an arrow from the quiver on my back. As I lifted the arrow and knocked it into place, I watched Rochelle do the same.

Behind us, there was a shuffle. Marian and Madawi had each picked up bows now. I watched in wonder as they appeared at either side of me—lining up with the targets in the distance.

"It usually takes at least two arrows to take down someone in armor down. Of course, that depends on where you hit the person." I released my arrow and watched it soar across the field into the center circle in the distance.

The soft thud was barely audible, but a flurry of dust from the hay settled against the ground. On my left, Madawi's arrow flew a few feet and then dropped. Marian drew her bow and pierced just outside the target in the distance.

"My people starve. They fight for food, while the king hosts lavish parties. The queen is pressuring my father to marry me off to my cousin in the east. They're all so busy complimenting one another, that no one is listening to what I want or what our people need."

My heart pounded as I listened to the woman's treasonous words. Never had I imagined Lady Rochelle might care for anyone except herself—so few in Court did. To hear of her speak of it so near to the castle, and with the princess present, was a dangerous game to play.

From my periphery, Marian approached Rochelle. Her face was solemn as she stood at her side. I walked closer too. Guilt sat in my gut. There was so much I could share about the rebellion and our efforts to thwart the king and to get food to the people of Notting.

"I will do what I can to help." Marian's smile was weak as she placed a gentle hand on Rochelle's shoulder.

Rochelle's pale cheeks were stained with tears. Her long, black hair had begun to fall from its pins.

Tell her. Tell Marian. Let them know what's going on, the voice pounded and screamed inside of my skull.

The image of the messenger who had been killed for my foolishness and left to die in Sherwood flitted through my mind. I couldn't tell them. Not even Marian. Too many lives were at risk.

Rochelle's aim was steady as she nocked the arrow in place once more.

"For the queen," she whispered as she released the arrow.

Marian

With great fanfare, the tournament had begun. A grand procession paraded through the capital and down to the fields. All of Court had arrived to ride to the opening of the tournament.

I rode Marengo at the very back of the caravan. When the parade had first been announced, I had intended to ride more center to the ladies of Court, as the queen suggested, but now, for some reason, I couldn't quite stomach it.

Despite the heat of the day, each family had come dressed in absolute finery. Though the prize for the winner was to be a fortune of food and supplies, you would never guess that the royal houses were starved or that their people suffered.

Jewels and gold dripped from every neck, finger, and bodice in the caravan. Though the families would fight and kill for this opportunity to best one another, it was clear they did not want to seem too desperate.

As they finally entered the city, I could not help but sigh as my frustration grew.

"Though it is not required for her to *love* all of her charges, I believe it is customary for the Royal Healer to at least not *loathe* them."

Gawayne's deep laughter brought a smile to my face, and I felt my cheeks flush with embarrassment. Though I was happy to see him — we hadn't seen any of each other since arriving back at the castle — I was embarrassed that once again my feelings were written so clearly on my face.

"I do not *loathe* anyone. I love my country. I love its people." I looked at the faces popping out of the windows high above us. The laughter of children filled the streets as some of the nobility threw coins and sweets to the ground. Although some citizens of Notting had shown up to see the royal parade, I knew many of the sick and starving were not present. "I just wish things were better. I wish things were different."

I looked at where Gawayne rode next to me. A strange, puzzled expression had fallen over his face. He opened and closed his mouth a few times--as if struggling with what to say.

"You can love your country and want it to change. You can love your people and want some of them to do better, act better--especially to one another. You just have to know when it's time to fight, and you have to be sure you know what you're fighting for."

I thought about what Gawayne had said for several more minutes as we rode in silence out to the fields. I thought about Asher and Madawi sitting together. They were the future of the kingdom. They were the future king and queen—whether we wanted them or not.

Asher had long ago been my friend, but he had put me through hell since then. Madawi was kind and patient—the complete opposite of her betrothed.

I thought back to the patients I had treated and the reports that had come in from our healers across the kingdom. Things had been bad before, but now it seemed they were only getting worse.

"Maybe Madawi will be good for the kingdom," I whispered as I looked out over the parade of nobility before me and thought of my friend destined to marry my enemy.

"But can the people afford to wait for a 'maybe?'" Gawayne's voice was soft as he rode ahead.

The tournament would take an entire month to finish. I listened as Sir Sampson explained the rules. Every man or woman who wished to compete was present. Their haggard faces looked up into the royal pavilion as the rules were explained.

I stared at the sight of the older man's balding head as my stomach rolled with disgust. Yesterday he had been insufferable all throughout the morning. He had clung to my side, offering me his hand more times than I could count. Just as with Asher, neither man seemed to mind staring at a woman's breasts during a discussion instead of meeting her eyes.

"There would be four events—wrestling, hand-to-hand combat, swordsmanship, and the queen's event, archery. Each event will take place over the course of several days. Each day will consist of three different matches. The winners of each match will move on to the final matches later in the week. Each of the five great houses is allowed five contestants per event."

From the field, several of the men bristled. Allowing only five contestants per house put a tremendous amount of pressure on who was chosen.

Lord Sampson waited as the contestants settled down. The surprise and the anger in their eyes did not quell as he continued. "The champion for each event will be awarded a point for their house. The house with the most points at the end of the tournament will receive the grand prize to take home. In the event of a tie, an event will be randomly chosen, and a contestant will be chosen from the two houses."

A few minutes later, the men were dismissed. Somewhere nearby, musicians began to play. Brightly-colored entertainers entered the field, flipping and cartwheeling across the grass.

Despite the breeze, the summer heat was positively oppressive. The thin canvas of the tent offered shade to the royal pavilion, but not much. Sweat had begun to pool along my brow, and I knew it would only get worse.

I soaked cloths in water bowls to give to the ladies, but I knew it was not much relief.

There was a cheer as the entertainers left, and a louder cheer as Sampson stepped toward the edge of the royal pavilion. He held a piece of parchment in his withered hands as he read the names from the list.

The king had ordained that all wrestling matches were to be clean. No hitting, no punching, just brute force. A count of five with the opponent pounding on the ground meant a win.

A large, muscled man with white hair emerged from one end of the field. He wore no shirt over his broad shoulders, and the crowd cheered as he raised a fist to the air. From the opposite end, a smaller man appeared. He wore a dark-green tunic with a fish embroidered on his chest. The fish's mouth was open wide with long, thick teeth jutting outward.

I had just brought another damp cloth to the queen when the crowd around me gasped and I jumped in alarm. With every injury on the field and every sigh from a member of Court, the anxious feeling I needed to return to the healer's tent grew.

I watched as the man in torn, black trousers ran at his opponent. The other man fell back to the ground, and the sound of his skull hitting the earth shook through me like thunder.

When the man did not rise again—even as his attacker stood above him, raising his fists to the air, I knew that Kira would need help.

As I handed the queen her cloth, I motioned for one of the young acolytes to take my place. Silently, I slipped down the staircase and made my way to the white tent on the other side of the field.

An acolyte ran past me, carrying a large bucket of something foul-smelling. I hoped it was water as it splashed all over the boy's clothes.

"The next one will be bad," I spoke to Kira as her face filled with alarm.

"I heard the crowd gasp. Several watching from the stands were sick at the sight of it."

I nodded as Kira and I waited at the table in the center of the tent. A few moments later, two men carried the injured man into the tent. A trail of blood followed behind them.

"We need fresh water and clean cloth."

The two men heaved the injured onto the table, and the smell of sweat and blood was almost too much to bear.

To my surprise, the man was much older than I had expected for someone competing in the tournament. His grizzled face was covered in hard lines and wrinkles. His beard was a dark gray. Though it dripped with blood, I could see his hair was the same color.

A gasp escaped his lips as I looked at the wound on the back of his head. The man tossed and turned as he fell in and out of consciousness.

"Hold him down," I ordered the two men now staring at me in shock. "What's his name?"

"Rolfe." The younger man with the startling blue eyes spoke. As I looked him over, I could see the fear and concern written across his features.

"I need hot water so I can see the wound." I had barely turned around before Kira handed me the small pot. I looked at her quizzically, as I struggled to remember if I had ordered them to keep water boiling.

"We set a fire up nearby. Every pot used is instantly replaced. It's allowing us to keep up with the demand."

I smiled for a moment at Kira's preparedness. She had really come into her own these last few weeks.

Rolfe groaned from the table, bringing my thoughts back to the problem at hand.

"This is going to hurt." I poured the water across his head, trying desperately to wash the blood away. I breathed a sigh of relief at the size of the wound. Despite the blood that often came with head wounds, this was not one of the worst she had seen. Though, that didn't mean the man wouldn't need care.

"I'm going to have to sew this wound. You will have to keep him very, very still." I watched the two men before me pale as each of them lay across the man's wide chest and legs.

After more than an hour later, I had finally sewed the man's wound closed. Thankfully, he had stayed unconscious for most of it, but I still felt guilty as he moaned from the table.

"You must keep giving him water. Do not allow him to sleep for too long or he might not wake up. Do you understand?"

The men nodded, and I was satisfied that they would take care of him. As they left to fetch a litter, I checked the cloth now covering the thin thread.

"Thank you." The man's voice was hoarse, and I placed a hand on his shoulder to still him. "We have missed you, Lady Reya."

I felt the blood drain from my face as the older man called me by my mother's name. I looked over the man's clothing. There were no insignias or colors to signify where he had come from, but I realized he must be from the northern province--or even further north, in Aicias.

The men returned before I could ask any questions, and as they disappeared with Rolfe, I wondered how many others had known my mother.

Once I had washed the blood from my hands and changed into a spare dress brought by Kira, I trudged back to the royal pavilion.

Many of the ladies had retreated back to the castle, but I wanted to check in on the queen.

Queen Naomi's droll voice carried over the scurry of the servants as the match below continued.

"You have a younger sister? How nice for your mother. I was never able to supply the king with a spare. It must be a relief."

I stopped in my tracks, looking between Madawi and the queen. Shock swept over me at how casually the queen had mentioned the princess' death. Next to her, Joppa bristled. I watched the guard's hand fall to the weapon at her side. I ad no doubt that if anyone else had made such a veiled threat against Madawi, that person would no longer be breathing.

Madawi seemed to recover from Queen Naomi's rudeness. I handed my friend a glass of water, squeezing her hand gently as we passed the cup between us. Then I stepped back next to Joppa. With the heat and the exhaustion from running around the last few days, the last thing I wanted was the queen's unwanted attention.

"When will your event be, Your Majesty? At the end of the week?"

I watched the queen take a long swig of her goblet. From the red staining the delicate skin around her mouth features, it was certainly not water that had made her speak so loosely.

"Yes. At the end of the week. Your girl had better practice. If so many women are going to compete, we wouldn't want anything embarrassing to happen." A male servant leaned forward, filling the goblet again as the queen waved it in the air above her head. "So many women embarrass themselves. Dressing like a man. Laying with women. They forget their place and their duties to the kingdom."

I steadied my breath at the queen's contempt. It was clear who she was discussing, and I felt my anger rise. Though the war between Aicias and Notting had resulted in women finally earning their place amongst the king's soldiers, there were certainly women like Queen Naomi who wished for the old ways.

It was all I could do to focus on the wooden pavilion beneath my feet and keep my comments in check. It seemed the tournament would be unbearable for a multitude of reasons. . .

Chapter 26

Robyn

The first two weeks of the tournament seemed to fly by in a blur. At the end of the first week, the champion for Colch had dueled the contestant from the western river. Colch had triumphantly ended the week with the first point and was one step closer to winning the provisions.

That night a fight had broken out in the field where the contestants had made camp. Apparently, some bets had been placed on who the winner would be, and those who didn't have the means to pay up were dealt with quite severely.

A week later, the same thing happened when the contestant from Eastern River won. Samwell had competed for the Loxley house but lost to some rather shady tricks from his opponent. Gawayne and I had kept an eye on him the entire night to keep him from chasing after the man.

By the time the championship match had begun at the beginning of the week, the unrest in the camps was at a tipping point. The king's guard had taken to patrolling both the camps and the city streets—and they seemed to have expended the rest of their patience.

I couldn't be sure what was worse—the crowd or the men trying to control it.

It was evening when the match began, and it seemed everyone from the castle and many from the capital had arrived to watch. Not that I could blame them—Danyeil was the first woman to compete in the tournament, and she was sure to put on a show.

Samwell was tight at my side as we slipped through the throngs of people. Up ahead, the healer's tent with its white flag flapped in the evening wind. Samwell's blond hair disappeared for a moment, but when I looked back again he was ahead of me. I couldn't help but smile at my sly friend. Despite his defeat, he was eager to see Danyeil's fight. We had both come to know her skill the last few weeks in Colch.

If all went well, Duke Inglis would go home with rations tonight—and hopefully, a portion of those would feed those camped at his gates.

After the first skirmish in the camp, I had posted two squires at the back of the tent. Tedric and Gabriel nodded to us as Samwell and I walked into the back. Both Samwell and I had taken to hanging around and helping out throughout the tournament. Not only did it give us Samwell a chance to see Kira, but I also found it difficult lately to leave Marian's side. Every time I did, I remembered back to the way Sampson and Asher had looked when I caught them watching Marian.

Anger filled me as I wondered again what the prince had said to Marian the morning he had summoned her.

The crowd could surely be heard throughout the corners of Notting. The sun was waning in the distance, leaving a soft-blue glow to the evening. I walked with Samwell across the tent, and my breathing increased as I found myself looking for Marian.

Acolytes in their gray tunics walked in-between the long tables that typically held patients. Their steps were hurried as they prepped the different materials and supplies the healers might need.

A young, blond woman scurried past me with a basket full of bloodied strips of cloth. My stomach lurched a bit at the sight of it. Others hurried to light candles and oil lanterns. The soft, yellow glow transformed the tent. I released a sigh as we approached the front opening. It was strange that a place that had seen so much blood and carnage had come to bring me a kind of peace.

Or was it Marian who brought me peace?

Kira stood at the opening with Marian right beside her. I stared at the back of Marian's head, fighting the urge to walk up and run my hand down her long, silky braid. The sound of her laughter filled the air, and I found myself jealous that I had not been the one to cause it.

"Jaspar is a close friend of Prince Asher. It will not win you many favors to best him."

"It will not win me many favors not to," a soft voice whispered, and I recognized it immediately as Danyeil.

"It will probably do him some good though—to be bested by a woman. It might be good to knock the confidence out of him a bit." Marian spoke as we approached the three women.

"He will not go down easily, and I would not put it past him to do something devious." Samwell walked next to Kira, who immediately wrapped her arm around his.

I walked next to Marian, and the ache in my chest grew as she did not do the same. Her warmth seemed to reach out to me, and I fought the urge not to place my arm around her waist and pull her closer.

Danyeil nodded to us as she walked off toward the field. I knew she would want to stretch for a bit before the fight began.

Marian released a long sigh and when I turned I could see the worry written clearly across her features. I brought her hand to my lips, kissing the back tenderly.

"Danyeil will be okay. She is faster than anyone I have ever seen. Jaspar will be lucky if he gets a single shot in."

Marian's smile was weak as she stared back at me. This time I didn't hesitate as I wrapped my arm around her waist. She leaned into my shoulder as we watched our friend walk onto the field.

An army could have marched on us, but I wouldn't have moved as long as her head rested on my shoulder.

Nothing short of a dull roar erupted from the royal pavilion as Jaspar walked to the center of the ring. I watched with disdain as the pompous fool spun in a circle, raising his outstretched arms to the crowd. Now I could see why Jaspar and the prince got along so well—they were both fond of adoration and no one would ever adore them as much as they adored themselves.

The short, brown curls bounced on Jaspar's head as he walked back and forth across the center of the field. Though Jaspar's house was from the western river, he wore the colors of Notting.

Behind him, Danyeil waited silently. She was dressed in blue and white for Duke Inglis' house. As she walked closer to the center, I watched the crowd bristle. Jaspar was the first to wear the colors of the crown, and it was hard not to miss the implication.

To anyone watching nearby, it felt like something else. It felt like a symbol of something more.

This was not good.

Father had been working on his carefully-laid plans, placing support where he could, sending his spies to whisper in the ears of wealthy merchants or houses who might turn to our cause. I wondered for a moment what the Baron of Loxley thought of this sudden display. I peered up into the royal pavilion, but I could not see his face among the crowd.

From the front of the pavilion, a young boy I didn't recognize held a flag aloft in his hand as Lord Sampson approached the wooden rail.

"This will be a match of hand-to-hand combat. No weapons shall be permitted. This match between Lord Jaspar of the Western River and the champion for the house of Inglis shall go until one opponent can no longer compete."

Again the crowd either cheered or booed. All the other fights had ended when a contestant decided. It seemed the choice to walk away had been stolen for these fighters.

The crowd watching from the ground protested the change in rules, while the royal pavilion clapped. My eyes darted between the two sides as the divide between our country grew wider with every cheer.

Next to me, Marian grabbed my hand tight in hers, pulling my focus back to the field and the others around me. Samwell held Kira's waist. My friend nodded to me as I continued to sweep my gaze around the tent. Acolytes stood behind us. Some clenched their medical supplies tight in their hands. Their faces were filled with horror.

I squeezed Marian's slender hip tighter against me. Her eyes were wide as she looked up at me. The tension around the field was palpable and I had a feeling Danyeil would not be the last to face an opponent tonight as the sun set behind the trees.

The young boy dropped the flag—the signal to begin—and silence fell around the field. Danyeil's gaze was steel as she watched Jaspar.

Danyeil stepped to the right and Jaspar began to circle as well. Despite his bravado, Jaspar was still a worthy opponent. He may have learned his studies in the castle, but it was well known that the men of the Western River trained their boys young and that they trained them hard.

Danyeil's braids were pulled back tight against her scalp. The arms of her tunic were cut, revealing her muscled arms. She moved effortlessly around the field as she dodged Jaspar's first attack.

His right arm swung wide through the air as she ducked out of the way. He was quick though, using the momentum of the swing to spin himself around. Danyeil took a good punch to the gut before stumbling backward.

The pavilion roared for a second, but it was short-lived as Danyeil recovered. She feinted to the right, and Jaspar took the bait. He sent a fist out, but Danyeil was fast. She bobbed to the left, bringing her knee to his chest. The moment her knee made impact, she brought both elbows down into his spine--hard.

The two stopped just outside the healer's tent, barely an arm's length away. I felt Marian gasp beside me as the crowd roared. I watched several men of the men who had been cursing Danyeil only hours before now cheer her on.

Jaspar was down on the ground, and I watched as he fought for breath. A smarter opponent might have given up at that point, but the rules of the fight had been clear.

"Bitch. You're going to pay for that one." I could barely hear over the sound of the crowd, but the look on Jaspar's face quickened my breath.

Danyeil's smirk grew as she motioned for him to continue.

That was when I saw the glint of silver in the light of the torches placed along the edges of the field. Just barely visible beneath the long sleeves of his tunic, Jaspar had tucked away a blade.

He rushed Danyeil and I saw the surprise on her face as he barreled toward her.

"Danyeil!" Marian stepped toward the field, but I grabbed her tight around the waist.

Jaspar swung with his left hand—a surprise since he had primarily been using the right. It wasn't the fist with the blade, but it made a crack as it met with Danyeil's cheekbone.

Danyeil staggered for a second, just out of reach of the second blow. I held my breath as she dodged his fist. She held one hand to her face, the other was still tight in a fist. Jaspar walked closer—no longer even bothering to hide the blade in his hand.

"I see you, boy. So does everyone here. We see that the men of the Western Rivers must cheat to gain their advantage. We see your treachery and we will not forget." Danyeil's voice rose as the crowd went silent.

As if my mind knew what was about to happen, I watched as Jaspar ran at Danyeil again. She dipped to the right, swinging her fist back toward his face. Jaspar took the hit to his face, and I watched the blade in his hand disappear into Danyeil's side

Marian

Chaos erupted as blood sprayed onto the ground. All I could think about was the morning training sessions where Danyeil had been so kind, and her sweet smile as she encouraged me to keep training when I thought my legs might truly give out.

I pulled from Robyn's grip, running toward the field. I had to staunch the blood pouring onto the dirt.

The crowd on the ground began to rush the field, but they were quickly stopped by the king's guard, who seemed to pour from the edges out of nowhere.

My knees slid into the dirt at Danyeil's side as the puddle of blood grew around her.

"Get out of the—" A rough hand touched my shoulder for a split-second. Then I heard an audible snap. I looked up in shock to see Jaspar's face contorted in pain. He screamed as Robyn gripped his wrist. It took me a second to realize the sound I had heard was Jaspar's bone cracking.

Robyn's golden eyes promised Jaspar a slow death as she stood above me. People from the crowd were pushing around the guards. They screamed Danyeil's name, but what I heard above all else was the word 'cheater' yelled over again and again.

"You can stay and deal with us and the angry crowd that just watched you cheat to win, or you can leave before they arrive. The choice is yours." Robyn's voice was barely a whisper as Jaspar looked between us and the increasing crowd. Robyn released his wrist and he took off at a run.

"Grab her feet." I wrapped my arms up underneath Danyeil's arms, pulling her back tight to my chest as I struggled to lift her.

Robyn did as she was told and we headed to the healer's tent together.

The moment we entered the tent, I yelled at the acolytes to run for the tower. Several of them had already moved to action. A young girl named Cherise brought a large pot of steaming water to the table. I nodded to her in thanks. Another girl, named Tierry, who was barely older than I was when I entered into training, began to pile strips of cloth at the edge of the table.

"You all need to get to the tower, now. We will do no one any good if we get hurt by this chaos. Go now. I will leave when I can."

To my shock, none of them moved.

Though their faces were full of shock as Robyn and I placed Danyeil on the table at the center of the room, no one listened to my command.

Confusion filled me. Everyone had been so accepting when I took over for Genevieve. I had not had a single problem since I had returned to the capital.

Why would they disobey me now?

Adrenaline coursed through me as I tried to understand what was happening. The angry shouts of the crowd had turned to clashes of metal as the riot grew to new levels.

I held my hand over the wound in Danyeil's side. Her warm blood pushed through my fingers. I looked back at the acolytes around me. Robyn grabbed another cloth, and I allowed her hand to replace mine as I faced the faces of my apprentices. I had known most of them for years. . .

"You are all under my care. I cannot move her, but you must go now. You must get to the tower and wait until this settles and we can see to the injured."

"We will not leave you." Kira's soft voice startled me as she walked up behind me. Her hair was tussled, and she carried the kit Robyn had made for me. A bruise began to swell on one of her cheeks, and worry filled me as I examined her injury.

"Don't worry. A guard struck me when I yelled at him to allow me near the horses. Samwell didn't take kindly to that."

Kira passed the box over to me, and I stared at her for a moment. Danyeil would be in far less pain thanks to Kira's forethought.

A low moan sounded on the table, and I turned my attention back to my patient.

"What do you need?" Robyn's voice whispered from next to me, and I slowly processed the reality around me.

I looked around as the tent shook.

"Cherise and Tierry wash up in case we need you. Robyn, you and the others keep the mob out while Kira and I work."

Robyn nodded as she motioned for the others to follow. I took a breath to steady myself as I prepared for what came next.

I wasn't really sure how much time had passed, but my shoulders were heavy as I sank onto the stool Cherise had brought over.

Beneath us, Danyeil had grown cool to the touch and there was nothing else we could do. I had tried to staunch the bleeding with hot pokers, but it seemed Jaspar had turned the blade. Several of Danyeil's organs had been punctured. Every time I stopped one bleed, another started.

I fought back the hot tears as I drew a long breath. I turned from the table, knocking into the one behind me. Cherise had placed vials along the edge, and grief filled me. I knocked several to the floor. The rest I threw furiously against the edge of the tent. The sound of the glass hitting the ground nearly brought me to my knees.

It was all such a waste. Danyeil was so skilled and so determined, but it hadn't meant anything in the end.

Once I could force myself to face them, I turned back to the others who had fought so hard alongside me through the night. The sound of the skirmish faded into almost nothing as I washed my hands in the hot water Tierry poured from the pot. The water was almost unbearably hot, but it was a welcome feeling compared to my friend's cool skin.

There were no more cloths to dry my hands, so I shook the water from them as I walked from the tent. It was hard to force myself to face them, but my vision finally adjusted to the scene before me.

The acolytes stood in a circle around the tent. None of them bore a weapon, but neither did they bear any signs of injuries. Their sallow faces stared back at me.

It was the rest of the people outside the tent that brought me to tears.

A warm hand gripped mine as the sobs fell from me in waves.

"Nearly everyone from the camps arrived just as the guards were losing control. Everyone was so shocked by their sudden appearance that the fight just ended. They've been waiting for you."

I tried to process Robyn's words, but I could not shake the image of my friend now dead on the table from my mind. My hands were still stained with her blood and I looked at my hand intertwined with Robyn's.

Robyn's hand was warm in mine, but it did nothing against the blood that was deep beneath my fingernails. Blood was supposed to be warm, but Danyeil's was chilled now.

I looked around at the crowd again. To my surprise, Duke Edward and Duchess Elsie stood at the front. The duke's face was stone. I watched his chest rise and fall as he looked back at me. Next to him, Queen Elsie's eyes reached for me, and I could feel the hope pouring out of them. Hope for our friend. Hope that she had made it—but she hadn't.

I could read the question on their faces, and it took everything inside of me to stay standing as I shook my head.

The sounds of crying erupted around me as Elsie squeezed my shoulders tight.

I muttered my apologies against the soft fabric of her dress, but her gentle hand patted my back. My heart ached as part of me wondered if this was what it was like to be held by your mother.

"It's not your fault. It's mine." The duke's voice surprised me, and I turned to face him.

Duke Edward rubbed his brow, and I could see the grief on his face. Danyeil had been his captain. He had made her his champion.

"It's not your fault Jaspar cheated." Robyn's voice was ice, and I stepped back toward her, wrapping my arm with hers. I gripped her arm now, desperately needing her comfort.

"I spoke out against the Western River being allowed to compete. The rations came primarily from their land. They are the only House not affected by the plight killing the crops. Except for some rations destined for the castle that was stolen by bandits, their people have not suffered as others have." Duke Inglis' face had once again turned to stone, but his hand had fallen to the hilt of his sword. His internal battle was clear, and it seemed he was barely keeping his fury in check.

"The king's poor decisions are not your fault, my love. We cannot know for sure that Jaspar simply didn't want to lose to a woman." Elsie squeezed her husband's hand tight. "We must take Danyeil home. We must bury her by the shore."

Robyn took my hand as the duke and duchess walked toward the tent. My heart was heavy as I allowed Robyn to lead me to the horses.

I did not recognize the two guards from Colch who entered the tent and emerged with Danyeil's body on a pallet strung between them. Once again, I felt the world around me shift slowly.

Everything was passing by in a daze, and it was some time before I was able to force my feet to move again. The sticky feeling of blood between my fingers reminded me that I still needed to wash my friend's blood away.

Focusing on one step at a time, I walked into the tent, looking for water to rinse. Like a faint echo, I registered a familiar face as it passed me a pot of boiling water. The steam coming from it reached for me, and I reached back.

"Marian!" Robyn's voice startled me from my stupor, and I look up to see her face filled with alarm. "Let it cool." Her hand rubbed at my cheek, and I felt myself nod.

A different pair of hands pulled at my clothes, and I realized Kira was trying to help me change. I forced a smile as I allowed her to pull the fabric, heavy with blood, over my head. Like a babe without a mother, I stood still as Robyn and Kira washed the day off my flesh.

As I stood nude inside the cool tent, I felt relief spill from me. Warm tears fell down my cheeks, and I feared they might never stop.

I dressed with their help, donning a gray tunic belonging to some kind stranger.

Some time later, I was riding atop Gold, leaning my cheek against Robyn's firm back. My tears had finally stopped, but it wasn't until we crossed the fields that I felt myself truly sink back into reality.

Awe filled me at the sea of tents that had already been erected. The people of Notting had finally shown up to the Capital. They waited outside the city gates and, like my own, their desperate cries for justice would no longer be ignored.

Robyn

Marian and I rode atop Gold as the sounds of the camps slowly enveloped us. Next to us, Kira rode Marengo, with Samwell and Gawayne close by on their horses.

Every moment that passed felt like an eternity as I watched the look of horror on Marian's face. Every part of my body was screaming at me to hold her and comfort her, even as she squeezed my waist tighter. I knew the pain she was experiencing. I knew the guilt she lived with, and I hated that I couldn't take it away.

Once again, I rubbed at the smooth skin on the back of Marian's hand. Whether I was comforting her or myself, I didn't know.

As we rode it quickly became apparent that though the rioting had calmed, the atmosphere in the camps was thick with tension. Like a rope pulled taut, it would not take much to unravel or snap.

We were finally nearing the city gates when the sound of angry shouting reached my ears. A mass of black shapes ahead in the darkness told me there was a group of people blocking the narrow path.

"Get this godsdamned cart off the road or I will set it on fire!"

"Please. We are trying. The wheel—"

"I don't fucking care, just get it off the road."

Beside me, Gawayne and Samwell moved immediately closer, urging their horses to a slow trot.

"Perhaps you could pull your head out of your ass and offer to help." Samwell's voice was a low growl as he approached the angry guard.

"What's it to you—" The furious guard stopped short as he looked at those suddenly approaching. His eyes seemed to take us all in, and for a moment I watched him briefly reconsider his words.

"Sirs, we were instructed not to aid anyone in the camps...and— and to keep the road cleared." The guard fumbled with his words as his arm swept toward the cart.

I did not immediately recognize the man, but I had surely met many like him. Someone who used the smallest bit of power they had to make those around them feel small.

Anger built in my chest as I stared down at the fumbling guard. Around my waist, I felt Marian's grip loosen.

"We can help." Her voice shook and I felt her straighten in the saddle.

I turned a bit, straining to see her.

"Marian..."

"It's fine. Let's end this day with something good."

Once again, I felt my chest fill with pride at her words. She was always, continuously surprising me.

"Hop out for a moment, Layla."

A small, brunette girl leapt from the edge of the cart. My smile broadened as her loose dress filled with air momentarily.

"Layla!" Behind me, Marian's voice was filled with delight. As if she had not just spent an entire day tending to the wounded, and as if she had not just had a friend die on her table, Marian smiled at the child as she dismounted.

Layla's small feet worked faster than the rest of her, sending the squealing child forward, and toppling her into the rough terrain of the path at our feet.

I lunged for her, but was not close enough to catch her as she fell. There was a moment of silence before a cry erupted from Layla. Tears streamed down her face as she held her scraped hands up in the air.

Marian and Layla's mother were there in seconds, comforting the child and dabbing at the wounds.

For a moment, I stood awkwardly beside them. I looked back at Samwell and Gawayne, but they were already at work fixing the wheel. The guard had apparently been instructed to help, as he too was grappling at the cart, trying to lift it enough to right the wheel.

Suddenly, I realized Kira was standing beside me. We stood together in silence, watching as the wheel was quickly fixed.

I turned back toward Marian. The weight of today was heavy on my shoulders, but she seemed unfazed.

The small child was already laughing at something Marian had whispered in her ear, and I suddenly longed to hear whatever it was.

"She was truly shaken tonight. In a way I've never seen before." Kira's voice was barely a whisper beside me. "I don't know how she can smile after a night like tonight."

I nodded in agreement as I stared at Marian, reveling in the way she seemed to never break--no matter what was thrown at her. Layla pulled gently at Marian's braid, rubbing at the length of silk wrapped around her blond locks.

An ache filled my chest as I too longed to wrap my fingers in Marian's long hair.

If it had been difficult to be away from Marian before, now it was simply impossible. As we both processed our grief over Danyeil, we simply stayed by each other's side.

It had been two days since Danyeil had passed. There were supposed to be a few days before the next event would begin, but the king's guard was busy trying to keep order while the people outside the city gates made the field around the city their new home. It seemed there would be even more delay as the castle tried to settle.

Word throughout the healer's tower was that Duchess Elsie had left that night to ride with Danyeil's body back to Colch. Duke Edward had spent the last two days locked in the king's council chamber, demanding justice for his champion.

I knew the verdict long before it spread through the castle. As one of Asher's closest friends, there would be no punishment for Jaspar's crimes.

I had followed Marian back to her room that night, and though we had not kissed again or made any attempts to further things between us, we had held each other each night since.

This morning I had once again awoken to the smell of lavender and the feel of her hair in my hand. Marian had taken to sleeping with one leg draped over me, burrowing herself in as close as she could to my side.

As the sun streamed in from her bedroom window, I felt her stretch beside me. As she had the morning before, she blinked awake a few times, before nuzzling her nose against my side—and just as with the morning before, I was relieved to see her wake peacefully despite the trauma she had endured.

My body jerked in response as the tip of Marian's delicate nose tickled at the side of my breast.

"You had better keep that frigid nose from me!" I teased, pulling away from her.

"That is nothing compared to your icy feet!" Marian sat upright in the bed, smiling down at me as she made to dress.

The sight of her leaving twisted my gut into something unpleasant, and I immediately regretted pulling away so quickly.

As if sensing my thoughts, Marian looked back at me with a sly look that sent waves of desire across my body. But I resisted the urge to push her further. We had both lost a friend, and neither of us was ready to move forward when that grief was still so new.

In the daytime, I found myself glued to her side. Though I could see the exhaustion written all over her, she was out each morning with her acolytes treating anyone who asked.

Marian and her acolytes visited the barracks, tending to the different guards. Each time she went inside, I felt my guilt grow. I recognized many of the men she treated. I had fought alongside them, had commanded them. But soon, much sooner than any of these soldiers realized, they would have to make a choice.

As we left the barracks and made our way through the city and out to the camps, a young acolyte stopped short on the dirt path.

"Why are we helping the soldiers and also the people who the soldiers have harmed? What good is it?"

To my surprise, I watched Marian's face flush with anger.

"We do not choose sides. We are healers. Our duty is to help those in need, no matter who it might be."

The young girl nodded, and Marian's eyes fell to all the others who had followed her into the camp. Her blue eyes were icy as she waited for each of them to nod.

Each acolyte seemed to think over Marian's words, but as I considered what they meant, I felt my anger take hold.

Frustration rose in my chest, and for the first time in two days, I walked away from Marian.

The ground crunched beneath my feet as I walked across the fields, heading for the shade of Sherwood in the far distance. I couldn't be sure if it was the grief from Danyeil's death or the increasing tension in the castle, but I felt myself reach a tipping point.

Father had been waiting years for the rebellion to be able to make its move. I had obeyed him every step of the way. I had waited as the people of Notting suffered.

I am tired of waiting.

Marian appeared at my side, but I couldn't bring myself to slow my angry steps.

"Robyn, what's wrong?" Her gentle hand grabbed my arm, but I pulled away. I couldn't look at her right now. Not until I got the fury building inside of me in check.

The heat of my anger flushed over my cheeks as my breath came in deep bursts.

"What's wrong?" Marian's voice shook a little, and I finally turned to face her, spinning on my heels.

"How can you tell them that?" I felt my anger loosen, and despite the alarm on her face, I couldn't stop myself. "How could you expect them to treat people who are starving and in need of care *and* treat the ones who have forced them to be this way?"

"It's not our place to question—"

"To question *who*, Marian? Not our place to question the crown? The same man who tried to force himself on you will one day have sole power over every person in Notting!"

Marian winced like I'd struck her, but I couldn't stop myself. I couldn't keep myself from spewing the angry words I'd been holding in for so long.

"Aren't you tired of it? Aren't you tired of wondering just how much worse it's going to get? How much more can the people take? How many more people need to die before something is done?"

We were far from the camps, but Marian still looked around us—clearly alarmed by my treasonous words. I watched something change inside of her as her shoulders straightened and her chin jutted outward. I felt my anger deflate a little as her chin quivered.

"Yes, I'm tired. Of course, I'm tired, Robyn! I'm tired of seeing the sick and starved while the queen asks me to bring her cool cloths, so she doesn't overheat. I'm tired of looking over my shoulder, scared that Asher or the man he wants to become my husband is there lurking." —I started at the word husband, my mouth falling agape-- "I'm tired of spending every night hoping—praying to any gods that might listen that Madawi can make Asher a fair and just ruler when I'm not sure what will happen once the crown is on his head."

I watched Marian throw her arms up in the air as her voice rose. My breathing calmed a little and I was thankful her acolytes had had the sense not to follow us.

"But I'm one person. I'm one person and all I can do is help those who need it."

"You could do more," I whispered. I felt the confession start to stumble out of me and I was helpless to stop it. "You could help us take them down."

Marian's hand flew to her mouth as she stumbled back a little, nearly tripping over the stones at her feet.

"It has already begun, Marian. It started with raiding the royal caravans traveling through Sherwood and giving the people of the forest what they needed. But, now it's more. We have seen the banner. We hear its call. The people are ready. Soon you will have to make a choice."

I knew there was nothing else to say, so I turned and left Marian standing. I had done it. I had told her what was coming. Now, it was up to her to decide.

Marian

More than a week had gone by since Robyn had left me standing near the edge of Sherwood. The Queen's event was the last in the tournament—and it seemed it would be the most violent so far.

Two of the provinces were tied. Colch had won wrestling, but the western river province had won hand-to-hand combat with their contestant's cheap trick. Now we would see if the northern province would best their competitors with their superb swordsmanship.

To my surprise, the king and queen had invited Rolfe to the royal pavilion to watch the championship match.

It was well into the evening before the match began, and the field was positively buzzing. Neither province had won a point yet in the tournament. Whoever won this match would make the queen's event the next week even more crucial.

A chill had entered the air, and I shivered a bit. The cold had come early this year—a promise for a harsh winter. The weight of it sat heavy on my chest. The kingdom could not afford to lose any more crops.

Something soft fell across my shoulders and warmed my skin. I was startled to find my white cloak resting there—and even more shocked to see that it was Robyn who had placed it around my shoulders.

A sly smile peeked at the edge of her mouth as she walked closer to the end of the pavilion. I wasn't sure which had surprised me more—that she had such forethought about my well-being or that she had joined the royal pavilion.

Robyn stopped just behind her where her father rested. She leaned against one of the thick poles that supported the canvas overhead. In front of her, the Baron of Loxley was watching the field with feigned interest. I clutched at my cloak as I felt the tension between these powerful people with new understanding.

"Who knew how chilly it would get tonight!" Queen Naomi exclaimed nearby. As was expected no less than three suitors and four ladies nearby offered the queen their cloaks.

"We must seem like such frail things to you, Rolfe. You northerners are so used to the chill."

I walked nearer, surprised to find my former patient seated by the queen and king.

"I would never call any of these women frail after all I have witnessed." Rolfe's low voice boomed across the space. "Why, your royal healer saved my life after that first event. I shall owe her strength and fortitude a debt I may never be able to repay."

My cheeks burned at the mention of my name. I tried unsuccessfully to blend into the background of the pavilion, but Queen Naomi waved me forward.

"She seems to possess a fair amount of skill." Naomi's smile was sweet as she looked me over and it was the kindest words she had ever spoken to me.

"Yes. My betrothed is skilled and beautiful." Lord Sampson's voice was filled with a sense of pride, and I felt my stomach churn. My heart raced as I watched from the corner of my eye as Robyn's mouth fell open.

"Oh! I had no idea!" The queen practically squealed her response, and I knew I had to end this before it got even more out of hand. Rolfe's thick brows pulled together as he looked between the older man and me.

I looked guiltily at Robyn. Desperation filled me. I should have told her immediately, but I truly hadn't expected something like this. It was a trap, and by the look on Sampson's face, he knew it too. I hurried to right the trap I had fallen so easily into.

"Lord Sampson flatters me," I stuttered. "To think that someone like him would marry someone not of noble birth like myself. I could not do such to him, and I have assured him that with my new responsibilities I plan to follow in the steps of Mistress Genevieve and may never marry."

I watched the older man's face flush with anger. His balding head soon matched the deep red of his ears. I had denied him—and I had done it in front of the queen.

"Of course, you have many responsibilities, Lady Marian." Rolfe's voice was gentle as he continued. "Ah! Here comes my Lord Aren! Queen Naomi, you are in for quite a treat."

I breathed a sigh of relief as Rolfe tried to divert everyone's attention once more to the field. I took a nervous step back, trying my best to shy away. When I looked back two furious faces were staring at me now. I wasn't sure which was worse, the angry, red face of Lord Sampson or the cold, lifeless stare of the queen.

The match began, though the talk was that it was to be short-lived. Baron Maxwell's heir, Lord Aren, had a well-known and respected reputation for his skill with a sword.

I walked once more down the steps and off into the night. I stepped into the darkness that had gathered between two torches, allowing my breathing and my stomach to settle. The soft crunch of footsteps approached from behind me, and I was shocked to see Robyn standing close.

"Lord Sampson, really? You could have told me."

I opened my mouth to explain, but that was when I noticed the glint of humor in her eye and the lift at the edge of her mouth.

"It's Asher's way of trying to control me. He wants to keep me near." My shoulders drooped, and I shrugged.

Robyn stepped closer to me now. I looked up at her and my heart began to pound.

She watched me intensely for a moment, leaning closer as if waiting for me to pull away. Her hand slid under my cloak, wrapping around my hip, and pulling me close. Before I knew it, her other hand was around the back of my neck, tangled in my hair as her lips crushed against mine.

Our tongues danced together as my breath caught in my throat. A deep need flooded my core. I throbbed almost painfully as my breathing came in short gasps.

In the back of my mind, I knew there were things we needed to discuss. There were questions that needed to be answered, but that could come later. All that mattered right now was the feel of her against me and the fire she ignited inside of me.

Something snapped inside of me, and I felt the world around us fall away for a moment. The heat of her skin pushed me forward and I followed the hard curve of her hip down into her breeches. When she didn't pull away, I searched lower until my fingers were deep inside her core.

Robyn moaned against my lips, and I felt her chest press against mine.

I rubbed my thumb against her sensitive skin, delighting in every catch of her breath. Her tongue explored my mouth as I felt her lips crush against mine.

The sharp intake of breath startled both of us from our heated stupor.

My eyes flew open as Robyn pulled away abruptly. I felt the heat of her slip away like a warm blanket falling to the floor. It took a second for my mind to focus as I struggled to ease the blood pumping through my veins.

The world around us focused and there, standing in the flickering light of the torches, were Asher and Lord Sampson.

I felt my heart drop into my stomach as both men stared at us for a moment before walking away.

I couldn't be sure which of us had been more shocked, but it was enough to throw ice across us both. We retrieved our horses and rode back to the castle in silence.

Over the next few days, Robyn and I were once again nearly inseparable. Though I knew things with Asher and Sampson were far from over, it was hard to keep the smile from my face when Robyn appeared at my chamber door each morning.

She had not stayed over again, and I had not asked. Though, with each passing day, it got harder and harder not to beg her to stay.

The queen's event had finally arrived, and I had not expected to see Robyn that morning as I rolled out of bed. She would be riding as Loxley's champion, and though I had no doubt of her skill by now, I worried for what might come when she was alone in the field.

To my surprise, she was, indeed, standing outside my chamber.

"I did not expect—"

My words were quickly cut off as Robyn pushed me back into my room. Her hot lips crashed against mine, and I heard the clamor of my door as it slammed closed. Her deft hands spun us around until I was pressed against the cool wood. I struggled to think as all sense seemed to fall out of me. Robyn pulled my bottom lip between her teeth, pulling gently.

I struggled to stay upright as my knees threatened to buckle.

Robyn pulled away abruptly and I felt the absence of her lips on mine like a hole had been punched through my chest. Her breath was warm against my skin as she spoke, "No matter what happens today—win or lose—I will come back tonight, and we will not leave this chamber for days."

Robyn pressed her lips lightly against mine once more, and I knew our brief moment was over, but I also knew that she would keep her word. Suddenly, I could not be happier to begin—and end—this tournament.

We walked down the cold, stone corridor. The castle was slowly waking and soon the sound of hushed, angry voices echoed toward us.

"Shame? How could I possibly bring shame to our people, Father? We haven't won a single event so there is literally nothing to lose. Regardless of whether or not I win today, our people will still be starving in the streets while we attend another lavish party!"

I recognized Rochelle's voice immediately, and I was shocked when Robyn and I found her staring up at a tall man with short, thinning, black hair and a long, black beard.

"You will not say one more thing. You will remember your place and your family."

They both turned to look at us as Robyn and I hurried past.

Once again, I was reminded of the things left unsaid between Robyn and myself. Rochelle's words were near treasonous. Was she part of Robyn's plan?

The thought was still on my mind as Robyn and I said our goodbyes until we would unite again after the event.

Robyn

The first surprise of the morning was that this event would have no spectators. The queen had set up a course far from the peering eyes of the camps, leaving only the members of Court willing to ride out with her to view the match. Of course, that was nearly all the members of Court.

The competitors rode next to the queen, and I suddenly found myself riding between Prince Asher and Lord Sampson. Neither man said anything as we crossed the fields in silence.

Finally, the course appeared before us, and the queen pulled to a halt. Gold nickered nervously beneath me as Prince Asher rode at our side. I threw him a furious look that he ignored as I realized the pointed edge of his sheathed sword rocked against Gold's round stomach. For once, as if sensing the intensity around us, the members of Court were silent.

Lady Rochelle pulled up her black stallion beside Lord Sampson. Her face was stone as she stared ahead at the queen. To my surprise, she had removed her typical long, flowing dresses and replaced them with a pair of leather breeches so tight they appeared to be melded with her skin.

I had seen her many times these past few weeks at the ranges. Though she was good for a beginner, she did not stand a chance against the seasoned archers around me. I looked again at the tight pull of her corset and the slick leather clinging to her legs. Perhaps her intent was to distract the competitors so much that she would be able to stay in the contest longer.

I smiled a little. I didn't know Rochelle that well, but from what I knew it felt like something she might do, and I could appreciate the effort. Now if Marian were to do the same, even I might miss a target or two.

Queen Naomi looked us over. Her nose rose to the air as she

searched the faces before her. For the first time, I realized several male members of the nobility were not present. It seemed not even the king could be bothered to come out from the castle to see his wife's event. For just a brief second, I felt a twinge of sympathy for her at the obvious slight.

"Each contestant will ride through the course, hitting each target as they go. Each target must be struck before the contestant can continue. The first rider out will be the winner. Lord Sampson will ride along, ensuring that each contestant hits the target."

The rules were simple enough, but as I felt Sampson's horse press against Gold from the other side, I knew nothing about this event would be simple.

"I will compete for the western river province today." Prince Asher made the statement like he was saying something as simple and not a blatant show of favoritism. Members of Court began to murmur and, to my surprise, several of them called out against it.

Queen Naomi's sharp gaze peered over the crowd, and when she raised her hand there was silence once more. "If the contestants from Colch, the eastern river, or the northern province win today, they will have won the tournament and its prize for their people. As it stands, there will be an additional prize for the winner of today's event. A cart of food will be delivered to every village in your province to help your people through the winter. The king is preparing it now."

Several people applauded. A few called out to thank the queen for her generosity, and I had to fight the urge not to roll my eyes. The prize would help some people, but it wasn't a solution to the repeated extravagance of the castle and the crown.

I looked at the faces of the contestants around me. Rochelle's face showed no expression at all, and Lord Aren was barely hiding his contempt as he studied the back of his horse's head.

A thought occurred to me just then. I realized that it was truly a gamble, but I thought back to the unrest throughout the castle and all of Notting. It would surely make enemies, but it was time I lived up to my word.

"Queen Naomi is so incredibly generous to offer the people of Notting such a prize." I allowed my voice to carry so all could hear it. "I will follow the lead of her and Prince Asher. Since the people of Loxley are not in need of such generosity, I pledge my winnings today to those in the camps just outside the city gates. Let my winnings go to them."

A few members of Court dared to clap. I watched the queen's jaw tighten and her thin lips purse into a straight line. She opened her mouth a few times as if to mutter something but did not speak.

My heartbeat quickened as the weight of my words settled over everyone present. Not only had I claimed that the Loxleys could take care of their people in a way that the crown could not, I had subtly acknowledged that the crown was knowingly ignoring the people right at their feet.

"Let us begin," was Queen Naomi's only response as she turned and rode away.

The crowd dispersed as people spread along the course to try to find the best vantage point. I knew Marian was with them somewhere, watching, but I tried to focus instead on the task at hand.

Marian

Robyn's challenge was clear as I listened to her promise her winnings to the people at the gate. If I had not known that she was part of some plot to rebel against the crown, it was painfully obvious now.

The contestant trotted to the starting line, and I watched as Robyn rode silently between Asher and Sampson. Fear and worry ate at me as I moved Marengo further down the course. Large, wooden barriers had been erected along the way, obscuring parts of the course. I strained to see the various targets inside, but it was impossible from this angle.

The flag was dropped only seconds later, and the race had begun.

The sound of thundering hooves shook through the air, and I stood higher in Marengo's saddle, trying again to watch as the blur of horses sped past. There were several thunks as arrows hit their targets in the distance.

My heart raced as panic began to overtake me. The memory of Prince Asher and Sampson's shocked faces when they saw Robyn and I entangled flashed across my mind. They hadn't said anything that night, but something told me that there was more to this event than simply another contest to see who was the best archer.

Chapter 32

Robyn

My first arrow hit the small target hanging from the straw bag inside the wooden platform. The first of the prince's arrows whizzed by, barely missing my ear before shooting right into the target.

Already the sound of the other riders had fallen away. The second target approached quickly. This one was near to the ground, and I had to maneuver atop Gold to get the arrow in the hay. Once again one of Asher's arrows narrowly missed me.

I looked ahead toward our 'judge' but the look on Sampson's face told me everything I needed to know. He and the prince had planned this. I would be lucky to leave this event alive.

The course shook a sharp left turn and Sampson blocked the path to continue. I knew immediately he meant to stop me so the prince could take aim. I whipped Gold again. This time I headed toward Sherwood. As I leaned, an arrow tore through my shirt, grazing my skin. I winced at the pain. It appeared that now we were far enough away from the other competitors, Asher had given up any semblance of pretending he was aiming for the targets.

"You're a shit shot, Your Majesty," I called back to my pursuer.

"You know you won't leave here alive."

I did know that, but it didn't mean I would make it easier for them to take me down. I ducked tight against Gold as arrow after arrow whizzed by. We rode blindly through the thick trees, and I realized too late we had neared a shallow ravine as Gold reared back. I heard the arrow only a heartbeat before it embedded in my leg.

The world blurred around me as I hit the ground. Pain sliced through me, knocking the air from my lungs as everything went black.

The first thing I saw when I opened my eyes was the dark silhouette of an absolutely stunning woman. The sun was barely shining through the branches as I struggled through the pain to stumble back into reality. Even through the haze of pain, I knew it was Marian who looked down at me now.

"Where is Gold?" Images of the horse rearing unexpectedly, followed by the memory of sharp rocks rising to greet me filled my mind.

"She is being seen to. Lee will look after her." Marian's voice reached out to me through the pain, bringing with it a sense of comfort. "We have been looking for you for hours, Robyn."

A soft breeze tickled at my sensitive skin, and I realized that Marian had lifted my shirt. Her soft touch pressed against my ribs, sending shooting pain through my chest. I winced, pulling away with a deep gasp--which only made matters worse.

As my vision cleared, I watched Marian retrieve a small knife from her side. I smiled when I realized it was the one I had given her. My joy was short-lived when I realized her intent. She brought the knife toward my chest, and I knew she meant to cut through the bindings around my breasts.

Panic filled me as I looked up at the faces around me. Rochelle and Samwell knelt into the mud beside me.

I grabbed Marian's hand, squeezing it tight. For a moment she looked down at our hands, then back up at me. A look of understanding passed over her face as she pulled back.

"You didn't see it. The prince was out for blood the moment the contest started," Rochelle's voice shook as she whispered.

"We need to get her somewhere I can examine her wounds."

I had never heard Marian be so forceful. Despite the ache in my ribs, I found myself laughing as the reality of the situation dawned on me. "The prince will be so disappointed to find that I am not dead."

"Robyn. . ." Marian began, but I watched as Samwell placed a hand on her shoulder. He shook his head and I watched something pass between the two of them.

"What? I'm fine, truly. Bring me some wine and I will be much better."

Once more, Marian's furious stare greeted me as the world swirled around me. She brought her hands to her hips as she huffed toward me. The look sent flips through my stomach.

"We need to get her somewhere safe," Marian spoke directly to Samwell now.

"There is a small cottage…" Samwell replied quickly.

Without another word, Marian ducked underneath my arm. Her warm body pressed against mine, allowing me to lean on her. On the other side, Samwell joined her. Together, we made it slowly through the thick brush of Sherwood.

After many, many stops to catch my breath or allow the world to come into focus again, we finally arrived at the small cottage. My rescuers placed me on the small cot and once again I felt my stomach protest as my head swam.

"Come back to the castle when you can." I was surprised again to hear Rochelle's concerned voice.

"The prince and the king's guard will be looking for her." Samwell's voice was filled with concern.

"Can't the baron do something?"

"I'm sure he will. Give it time. We will bring you supplies soon."

There was a pause and the creak of the door closing, followed by the distinct sound of a lock sliding in place.

I felt Marian's gaze pass me before I felt the soft caress of her fingers as they assessed my wounds.

I felt myself slide off into slumber, content to have Marian watching over me once more.

When I woke sometime later, I knew it must be very late in the night, or perhaps even early morning. Marian had wrapped my wounds while I slept. I felt the pinch and tug of stitches across my brow as I pulled them together.

"You need to sleep," I whispered to Marian. I wasn't sure what had happened, but the pain was certainly easing a bit.

Marian sat next to me with a long sigh. According to her, I had at least two broken ribs and several long gashes up my arm from falling onto the rocks. I closed my eyes as she continued to pester me with questions. Marian seemed intent on checking my mind as well, asking me questions about what my name was, what kingdom did I serve, and her name.

When I answered her name was 'delicious' she huffed at me again. I peeked open one eye, happy that I had at least made her smile.

"You are lucky I have sworn an oath to protect anyone in need. Even those who are irritating and behave as children goading on powerful members of Court."

I tried to hide my smile as Marian paced the room again. Her brows furrowed together as she grabbed small glass vials and bandages from the box I had given her. It felt like lifetimes ago that we were in her room in Colch. Marian moved the vials mindlessly around the room. She had already had me chew on some foul-tasting herbs to help with the pain—something I was not eager to do a second time.

Marian continued to chastise me, murmuring irritated words under her breath. Several times she turned back toward me, pointing a finger or vial menacingly at me. I could do nothing but grin as I watched her hips sway in the sunlight.

"Why, Lady Marian, am I so irritating?" I asked her again.

Her keen, blue eyes turned toward me. She crossed her arms tight to her chest and I fought to keep from staring at her ample bosom. I had always been thankful for my small chest, but suddenly my hands were itching to explore.

"I knew we should not have underestimated Asher or Sampson. I should have known they would retaliate."

It was her turn to rake her eyes across my body. She assessed my wounds, taking in each and every one. This look wasn't as cold and calculating as before. This time, her sapphire gaze felt warm against my skin.

My breath came in short bursts now, and Marian noticed immediately. She stalked back to my bedside. Her warm hand pressed against my chest, pushing me firmly against the bed.

She knelt against the pallet, head cocked to the side as she listened intently to my breathing. Her long strands had come loose of their braid, falling to the side of her face.

"Are you having problems breathing?" she whispered, leaning closer to me.

I felt the heat radiate from her, warming my side. The same heat spread throughout my body as I reached for the wisp of hair.

I tucked the hair back onto her slender shoulder as she startled at my touch. She tracked my movement, but when she didn't pull away I found myself running the pad of my thumb across the slope of her cheek. In all the times we had kissed or slept in a bed together, I knew I would never get used to the touch of her skin.

I have never felt something so soft.

I watched her look of concern grow.

"I am suddenly having pain in my chest. . . "

Marian's eyes filled with alarm as she made to pull away. I grabbed her arm gently, keeping her in place.

Terror filled me. I wondered at first if I had truly damaged my head, but then clarity fell over me and I had never been more certain of anything. I knew I must say what was on my mind now, or I would never be able to say it. "It is not my chest. It is my heart, wracked by guilt I cannot live with, knowing that I have caused you pain at any time."

Marian blinked several times. Her eyes never strayed from mine as I pressed against the cloth bed beneath me to sit up.

"I am sorry for what I have said and done. I am sorry for being cruel and irritating at times." Marian bit her lip, once again sending heat coursing through me. I stared at her delicate, pink lips.

Marian's brows pulled tight together, distracting me from my intrusive thoughts. I brought my hand once more to her cheek, settling my fingers along her chin.

"But I am afraid you have broken your oath to harm no one long ago."

Her chin quivered beneath my touch, and I recognized the stubborn, playful look return. "I have not."

"You have, since that first night you rode toward assassins to save Gawayne. You have broken your oath every day since--because every moment that your lips are not on mine is pure anguish."

A soft 'oh' floated from her, and I could no longer resist. Her lips were exactly as I had been seeing them in my dreams every night since we first left for Colch. I pressed my lips against hers, and I knew no amount of pain would keep me from the promise I had made her that morning.

At first, she hesitated, and I feared she might pull away. For a heartbeat, I worried I had misjudged. Perhaps she was truly furious with me.

All worry was washed away as she returned my kiss. It was my turn to release a sigh of gratitude as she kissed me with hunger and need behind her touch. Her hand on my chest traveled up and around the back of my neck, pulling me deeper. I felt her fingers stretch through my hair as she tumbled onto the pallet, struggling for balance.

I caught her slender waist in my free arm, ignoring the protests of my freshly-bandaged skin. I felt her smile against my lips as I pulled her tight against me.

Her tongue danced with mine as our hands continued to explore each other. One hand traveled achingly slow down my arms, settling at my waist. *Well, if she could, I could too. . .*

A wicked thought passed over me as I trailed my fingers down her back, running my nails along the thin cloth of her shirt. Her chemise was shorter today than normal. I quickly found the hem, placing my hands underneath to settle on her voluptuous backside. Images of her walking around in those breeches during the tournament flashed in my mind.

I gripped at her luscious behind. A newfound desire swept through me. My thoughts were once again a blur as our tongues continued to collide and her fingers found the strings of my trousers.

Trailing kisses across her cheek, I nibbled at the tender flesh of her ear lobe. "I have been thinking about you in these pants for *months. . .* " The feel of her ass in my hands was almost enough to melt me, but I felt her muscles flex in response and knew I needed more.

A low whine escaped her as I pulled my hand free of her pants. I could feel her breath quicken as I rubbed the back of my knuckles along the curve of her waist. Her hip raised up and her leg wrapped around my hip as her lips found mine again.

I didn't need any more of an invitation.

Marian gasped as I dipped my hand below her waistband, rubbing palm my along her soft mound, before plunging two fingers inside of her. Her slender neck arched back as she leaned into my touch. I trailed my tongue up her throat as she rode my hand desperately.

Her hands were in my hair, but they quickly dipped lower. I grabbed one with my free hand as I continued to tease and play with the bundle of nerves at Marian's core.

She tossed me a heated glare as she tried to pull her hand free.

"You kissed me first that night in the garden. It seems I have a debt to pay." Despite the protests of my body, I managed to flip our positions. Marian's blue eyes were filled with surprise as I perched above her.

I brought our entwined hands closer, kissing the back of her knuckles and watching her shiver as I kissed the underside of her arm. I placed them above our heads, pinning her to the cot.

This time I rubbed my fingers along her clit while I kissed my way down her neck. Her breath was fast and uneven as I nibbled and bit at the tops of her breasts. She continued to moan, arching her hips against my fingers until I was wet with her.

Her body tensed around mine, and when she called my name out, I knew my debt was paid, and I would gladly pay it again.

Marian's body relaxed against mine on the cot as my heartbeat eventually slowed. The smell of her lingered in the air around me, lulling me into bliss. I buried my face against her hair, finally allowing myself to think about everything that had happened over the last few months and everything that was still to come.

The last thought I had before sleep took me was that absolute anarchy could fall over the kingdom, but I'd never find something I wanted to fight for more than a pair of big, blue eyes and the smell of lavender on my skin.

Marian

Robyn was not in the bed when I woke up. It took me a moment to realize where I was, as my vision adjusted to the dim light of the cabin. Someone had lit the small stove in the corner. The soft glow of the embers reached for me through the darkness.

I had no idea how long Robyn and I had slept, but nighttime had fallen.

The wooden floor was chilly on my feet as I stood. Panic filled my chest for a moment as the quiet of the forest fell around me. I fought back the urge to go screaming from the cabin in search of Robyn. The door before me was unlocked, but there were no signs of a struggle. Surely, I reasoned with myself, if Asher or the guards had appeared I would have woken from the skirmish.

I pulled the door open gently and the warm breeze swept over my skin. Autumn was approaching, but I was thankful for the last bit of summer. In the trees above me, an owl called out. I peered up into the branches, but the darkness was too heavy.

I wondered again where Robyn might have gone. Then I heard the soft sound of splashing nearby.

I followed the sound of the creek until I could see the flow of the water reflecting in the moonlight above. My heart skipped a beat as my eyes fell on the image of Robyn wading naked in a shallow pool of water.

Her skin was positively luminescent as she splashed water up over her thighs. I watched, mesmerized, as she continued to wash. Her tight, lithe muscles flexed as she continued, and I found myself suddenly breathless. A twig snapped beneath my feet as I took a step forward.

Robyn's golden eyes looked up abruptly, immediately meeting my own. The sly smile I adored peeked again at the corner of her mouth.

She made no move to cover up, and I did not stop as I walked toward her.

We watched each other as I continued up the side of the small creek. An ache grew deep inside of me, making me feel brazen and wild. I pulled at the strings across the front of my dress, loosening the long, heavy fabric. I stopped for a moment, allowing the dress to pool at my feet.

Robyn's hand fell to her chest as I stood naked before her. To my surprise, the water was warm at my feet as I walked nearer. As we both stood wordless in the water, I watched as Robyn shifted uneasily for a moment.

Panic surged through me for a second, and I stopped short. It took me a moment to register her sudden discomfort, and I felt my brave facade slip a little.

Goosebumps traveled down my arms as I waited, trying to judge what to do. Slowly, Robyn's hand fell to the flat of her stomach, and for the first time, I realized the sudden cause for her unease.

Covering parts of her stomach, legs, and arms were a series of white lines. Across her body were scars that told the stories of the battles she had won.

My heart swelled a little as I briefly scanned the scars, suddenly understanding her embarrassment. Robyn was bare before me. Nothing more than the warrior I had come to adore.

I grabbed at her hand first. Pulling it away from the wide scar across her abdomen and intertwining my fingers with hers. I leaned closer to her as the water rushed around us. With my other hand, I touched her chin gingerly, placing soft kisses at the base of her ear. She trembled under my touch.

"Tell me about them," I whispered against her neck.

A small, jagged, white line shone in the moonlight, right atop the curve of her collarbone.

"What is this one from?" I placed my lips tenderly against the white line, trying to ignore the intense desire sweeping through me. Every part of my body urged me to move faster.

"First time I rode Gold. She ran straight into a pine tree." Robyn trembled a little as I ran my tongue across the first scar. Her body was sweet and salty beneath my lips, and I took my time devouring it.

I leaned back for a moment until I found another white line. This one ran just along the outside of her left breast. The skin had obviously torn open and was now healed into a jagged line.

I made my way to the scar slowly, allowing my tongue to trail across the flat expanse of her chest, grazing her taut nipple with my teeth, and then following the faint outlines of her marred skin.

"Got. . . that one. . . " --I smiled as Robyn struggled to focus. I returned to teasing the soft skin of her breast, gently kneading it in my hand— ". . . trying. . . to climb a mountain. . . "

Her hand squeezed mine as I continued to make my way down her body. A thick, pink scar stretched across her flat, muscled stomach. I knew where this one was from. I was the one who had stitched it.

Images of Robyn coming back to the castle in Colch flooded through my mind, but I kept them at bay. Now was not the time to focus on what might have been or what almost was. All that mattered now was Robyn's gorgeous, toned stomach and my overwhelming desire to explore every inch.

I knelt in the water before her. My knees sunk into the deep clay of the banks. I followed the curve of her hip with my tongue—well past where the scar had ended. I didn't stop until she was moaning in delight and I could taste exactly how much she needed me too.

Robyn buried her hands deep into my hair, and this time it wasn't with the gentle touch like when we were sleeping. Her touch was filled with need.

I delved my tongue in and out of the folds of her skin until her moans filled the forest around us, startling the birds from the trees.

Far sooner than I would have liked, Robyn stopped me. Though I could feel the way her body shook with desire, she lifted me off my knees with a gentle tug.

We retrieved our clothes from the grass, but Robyn surprised me by grabbing at the dress now in my hands.

"Do not even think of putting that on." A mischievous look sparked in her eyes, and we walked quickly back to the cabin.

The door had scarcely closed behind us before Robyn's mouth was once again on mine. The cool wood of the door pressed firmly against my backside as Robyn's grabbed at my wrists, bringing them high over my head.

Her lips left mine as she trailed her teeth gently across my jaw. One hand held my wrists, while the other drifted to my core. My body was ready as she plunged her fingers in and out.

My senses were truly overloaded, and I felt myself build until the pleasure was almost unbearable.

Robyn's mouth continued to tease along my neck and down to my breasts. The world seemed to blur around me until I finally fell over the edge.

Robyn and I spent the rest of the night in the cabin and didn't stop our exploration of each other's bodies until the sun was beginning to peek over the horizon. I had never felt such pleasure and had never found myself so determined to help a lover find theirs as I had that night. When we were both truly spent, sleep found us tangled together in a pile of blankets on the floor of the cottage.

When I awoke once more, it was to the feel of Robyn's gentle fingers running through my hair. Despite the tangles we had created last night, I loved that she was always playing with the long strands.

I looked up at her locks. They had grown longer than I had ever seen them, and I ran my fingers through them.

"I'm thinking of cutting it shorter. Perhaps with a razor."

I tried to imagine how she would look with even shorter hair. Trailing my fingernail down her skin, I marveled at the steep slope of her neck and the thick muscles of her shoulders and arms.

"It would display some of my favorite parts even more." I placed a teasing kiss on her collarbone—which had quickly become my new favorite pastime.

"Oh? I thought there were other parts of me that were your favorite. . . " Her smile was positively wicked as wrapped her hand along my ass. She kissed me on the lips gently, but only a second later a shadow seemed to fall over us. "Perhaps I will cut it. Now that I no longer have the opinions of Court to deal with."

Robyn's words had cast a pall over our happy morning, and suddenly I knew it was once again time to face reality.

"What will we do about the prince?" I chewed at my bottom lip as I remembered how close Asher's arrows had come to hitting her. "Perhaps his anger will fade with time. We have wounded his pride and that of Sampson by publicly refusing him."

"I do not care about their pride." Robyn sighed heavily, running her fingers through her long hair. "I will go see father in the city. You must check on your people. We will meet back tonight?"

I nodded as Robyn looked me over. She chewed at her lip, and I found myself leaning in to kiss her tender lips. She leaned her forehead against mine, releasing a deep sigh.

We both dressed, and in only a few brief minutes we were once again under the shadows of the trees. Robyn would cut through and enter the city in disguise until we knew what was happening. I would weave through the trees too, coming out at the edge of the camps where we had fought only days before. If anyone asked, I would simply explain that I had stayed amongst the people.

Everything was fine until I walked through the camps and into the harsh, afternoon sun. Every tent once again sported the long, flowing, white ribbon atop it. As I continued my trek to the castle, I felt my dread grow.

It wasn't difficult to discern the temperament of the castle. Servants with frightened faces scurried past me the moment I entered. A thundering voice echoed through the corridor, and I realized it was coming from the grand hall. King Ruelle was furious.

Keeping to the shadows of the corridor, I did my best to avoid any unwanted attention as I listened.

"They're traitors! Find them and bring them to me or it will be your head I put in a pike outside the city gates!"

My hand flew to my mouth as I listened. King Ruelle's temper was legendary. He had once had a chambermaid whipped for leaving his slippers too far from his bed—but even this seemed something far beyond his normal fury.

There was the sound of a clamor, and it seemed that the king had dismissed his audience. Members of Court scurried from the room, and I did my best to blend into the crowd. A soft arm wrapped into mine, pulling me down a side corridor. I looked with alarm to see Madawi and Joppa suddenly at my side.

"Where have you been? They said you went into Sherwood and never returned!" I could see my friend's panic. I struggled for an easy explanation, but there was none. I couldn't tell her where I had been. I wasn't even sure if she would believe Asher's part in it. "Marian. I am your friend. Let me help you." Madawi squeezed my arm, and the guilt of withholding so much from her began to truly eat away at me.

"We were all so concerned for you. . . " a shrill voice startled me. Madawi and I turned just in time to see Queen Naomi approach. Madawi did not release my arm as the two of us bowed low. "We were so worried for your safety."

"I apologize, Your Highness. I was tending to those in the camps, and stayed with a woman there." Queen Naomi looked me over slowly. I knew instinctively she did not believe anything I said.

"Then you will not mind joining me and Princess Madawi as we venture into the camps as well. We were just hoping to spread some kindness to them. King Ruelle has graciously offered not to raise this year's tithe and has even seen to it that some sweets be distributed amongst the little ones. We shall go tonight."

I wanted to argue. I struggled to find a reason that I could not attend the queen, but she was leading me from the castle before I could say a word.

Queen Naomi was quick in her preparations—far too fast for the trip to be as impromptu as she obviously wanted us all to believe. In far less time than I had ever seen a royal procession move, we were on our way and back through the city.

Nighttime had descended by the time we reached the city's outer wall. To my surprise, neither the queen nor Madawi had taken one of their carriages. In fact, the queen had insisted on riding atop her favorite stallion.

Madawi rode atop Asher's favorite stallion, with Joppa at her side on an impatient and irritable mare I had never seen before. I moved Marengo out of the way of the horse's angry teeth and flailing legs as it protested the sudden change around us.

Queen Naomi smiled prettily as we made our way along the outside wall. I looked at the worn and weary faces of the people as they poked their way out of their tents. I didn't recognize any of them.

More unfamiliar faces continued to pour in from every corner until there was an ocean of fury around us.

Something itched at the back of my mind, and my heart stopped as I suddenly wondered why the queen had chosen this route. We had ridden far from the gate and the center road running through the camp. Beside me, I watched Madawi shift nervously in her saddle, and I knew she sensed it too.

Something wasn't right.

I turned in the saddle, trying to think what Robyn might do. I needed to call the guards around us like I had seen her do on the road. When I looked around again, our guards had disappeared among the people now pressing in on us. Even Joppa was gone.

The queen slowed her horse, and I watched as she kicked its round belly with the heel of her boot. The horse nickered for a moment as more hands reached up, desperate to reach out and touch their monarch.

Queen Naomi kicked at the horse, and then I watched in horror as she began kicking at the people who were enclosing us. Behind me, darkness began to grow as the torches along the city wall were extinguished.

As the last torch blew out, I caught a flicker of light as a man in the crowd drew a dagger from his belt.

Robyn

Harvest time had this magical power to make even the humblest, most desolate citizens forget their troubles. As bonfires raged and crops were brought in from the fields, the city seemed to light up around me.

I kept the hood of my cloak tight around my head, careful not to allow anyone too close.

I wondered how long the temporary joy inside the city would last. As a special gift for such a fantastic tournament, the king had decided not to increase the yearly tithe for the providences.

It had been an absolute force of will not to roll my eyes when I saw the proclamations posted on every corner in the city. Like all the king's promises, they would soon float away in the breeze.

Asking for the same amount of an impossible fund was still asking for the impossible, I thought sourly.

The castle behind me glittered against the dark night sky. Each window, hallway, and otherwise flat surface of the castle had been filled with candles. Every year King Ruelle gave his queen a great gift for their anniversary and filled the castle with all manner of sweets and cakes—just as there had been on the night they had wed.

I wondered--not for the first time--if it wasn't the queen's doing. I had no doubt that the king had little to no part in the 'gift'.

All week servants had even been dispatched to the city children, distributing small treats and sweets. I watched as a young girl and boy in tattered clothing gathered at the corner of the narrow, cobbled road before me. Each face was covered in dirt and grime. The girl's dress was damp with water. Probably from washing someone's clothes that morning. Neither of the children wore shoes, despite the nip in the air. Still, their steps bounded across the street with their temporary joy.

My heart felt heavy as I passed a few coins from my purse to the hand of the older sister.

"Put some shoes on your feet and your brother's too," I whispered as the toothless little boy shoved the handfuls of sticky, red candy into his mouth.

"Fank you, sir." Once again the boy smiled in delight.

I walked once more toward my destination as the torches guiding the way became fewer and fewer.

Eventually, I found the inn where Father had summoned me in his letter. Piercing the dark wood of the doorway like an emblem blazing for all to see, it was there again. An arrow with a white cloth wrapped around its shaft. I watched for a moment as the tail whipped it wildly in the wind.

The small, wooden door creaked open. I struggled to close it, as it swung free from its hinges like it had been kicked one too many times. As the door shut behind me the familiar scent of booze, sweat, and something else I refused to consider greeted me. There were no windows in the small room, only the faint light of candles guided my gaze to the back table where Gawayne, Samwell, and the others were seated.

As I approached the table, the men gave off the air of a group of friends out for a pint in the low afternoon, but I knew better. The raucous laughter at the table might seem easy and relaxed, the men's shoulders might slouch, and their beers might spill, but their eyes were clear and their minds sharp.

Beside me, Gawayne's wrist was wrapped tight in a familiar, white cloth. I looked at him questioningly as I sat in the empty chair beside him, but he gave no response.

"Glad to see you up and about." Gawayne smacked me hard on the back, but I could see the pain and worry on his face. Gawayne was forever acting as the messenger to the different villages in Sherwood. No doubt he had been out doing something to help us all when the news of my accident reached him.

Though their smiles never faded, and the laughter seemed to continue, I knew the men were waiting on more information.

As if on cue, a barmaid wandered over to our table with a sway of her hips. Though I was sure many of the men around me had at some point paid for her company, I ignored her completely. Her voice carried above the noise of the other patrons as she came closer. Her engorged breasts hung remarkably close to me as the deep red of her dress dipped so low in the front I wondered how it contained her at all.

"Gentleman. I wonder if you'd like to join me for a drink? Some of the girls and I love to get together for drinks. . . "

Several of the men smiled—whether genuine or forced I couldn't be sure as the woman fell atop the table. There was a commotion as drinks were spilled and the men leapt to their feet.

"Well. . . we must take you lads upstairs and get you cleaned up." The invitation hung in the air as the blond woman turned to me with a smile. The men looked at me with bewildered stares, until at once we noticed the white band wrapped tight around her wrist, just under the sleeve of her red dress.

"I do think I could use someone, maybe a few, to help me clean up." I placed one hand around the woman's slender hip as she led us to the darkest corner of the bar. Beneath my sleeve, I pressed the tip of my dagger into her side.

"I do so hope the drinks in here are as good as you say." I nuzzled close to the woman's ear—giving the look of a lustful customer to anyone who cared to notice. I kept the knife at her back as we walked each step. I turned for only a second to see Samwell walking cautiously behind me. The others followed at a slower, leisurely pace, but their eyes were alight with focus. Each of them had a hand resting on the hilt of his sword.

In the crowded corridor, we watched as the woman pulled at a long chain that fell deep within her breasts. From the end of the chain held a set of keys. I gripped my knife tighter as she choose a key, pushing open the door.

I breathed a sigh of relief as father stepped forth from the dark room.

"Thank you, Kat."

I looked toward father for a moment as the woman nodded her head. Then, like a phantom, she walked off into the darkness.

The men and I filed in, crowding the room as we found our places. I eyed the bed suspiciously as I watched father enter too. Part of me gawked at how comfortable he seemed in such a place, but another part considered that there were some questions I probably did not want to be answered.

Samwell was the only one to dare touch the bed. He sprawled out along the mattress, sending a flurry of dust through the air. He looked the picture of relaxation until he met Father's disapproving stare.

I perched on the bedside table as Samwell moved to sit upon the edge of the bed. All eyes were on Father as he stood in the center.

"Obviously the king and queen are trying to garner some favor with all their 'good deeds.' But we will not forget as easily. I had a word with Lord Sampson, who swears he had no idea the prince's intent—"

"That's absolute bullshit—"

Father's hand rose abruptly, cutting off my protests.

"However, I believe he may have been compromised. Lord Sampson knows enough that the king could call for all of our heads at any time—if he hasn't done so already. My sources in the castle say that the proclamation was already being written by this early afternoon. The attack on Robyn and our people will not go unpunished, but it is time we left the capital."

The men made no sound, but I watched as Gawayne and Samwell both rolled their eyes. Father seemed to let his words settle before continuing.

"It is time to remind the people inside and outside the gates that winter is near. Soon the tithe will be taken, and providences will struggle even more to feed their people. The citizens of Notting are outside the city gates. We have brought their cries to the castle. Now we must remind those close by and those far away who their king really is."

Something cold and icy grew inside of me as father spoke. A memory formed in my mind. Father asking Marian who her father was. The way he looked at her--as if memorizing her face and studying her features.

"How will we do that?" Gawayne's voice was low as he spoke from the other side of the room. His stare was intense--a soldier and a spy, waiting for further instruction.

"It is well known that King Ruelle has a penchant for pretty girls. . . ." My heart began to race as I listened to father speak. His eyes were alight with mischief in only the way a former spymaster could look. "Perhaps it is time that the queen is reminded of this. Perhaps it is time she is reminded again of her husband's constant infidelity."

Once again father let the words settle, and I watched the men around me process the implications.

"But she knows already. What good will it be for us to remind the queen or the people of Notting something that everyone knows?" I watched as Samwell leaned forward—clearly intrigued.

This time, it was my turn to cut father off. I swallowed hard as I spoke the truth I had been considering for days now. "Because what we will remind her of is that her beloved Asher, her precious prince, might not be the king's firstborn." I took a calm breath as Father's gaze met mine across the room.

"I will not allow Marian to be hurt or become a target of the crown."

My voice was filled with ice as I stood up from my perch to stare down at my father.

"You see it now. You know who she is and what she means."

"What are you talking about?" Samwell spoke up. I took a deep breath as the men around me traded confused stares.

"Look at her. The next time you are with her, really look at her. She has his eyes, his chin. It is his mouth from which she speaks. It was only a matter of time until people realized the truth. Until they realized they might have better options than someone who ignores their hungry bellies and sick children."

There was a sharp intake of breath as the men realized the truth of Father's words.

"She is the firstborn," Gawayne's voice was barely a whisper. "She is the true heir."

I finally tore my gaze from Father's cold and calculating stare as I looked once more at my friends. Samwell and Gawayne waited patiently for me to explain.

"Lady Reya, Marian's mother, didn't die during childbirth. It is rumored, that Lady Reya brought her child safely into this world, intending on loving and caring for her, but when Marian so closely resembled the man who forced himself upon her that she killed herself with a vial of poison."

"Others believe the queen did it." Father's deep voice resounded through the room like cannon fire. "And even more women say that Lady Reya was not the only woman to suffer such a fate at the hands of the king."

All around us, the men shifted uncomfortably. Even during

wartime, forcing a woman was expressly forbidden among the king's army and punishable by death. It had been so for hundreds of years.

Despite their obvious disgust and discomfort at the news, I watched as behind the eyes of each man the wheels began to turn. The people of Notting deserved more than a king who would commit such an act. They deserved more than a queen who would stand idly by and allow it.

I paced around the room again as bile rose in my throat. It was too much. *Even if it were true, how could I ever tell Marian?*

"It is too awful. Too terrible, father." I rubbed at my eyes again--as if doing so would keep such horrendous images away.

"All across Notting, these ladies have come forward and now tell their stories far and wide. They are desperate for justice. It is time the people knew." Father's voice filled the air as the hair on my arms and neck stood on end.

"It is time the people knew." The men repeated back Father's words, but I could not.

"We see the banner. We hear its call," Father recited the mantra that was quickly becoming the thing that would bring the people together.

"The people respond," everyone in the room recited.

There was one person who deserved to know what the entire kingdom would be discussing by morning. I fled from the room, without another look at my companions.

The warm weather of autumn had given way to winter by the time I emerged from the inn. I pulled my cloak tight against my arms, but I knew nothing would keep away the chill that had settled deep in my bones.

I was brooding deep in my thoughts as I made my way toward the city gates. It would take a long time to get to the safety of the cabin, and if Marian was already there waiting, we had much to discuss.

Once again, I wished I could go and retrieve Gold from the stables. Marian had assured me she had directed Rochelle to take the horse to

Lee, and though I knew the old man would care for the horse, I longed for the mare's constant companionship.

I could not shake the weight sitting in my chest, and I allowed my feet to carry me as I neared the edge of the city. That was when I heard the familiar, terrifying sound of screaming and swords clashing together.

I jerked my head to attention, peering through the dark streets as two dozen guards made their way out the gates and toward the camps.

Chaos reigned as people rushed around us. I pulled my cloak tighter over my face as I squeezed between the river of people now filing in and out. A guard bumped me roughly, and my shoulder bounced against the hard, stone wall. A second later, I saw an older woman trip and fall. The guard who stomped on her frail hand didn't even bother to slow.

I pulled the older woman to the side, helping her to stumble from the stream.

"The queen. . ." The old woman wheezed as she clutched at her chest, gasping for air.

"The queen is out there? I'm sure her guards will find her." I tried to reassure the old woman. The old woman shook her head weakly, and confusion filled me. "Our Queen and the princess are out there."

Suddenly, I noticed the thin strip of white wrapped around her wrist. I grabbed at the woman's frail arms as panic threatened to overtake me. Dread filled me as I realized what the old woman truly meant. I knew who was lost amongst the crowd.

Marian

I kicked at the dagger in the man's hand as he approached, knocking it to the ground. I knew I was lucky to have caught him off-guard—but I also knew I probably wouldn't get so lucky again.

The dagger fell to the dirt beneath Marengo, and I did my best to keep the mare over top of it so he could not retrieve the weapon.

"Bitch!" The man spat at my feet as he neared. I felt his spittle fall against my ankle.

My mind reeled as I struggled to find the words to calm the crowd. I looked out at their faces, but these were not the same people I had aided at Colch. These were hungry, furious strangers who had finally had enough. "Now is your chance. Your queen is here among you. Tell her your needs! Share with her your sorrows."

A few faces looked up at me as they stopped. For a second my breath caught and I wondered if I had saved us all.

"We have brought you treats from the castle for your children." Queen Naomi's voice yelled across the crowd. I watched the curl of her nose as she looked out over the dirt-covered faces reaching out for her dress. As she glittered in her finery and her jewels beneath the light of the torches, her contempt for her subjects was written clearly across her face.

"We don't want your damn treats! We want food!" A furious man with a salt and pepper beard yelled from the back of the crowd. A chorus of yells resounded as those around him agreed.

"Get behind me, Madawi!" I fought back the panic threatening to overtake me as my heart pounded desperately against my chest. Across the throng of faces, I looked for someone, anyone familiar.

We need to get out of here.

Once again, I struggled not to panic as I looked for a way out. The tall, stone wall of the city pushed against our backs, and we would have to rush the crowd if we were to leave. I hesitated to allow

Marengo to push through. Hurting innocents as they slept in their bed would do no one any favors.

"Which of your maids will the king take to bed tonight?" A young, blond woman laughed as she stood before the queen. "As many as he wants—and whether they want to go or not."

My jaw dropped open at the woman's bold words. In front of me, Queen Naomi seemed equally stunned.

"You watch your mouth!" The queen began to kick at the crowd as her horse pushed against them. The girl fell as the queen urged the horse on. I watched in horror as the horse panicked and reared. There was a deafening crack as its hooves slammed back down, right atop the girl. Her scream filled the air and I knew our fates were sealed.

Angry hands reached for the queen, and then myself and Madawi. Their nails dragged across my flesh as I struggled to stay on Marengo. Someone tore the reins from my hands, and I hit the ground with a thud. In a flurry of dust, Madawi landed next to me.

"Where are our guards? Where is Joppa?" When I looked at Madawi's face again, I could see the terror written plainly across her face. Her eyes brimmed with unshed tears. I reached for her hand, trying to keep her close to me.

The queen's shrill scream filled the air as she was pushed and pulled to an empty space between two tents. Madawi and I followed as something sharp pressed against my back. I knew without looking it was the tip of a dagger.

"Stop it! I will have you hanged for this! I will burn this camp to the ground!"

Madawi and I were pushed until we too were at the center of the ring next to the queen. A sharp pain pierced my head as someone ripped at my hair. I stumbled for a second, scraping my palms against the sharp stones on the ground.

As I rose from the dirt I once again looked at our attackers. The woman who had been trampled by the queen was nowhere to be found. Instead, a ring of large, muscular men surrounded us. They all looked ragged as if they were used to days or weeks without bathing. Across their faces were scars and bruises. These were not simply people who had arrived at the camp by accident. These men were killers, and they had traveled here for this exact reason. They had come here for us.

A rough pair of hands pulled at my arm, dragging me away from Madawi and the queen. The man holding me sneered down at me as I pulled and kicked. I dug my feet into the dirt, trying to stay with Madawi. A voice in the back of my mind told me nothing good would come if we were separated.

The man squeezed my forearm so hard I thought he might snap the bone. His cold eyes looked at the leader again and then at me.

"This one?"

The leader gave a silent nod as new panic enveloped me. I felt the blood drain from my face.

Why are they here for me?

All coherent thoughts went out of my mind as I struggled to break free. Somewhere in my panic, I registered Madawi screaming my name. The man holding me tightened his grip when I remembered some of the brief training from Colch. Danyeil had told me to do whatever I could to get away. . .

Acting out of instinct, I turned and bit down hard on the man's hand. I could feel his blood in my mouth as he screamed and released my arm.

There was a moment of relief as I ran toward Madawi's outstretched arms. Just as I was about to graze her fingertips with mine, a sharp pain filled my head and the world went black.

Chapter 36

Robyn

I ran across the cobblestone as my hood fell back. Guards continued to fly by me in a hurry, but they were too busy to notice.

The sounds of swords clashing grew louder, and I watched as each guard headed off to stop the fight brewing in the distance.

"What's going on?" Samwell's voice was filled with concern as he appeared beside me. We paused for a moment, caught in our confusion. Gawayne appeared only seconds later. His thick brows were knitted tight together as he looked out over the camps.

Even from this distance, we could see the sparks flying as swords clashed together, but something itched in the back of my mind. The old woman's words played again in my mind. If the queen were surrounded by her guards, why had there been so much panic?

"Robyn." Gawayne's voice was filled with worry as he pointed to the ground. Fresh hoof prints had left a trail along the side of the wall—away from the skirmish where the king's guard had headed.

"Follow it." I took off at a run. Samwell and Gawayne did not wait as they followed me.

Within just a few minutes, I knew something was wrong. All along the wall, torches had been extinguished. Someone had gone to great lengths to keep the guards atop the wall from seeing what was happening below.

People were stirring from their tents now. I watched as their curious faces peeked from the heavy flaps of their tents. Again, my senses were set on edge as we ran. Someone had relit one of the torches ahead, and that's when I saw the pool of blood at the base of the wall.

"Stop!" I ordered my friends as we approached. Gawayne and Samwell immediately unsheathed their swords. I pulled mine as well. I chastised myself for leaving my bow at the cabin, but it would have been too easily recognized by the guards.

We followed the trail of blood with careful steps until we reached a small tent. Gawayne grabbed the torch nearby, and we entered the small space.

I blinked rapidly as my vision adjusted to the darkness inside the tent. A tremor of horror flowed across my skin as I looked at the bloodied corpse before us.

"Joppa. Its Princess' Madawi's guard," Samwell's voice was barely a whisper as he leaned down to inspect further.

"There's another over here—shit. No there's two." I flinched as Gawayne leaned over, lifting the dead, haunted faces of two more bodies toward the light. To my relief, I didn't recognize either face. "Looks like she put up a hell of a fight."

I nodded in agreement as fury filled me. The sight of Joppa's mangled corpse was almost too much to bear. I did my best to lay the older woman back and position her hands so she may seem at peace.

There was no use though. My stomach rolled and it was all I could do not to spill its contents onto the ground at my feet. Joppa's body was covered in blood. The silk of her shirt was caked in mud and a deep, red stain permeated the thin fabric. Someone had stabbed her in the side, but as I lay her head on the ground, I realized the true atrocities she had endured. Someone had snuck up from behind her and cut her throat.

My face flushed with anger that someone could be so cowardly. Joppa's throat had been slashed so deep that the bones had penetrated through the flesh.

Samwell passed me his cloak, and I covered her body until we could return.

I looked over at her lifeless attackers, they too had various wounds. One had blood pooling from his chest, while the other had slashes across his body. Joppa had clearly been outnumbered.

Samwell reached down, grabbing the curved blade from Joppa's side. I looked between my two friends, and I could see the anger on their faces now. I took a deep breath as we stepped out into the night once more.

We followed the trail of extinguished torches, and I suddenly heard the sound of shouting overhead. In the darkness, I could just make out a thin group of men.

They had all formed a ring around something—or someone— and my blood ran cold as I caught a glimmer of white.

Samwell, Gawayne, and I paused as we approached. I motioned for them to spread out at my side. The only way we would be able to take on so many would be if we managed to surprise them and fell a few before the others realized what had happened.

"You will leave the queen be," a furious female voice I didn't recognize came from the center of the ring. There was a cry of agreement, and my confusion grew.

One man stepped back, and that was when I realized that there were far more people at the center of the ring than I had expected.

Spread out across the captives, were faces I recognized immediately. They were citizens of Hazo, and they were protecting their healer.

"It seems you have a choice." I watched as the ring of men startled at the sound of my voice. They turned on their heels as they looked at Gawayne, Samwell, and me at their backs. "You can leave now before the king's guard arrives or you can stay and take your chances."

With the three of us at their back and the armed citizens guarding their captives, it was only a matter of seconds before the attackers realized their odds had changed desperately.

"You understand, Loxley, that we will not simply go peacefully."

I looked over at the man who spoke. I searched his withered and wrinkled face but found nothing familiar. None of the men seemed to wear the banners or colors of one of the noble houses.

Where had they come from?

We stood assessing one another for a few seconds. My family had many enemies. It wasn't uncommon for them to target me, but I shivered to think where this sudden enemy may have emerged from.

"I think, perhaps, you should reconsider."

This time the voice from the darkness startled me, but I did not let it take my focus from the man before me—even as my heart pounded in response.

A tall man in brown, leather breeches and a thin, white tunic emerged from the darkness. He held a sword in one hand. Next to him, three more men appeared. I recognized them immediately as the contestants from the northern province—including Lord Aren, the man soon to become Baron.

For a brief second, I allowed myself to search the crowd in the center for Marian. The people had formed a tight circle, making it impossible.

Then I noticed the drops of blood on the ground. Though I couldn't explain it, some instinct buried deep inside of me told me it was hers.

The leader of the attackers looked out over us all, and I could see his mind trying to determine if they could win. The people from the camps might not have put up much of a fight, but with the three of us, and the four men from the northern province, the odds were no longer in his favor. The leader had already lost two men to Joppa's sword tonight. Would he gamble losing more?

The leader lowered his sword, and the others followed. Like phantoms, they disappeared back into the sea of tents at a run.

Rolfe and Aren did not need an invitation. Their men raced to follow as Samwell, Gawayne, and I ran toward the center of the circle.

The people of Colch immediately parted, revealing the trio of women they had so bravely protected.

My blood ran cold and time seemed to slow as I stared at Marian's head laying in Madawi's lap. Blood had spread across Madawi's dress and tears fell from her eyes as they looked up at me.

"The bleeding has. . . slowed," Madawi's voice shook.

My stomach turned in response, and for a moment I thought I might be sick.

"I need a horse!" I yelled into the darkness. I didn't know if I could get there in time, but I needed to get Marian to the healer's tower as fast as possible.

Like someone had been waiting for me to ask, an older man brought forth a brown gelding. I lifted Marian in my arms, surprised at how light she felt. Wrapping my arms tight around her body, I walked to the side of the horse.

Panic had begun to take over me now, but Gawayne appeared at my side. His large, muscled arms reached out, and for a moment I hesitated. Letting go of Marian, even for a second, felt like I might truly lose her.

I climbed atop the horse, and Gawayne helped me tuck Marian tight against my chest. Her warm breath tickled at my neck. I focused on the feeling of the rise and fall of her chest, unsure what I would do if it suddenly stopped.

I raced through the city streets, guiding the horse around guards and carts, and anyone who might get in our way. The people around me turned into a blur as the chilly wind whipped across my face. The horse was unfamiliar to me, but it listened well enough as I pushed it to its limit up the hill leading to the tower.

I ignored those who cried out Marian's name as hot tears fell from my cheeks. The people of Notting called for her like she was already gone.

Marian's unconscious form leaned against me, and I could barely keep her in the saddle. I ignored the faces filled with concern as the horse stopped just short of the doorway.

Within seconds, dozens of hands reached for Marian. Acolytes in their gray tunics surrounded the horse, and they carried her away before I could even dismount.

My shoulders shook and my breath caught in my throat as I watched them disappear into the dark tower.

It had been hours since the acolytes had taken Marian, and I had been relegated to a workroom after my third screaming match with Kira.

I paced furiously across the floor, waiting for an update. The sword hanging from my side bounced against my leg again. My fury built as I released the strap holding it to my waist. I tossed the sword atop Marian's desk, where it skidded and fell to the ground, narrowly missing one of the candles that had been lit for me. Dozens of parchments fluttered onto the floor. They floated to the ground like feathers in the wind.

I ignored the mess I had made as I ran my fingers through my hair once more. The candle on the desk was already halfway to the size it had been when the acolyte lit it when I had been forced into the room.

I watched the flame flicker for a moment. Then I reasoned that I would wait until it burned down to the size of my thumb. If Kira or someone else hadn't given me some godsdamned news by then I would leave this office and hunt them down.

For the next few minutes, I alternated between watching the door, pacing angrily, and eyeing the burning candle.

I forced myself to take deep breaths, but the image of Marian's blood kept replaying in my mind. The candle had melted but a little, and I knew I could wait no more.

I let my feet carry me to the door, swinging it open wide. In the dark corridor stood a handful of acolytes. Some had tears in their eyes, while others wept openly as they held one another.

One young man pointed me down the corridor, and I raced as my heart beat against my chest. I rounded corner after corner until I realized they were leading me to Marian's room.

"You've got them all in tears. . . " I could hear Kira's soft voice whisper as I approached the doorway. "Robyn is beside herself. I had to have two acolytes drag her to your office."

I pushed the door open slowly as terror gripped me. The world seemed to spin a bit as my heart skipped a beat. Sitting at the end of her bed was Marian.

Warm tears fell as I walked into the room. I could feel Kira's wide, green eyes watching me, but I could not tear mine away from Marian's face. A bruise covered part of one eye, and Kira had covered the wound on Marian's head with a white cloth. It was such a stark contrast to the wrap she normally wore, that the sight of it hit me in the gut, and I felt myself crying harder.

"Robyn." Marian smiled at me and suddenly I was rushing to her. Marian stood but seemed to regret it. I could see the struggle as she took a step toward me. Kira reached out to help, but I was there first. My knees felt shaky too as I touched the warmth of her skin and we both dropped to the ground as we held one another.

Somewhere in the back of my mind, I registered the click of the door as it closed behind Kira. I drew a deep breath as my shoulders shook. The smell of lavender and blood greeted me as I buried my face in Marian's long hair. Her nails scored my back through the thin cloth of my tunic as she held me. I welcomed the sting, as it reminded me that she was truly alive.

Finally, we pulled back. Marian pressed her forehead gently to mine and we sat like that for several minutes.

"Thank you for saving me," she whispered into the air between us.

I fought against the surge of emotions as I heard her voice for the first time since that morning.

"Thank you for not leaving me." I leaned forward, placing the softest of kisses on Marian's lips as I placed my hands on her warm, wet cheeks. I was careful not to press on the bruise, but to my surprise, she deepened the kiss. I felt her tongue push into my mouth and her warm hands wrap around the back of my neck.

Marian pressed against me with a need I had never felt before, and as our tongues and hands danced together. By the time she pulled away, we were both breathless.

Marian rested her head against my shoulder as I wrapped my arms around her, gently pulling her against my chest. For the first time since I had entered the room, I truly noticed the state she was in.

Her white dress was torn in places and covered in dried blood and dirt. Her long hair was a tangled mess, and I could see the blood and dirt on her palms. Fury built inside of me once again for the men who had done this to her. I had not received news whether Rolfe and his men had caught up with the men, but if they were somehow still lucky enough to be breathing, they would not be for long.

I did my best to push the furious thoughts away. I would deal with them soon enough.

"What do you need from me, my love?"

Marian sighed against my chest. She stretched her long legs in front of her as she leaned against me.

"I feel disgusting."

"Draw her a bath," I ordered two acolytes waiting just outside the door. They immediately disappeared into the other room.

A few minutes later, steam filled the bath chamber.

"You are the patient now." I looked her over once more, internally cataloging all her bruises and scrapes.

"I'm fine, truly." Marian's face was weary and her shoulders slumped forward as she released a long sigh. I couldn't help myself. I brushed my hand along her cheek, pushing away the thin pieces of hair.

I stamped down my fury. There were people who would pay for what happened, but not tonight.

"I believe I shall decide that. Firstly, my sweet, a bath." I leaned forward, crinkling my nose in distaste. The smell of sweat and blood lingered in the air around Marian.

Her eyes sparkled as she brought her hand to her chest. A teasing look of offense crossed her face playfully. "It is considered quite rude for a healer to insult their patients."

Marian made to stand but staggered as she walked across the room. I reached for her, ducking under one of her arms and helping her walk.

A stool sat in the corner of the room, and I helped Marian to it. Once again her shoulders sagged forward. I released the strings of her dress, watching as it fell into a blood-stained puddle on the ground.

"Asher will know you are here." Marian looked at me with worry.

"I think he will find it difficult to storm the healer's tower. Besides, he has his hands full with Madawi and the queen to care for."

Marian nodded as she sank back against the copper tub. For a moment I watched the rise and fall of her chest. I grabbed one of the vials of oil from the shelf nearby. I opened the stopper and the smell of lavender greeted me. Slowly, I helped her wash away the blood and the dirt.

At her direction, I used a different oil in her long hair, gently washing and untangling it as she leaned back against the tub. I placed a kiss atop her head as I watched her relax.

The fear and I had been fighting and the relief I felt picked at my insides again until hot tears were falling from my eyes. There was so much more to be done. There was so much more still to come, but for tonight I thanked any of the gods who were listening that Marian was alive.

Marian

It did not take long for news of our attack, and of Robyn's rescue, to reach the castle. Though it had taken much persuasion, three days later, I finally coaxed her into going back to the cabin.

There had been an attack on his wife, the woman who was to be the future queen of the kingdom, and the Royal Healer, but true to form, King Ruelle would not allow something as trivial as an attack to stop the ball he had planned.

I had spent most of the day in the city doing what I could, but as nighttime fell, I knew it was time to get ready.

Tonight would be my last chance to try to convince Asher to stop his tirade against Robyn.

"If only the King and the prince knew that it was not simply the men who delighted in marveling at you. . . "

I jumped from my chair before the mirror, grabbing at the brush and brandishing it about me. My heart skipped a beat as Robyn whispered across the room. Hidden in the darkness, she emerged from the corner. The moonlight streamed against her short, brown locks. Her eyes sparkled with mischief, though her face looked worn and weary.

"I thought you had fled to the cabin."

"Why would I leave without you?" Robyn's words hung in the air between us as her brows furrowed.

My heart raced in response, and I knew what she was truly asking. I suddenly understood why she had come.

Closing the distance between us, I brought my hand against her cheek. "You don't have to do this."

"The king knows, or at least he suspects enough. It's only a matter of time. Father says we're waiting for the sign, and then we will make our move." Robyn stepped back from my touch, rubbing her temples in the way that told me she was really distraught. She paced toward the window. Her sword hung at her side, reminding me of the portraits of the great warriors that hung in the gallery. She was a warrior. She had proven herself time and time again — probably more times over than even the greatest warriors.

She was *my* warrior, but she was leaving.

"I cannot linger. The men wait for me at the edge of the wood. The king is too mistrustful and Father has made excuses. We need to go quickly."

Robyn thrust a small satchel at me as she gathered the items from around the room. A horrible feeling grew in my stomach as I realized what she meant.

"Robyn. . . " I whispered her name and already it felt like a betrayal. Her face was full of confusion as she stopped midway through placing my nightgown in the bag. "I. . . cannot leave."

Robyn's gaze met mine for a moment as her face fell.

"I cannot stay, Marian. The king has all but labeled us as traitors. It is only a matter of time. The people are ready. *We* are ready."

"Ready for what?" I resisted the urge to scream at her. I wanted to help the people too. I wanted the king to listen to his advisers, to listen to the noblemen, to listen to *me*. But he was the king. What more could we do?

"Ready to end this tyranny!" Robyn tossed the bag onto the floor, then closed the distance between us. "You have seen it all first hand. You have seen how the people suffer. You know how angry they are. It is time for the king to step down."

Her treasonous words fell over me as icy terror crawled down my back. I looked around the room frantically, running over and checking that the door was secure.

"Someone has to rule, Robyn. Even if the king stepped down, I'm. . . I'm afraid Asher wouldn't be much better. He is too. . . hot-headed. He is not ready."

"Then, perhaps, the people should rule." Robyn threw her hands in the air.

I considered her words. It was not unheard of. Smaller villages often elected their leaders. To see it on such a grand scale though? Surely it would amass to anarchy.

"Perhaps you are right, but who are we to say?"

"If we do not speak for the people, if their healer and the members of the most powerful family in the realm do not speak for them, do not demand change, then who will?" Robyn's shoulders slouched as she rubbed her temples. "It is coming, Marian. You must make your choice."

I listened to her words, though my heart struggled to process them.

"I have to go." Robyn stepped toward the door, walking past me. I grabbed at her hand, desperation filling me.

"You could stay for tonight. Come with me. You could wear a disguise." The words were out of my mouth before I could stop them.

Had I really just done that? Had I asked her to hide who she was? Had I asked her to put herself in danger over something so foolish?

Pain flashed across Robyn's golden eyes as she recoiled from my words.

"I could not."

I nodded, shame warming my face. I stared at the dark floorboards at our feet.

Robyn's gentle hand warmed my cheek as she brought my chin upward. "Not only because I cannot hide who I am anymore, but because there is no disguise I could wear, no matter how great, that would be enough to fool anyone from noticing how much I love you."

Robyn's lips were gentle against mine as tears began to flow down my cheeks. "Come with me." She whispered against my mouth.

Her breath was warm against my skin as her long fingers wrapped into my hair. She pressed her lips against mine again, pulling me in, deepening the kiss.

"I can't. Maybe we can get him to change. Maybe your father can talk to the king?"

Robyn's hand fell from my hair. She took a step back, eyes searching my face, and for the first time, I saw true anger flash. "There is no talking left to be done. You know the people are dying. You *know* it, Marian. The king has made his choice. Make yours."

We stood in silence for several moments, as a thousand thoughts and questions raged in my head. I knew something had to change. I knew something must be done, but could I do this? *Could I walk away from everything I had ever known? Could I abandon all I had worked for?*

Robyn's frown deepened as she shook her head at me. Her face seemed to harden for a moment, and, in a flash, the woman I knew was gone. In her place stood the Robyn I had known for years, but who was still a stranger. Before me was the woman desperate to prove herself worthy.

"Then you have made your choice." Robyn pushed past me in a flurry of brown hair, nearly knocking me to the ground as she headed once more for my doorway.

"Robyn—" I called her name, but she was gone as fast as shadows absorbed into nighttime. I stood silent for a moment as everything that had happened washed over me. For several moments I waited for her to return, picturing her standing in the space around me that was now devoid.

Finally, the reality hit me. I fell to my knees, hot tears pouring from me and sobs shaking my chest as I realized she truly was not coming back.

I could still feel Robyn's absence hours later as I stood before the dais.

I looked at the future of our kingdom and my heart sank. Madawi's face was sullen, deprived of its normal joy. She had lost not only her bodyguard and closest companion, but she had lost her only real tie to her kingdom—and now she was expected to dance and smile as if her heart was not broken.

King Ruelle was clearly already deep in his cups. I watched with disgust as he stared lustfully at every woman who came near. Beside him, Queen Naomi in her stunning, black velvet dress was pretending not to notice.

She said nothing to me as I approached. She showed no concern or surprise that we had nearly died together. The silver crown atop her head seemed to reach for me in the moonlight. She stared at me, sending chills down my spine.

Asher stood before me in all his finery. The golden hilt of his sword glittered at his side. He too showed no signs of distress that his mother and his betrothed had nearly died.

My cheeks warmed as I curtsied before the royal family. Queen Naomi continued to sneer at me from the dais. Her cold eyes assessed me, but for the first time, I realized that I no longer sought her approval. I had to force myself not to cringe as both the King's and Asher's gaze fell directly to my chest.

"Marian. You outshine the stars tonight." Asher's hand was cold in mine as he lifted me from the floor, kissing the tops of my fingers.

"Thank you, Your Highness." I pulled my palm from his, stepping back from where he stood so close. A look of confusion washed over Asher's face as I silently waited for their dismissal.

Around me, soft music played, but no one danced. It was as if the Court were holding its collective breath, waiting on what was to come next.

As each second passed, I felt my fury grow. This was the power they had over me. This was the power they had over us all. No one could dance, no one could even dare to leave the heavy scrutiny of the crown without fear.

Anger and frustration built inside of me as I waited. The Queen's stare darted between me and Asher. A cold sweat built on my brow as I wondered what my friend had shared with his mother.

"Enjoy yourself, Marian. I'm sure as our new Palace Healer this will be the last excursion for you before you are much too busy to attend such celebrations. . . " The queen's voice was filled with contempt as she waved me off.

Madawi looked shaken as she sat on her temporary throne. I could still see the faint bruises under her soft, brown skin and felt bad I had not reached out and talked with my friend.

I dipped my head politely at the queen and muttered my thanks. All around me, the nobility began to shuffle around the dance floor.

As I paced near the edges of the rooftop garden, it became increasingly clear that the king and queen had spared no expense. Beautiful, ornate topiaries shaped like birds stretched toward the night sky. Their feathers, constructed of stunning, yellow daffodils, swayed with the breeze.

I crept up to one of the enormous decorations, as something odd about its face caught my eye. My stomach rolled as I realized that an enormous ruby had been placed in the eyes of each sculpture.

Last week, the crown had all but told the freezing and starving people outside its gates that the coffers were empty, but tonight its true colors were shining through.

Anger continued to build in my chest as I watched servants begin to pour from the back of the room. Each servant carried silver platters towering with food. I watched several nobles reach for the food, completely unaware and apathetic of what this kind of splendor could do for the people just outside the city gates.

"Do not let the queen see you make that face." A deep, gruff voice whispered behind me, startling me from my anger and making me jump.

Trying to calm my wildly beating heart, I smiled at the older man. I struggled to remember his name, running through the long list of nobility I had yet to formally meet. "I'm sure I don't know what you mean, my lord."

"Please, call me Elijiah."

Something clicked in my mind as I suddenly realized — Earl Elijiah Griffith. His family was one of the oldest in Notting — and a favorite of the Court. He was also the father of the man who had killed Danyeil.

Elijiah sipped his drink without response.

"It seems the prince once again neglects his betrothed, though it is of no surprise. Prince Asher seems to be losing favor with many people as of late. It is one of many reasons I have sent my son Jaspar back home." Elijiah's brown eyes sparkled with mischief as they followed the trays of food around the room. His bulbous nose crinkled in disgust as one neared us.

We stood together for several moments as my heart continued to pound in my chest. I hadn't spent a lot of time with the nobility lately, except for Robyn. I needed to watch my tongue until I knew where the earl's loyalties truly resided.

Music played all around us as I shifted uneasily. The melody was soft and slow. Several couples had already entered the dance floor. Their elegant gowns seemed to reflect the golden glow in the light of the torches, reminding me painfully of a pair of stunning, golden eyes that I would probably never see again.

Emotion threatened to overwhelm me as I attempted to fade away into the crowd again. A glint of gold flashed on the dance floor, and I knew that Asher was headed for me.

What a fool. His mother will kill us both if he abandons Madawi.

As if sensing it too, the earl's withered hand reached for mine, squeezing my fingers gently and drawing my attention away from the prince. "Lady Marian, would you care to dance with an old man?"

Elijiah's gaze looked past my shoulder, and I knew without looking that Asher would not interrupt. To do so would not only insult the earl, but also Princess Madawi.

There were several murmurs of approval from other ladies, and a few members of Court clapped as Elijiah escorted me onto the dance floor. Despite the way his back had curved with age, I suddenly felt very small as Earl Griffith's towered over me. His cold hand rested on my lower back as he pulled me closer.

My heart threatened to beat out of my chest as we made a painfully slow circle around the dance floor.

"It seems to me that such a splendor must have been difficult for the crown to procure. . . " Elijah wheezed against my ear, ". . . since the coffers are so empty." I continued to allow him to lead me around the dance floor, listening intently as he whispered. "Our people starve, while its nobility sits around getting fat—something both my son and our prince seem to constantly overlook."

Elijah paused, and I knew he was waiting for a signal from me. I laughed loudly in his ear, flipping my hair over my shoulder. I had become the picture of a young girl enjoying the company of an older man with great stories to tell.

"My lord, you are full of such wisdom." I made a point to swing backward, bringing my hand up to my mouth as I batted my lashes for the entire Court to see.

Without missing a beat, the old man's smile grew. Once again, he pulled me in close.

"We see the banner. We hear its call. The people respond."

I didn't know what to say as Elijiah kissed the back of my hand and hobbled away.

My heart was heavy as I walked from the dance floor. Jaspar had killed my friend. How could a man such as Elijiah beget a man like that?

I could stand no more frivolity. No more dancing. No more plates of food whizzing by on their silver platters. The sight of it all made my stomach turn. I had come for one reason—to ask Asher to stop his tirade against Robyn.

Like something from a nightmare, it was only seconds later that the prince who had once been my friend appeared like a phantom at my side.

"Marian. I am so glad you are okay." Asher was much too close now as we stood in the shadow beneath one of the large, topiary birds. I fought the urge to flinch as his hand grazed the bruise on my face. It would do no good to offend him just before I was to ask him for the greatest favor imaginable.

"Kira has become quite the apprentice. She seems to have truly blossomed."

Asher nodded, though his gaze was cold and unfocused like his thoughts were far away.

"I don't know what might have happened if Robyn hadn't been there and taken me to the tower so quickly."

"As thankful as I am for her quick thinking, it doesn't excuse her treasonous behavior." Asher's nose scrunched with distaste as he clenched his fists. "She, and all the others who have put this kingdom at risk, will have to be dealt with quickly."

In that moment I knew any hope of reasoning with the man who had been my friend was gone. Asher stepped closer to me now until his chest was nearly level with mine.

I forced my breathing to calm as I spoke. "All she wants is what we all want. . . " —I watched Asher's lips flatten— ". . . the unity and care of our people."

"Are you insane? The Loxley's are leading a rebellion!" Asher's voice filled the garden. I felt my shoulders sag, even as my fury grew.

My feet carried me toward the parapet as I struggled to control my emotions. My jaw clenched and the edges of my nails scored the inside of my palms as I approached the edge of the wall. Ahead of me, the king's banner waved in the chilly wind.

"You are a fool, Marian!" Asher grabbed at my forearm. The same one the man had pulled at only two nights before. As I looked at Asher's icy hand and how it fit perfectly over the bruise, I felt the hope drain from me.

The similarities between the man who would one day be my king and the man who had nearly cost me my life were almost too much to handle. As my hope for Asher diminished, in its place, something else arose.

Robyn had been right, and I had been too stupid to see it. It was time for a change.

Despite the pain, I ripped my arm from Asher's grip. His eyes flashed with surprise. I let my voice carry now, even as I felt the dozens of eyes watching us. "They were saving *your* people."

"It's treason."

"Treason? What is the greater treason, hosting lavish parties while your people die of starvation and illness or helping them survive in any way you can?" Around us, I heard the nobles grumble.

Conversations stopped as people strained to listen. The music lulled.

"You will not disrespect the crown!" Asher's pale face turned red now. I watched as his shoulders shook with fury.

Total silence fell, as the queen and King rose from their seat on the dais. Asher approached, following me down the narrow, stone walkway. His steps were quick and intentional as he narrowed the space between us. His nose rose high into the air, and again he clenched his fists at his sides.

I would not allow myself to blanch as he hovered over me. The fury inside of me refused to quell. I steeled myself, unwilling to bow any longer. They had taken enough from the people of Notting. They had taken enough from our kingdom. They could take nothing else from me--because I had already lost everything.

Asher didn't bother to whisper, though he continued to seethe.

"Lady Marian. You are upset. Perhaps it is time for you to retire. You are disgracing yourself—"

"The crown is a disgrace to its people!" I spat the words I'd been thinking for months. Ever since the first day in the camps outside Colch, the words had been itching at the back of my mind.

The sting of the slap brought me to my knees. Gasps filled the garden.

Warm tears flowed freely down my cheeks now, but I rose to face my friend. The soft silk of my dress bunched tight in my hands as I stood before Asher.

Shock spread throughout his face as the light of the torch beside us shimmered off his black tunic. I stepped back instinctively as Asher's hand reached out for me, nearly toppling into the banner flapping in the breeze. I caught the thin pole, pulling it tight across my chest to keep him at bay.

Asher lowered his hand, stepping back from me.

Only a few weeks ago, this same man had nearly forced me into a loveless, abusive marriage. Now, he had called me a disgrace and struck me before the entire Court. The last piece of my pride fell away as the guards approached slowly. Their swords were drawn, and it took me a moment to realize why.

The end of the pole I was holding was steel, designed to dig deep into the hard rock. I analyzed the hard rod beneath my hands. It could easily be turned into a weapon against the prince. Despite the fact that it was he who had struck me, I had no doubt dozens of the king's best archers had their sights pinned on me now. They would strike me down before I even made a step toward Prince Asher.

"I have no desire to hurt you," I spoke directly to Asher, who signaled for the guards to halt with a wave of his hand.

Images of the sick and starving people filled my mind. The faces of children who hadn't felt full bellies in months, but still continued to smile and play, reminded me of what Robyn had tried for so long to get me to see.

My heart ached as I remembered their faces. I swept my eyes across the garden. The King and Queen had left the dais. Servants stopped pouring wine or carrying their trays. Noble men and women watched us. Their eyes were full of curiosity and fear as they watched the royal family's response.

I looked back once more to the man who had once been my confidante. Power and greed and unbridled hubris had morphed him into the monster before me. His brows still furrowed in anger, but I could see his uncertainty.

"Your people die in the streets. They die in the roads, headed toward a castle that will not take them in. Then, when someone *does* help them, you call those people traitors. You say they have disgraced our kingdom."

The green and yellow banner flapped wildly in the breeze, drawing my attention. The faint light of the nearby torch beckoned me as I stepped toward it.

"What is the higher crime? To befoul our kingdom with these symbols of hubris. . . " I leaned the banner closer to the torch now. The ends of the tassels began to simmer and smoke. "Or to allow our people to go without enough clothing or food to survive the winter?"

Asher lunged for the pole in my hands, but the weeks of training alongside Robyn had made me quick. I dodged out of his grasp. I dipped the flag into the flames, and it immediately caught fire.

The king's voice yelled for the guards as I flung the royal symbol over the wall. Rough hands grabbed me, pinning me against the stone. I peered through an arrow slit, watching the flames disappear into the camps below.

As the guards hauled me away, I could swear I heard cheering.

Robyn

I watched his hand strike Marian, and the arrow was free from my quiver and knocked into the bow before I took my next breath. *I would kill anyone who harmed her, even the prince.*

Father's hand was tight on my shoulder. The other hand gripped the arrow I held aimed at the prince's heart.

"I will *not* let him strike her again." Heat rose in my chest as wrenched my shoulder free from his firm grip. His hand did not leave the shaft of the arrow as his green eyes bore into mine.

"Neither will she." A smile curled at the edge of my father's mouth as he jerked with his head. I looked at the scene unfolding before us.

Every eye in the garden watched Prince Asher and Marian argue. Marian's long, blond hair swept around her face in the torchlight as she dodged the prince's outstretched hand. My fury was renewed at the look of fear on her face, but pride filled me as I watched that fear turn into something more.

Marian's chin jutted upward as she straightened her shoulders. I had come to recognize that look of defiance. *No.* A shiver swept down my spine as I realized, like all parts of her, I had come to love it.

My breath caught in my throat as Marian grabbed at the pole carrying the royal banner. Her mouth was moving, but I strained to hear over the roar of the wind. I watched in horror as guards approached on both sides. Panic filled me as I counted their numbers. *How many could I take out before they got to her? Even if I took them all out, I would never get to her in time.*

As if sensing my intentions, several of the men began retrieving arrows from their quivers. Beside me, the stares of Samwell and Gawayne met my own. They gave a silent nod. Neither of them looked to my father, but I did.

Sir Sebastion, Baron of Loxley, stood dumbfounded as he stared at his men. His mouth was now agape at this silent show of support. He had fought beside his men to earn their loyalty, but so had I. So had Marian.

"No. Look at them," Father whispered against the wind, sweeping his arm wide across the garden.

We peered down at the Court. All across the gilded garden, every person had stopped to watch. The King and Queen stood closer now, nearing the edge of the raised wall. As Marian spoke, several heads nodded. Servants and nobility alike wore faces filled with outrage.

Marian was one of them all. As Palace Healer, she had tended to all ranks. I had seen that first hand. She treated nobility and commoner with the same respect and care. It showed in the faces of everyone present. *Marian was beloved.*

"She is what we need." Father's words sent a new chill down my spine. I looked away for a moment to see his familiar cold and calculating stare. I could almost see the ideas growing as his brows furrowed together.

Several of the men gasped, bringing my attention back to the scene at hand. Even from this distance, I could see Marian as she stood defiantly before the royal family.

As she dipped the flag into the flames of the torch, I had never been so proud of anyone in my life. My heart nearly stopped as the flag hurtled to the ground. I knew the king would kill her for it.

Memories of Asher's hands hauling Marian away swept across my mind as I paced the small field inside the edge of Sherwood.

"We will get her back." Father had repeated the words for hours before disappearing deep into the heart of Sherwood to convene with Sir Godbert's force.

First, he had said it to me and the men atop the tower. His words had been biting as he explained that we would retrieve Marian as soon as possible, but we would also do it when it made the most sense.

I had nearly struck my father tonight. My hands were clenched into fists as he explained his plan. Samwell and Gawayne had to all but gag me as we spirited from the roof and out to the stables. Now we awaited news from father's spies about the King's decision.

No one was surprised when the news came, though I was certainly surprised by who it came from. Kira's red hair emerged from beneath the trees, riding Marian's horse.

Realization struck me. *Of course, she was one of my father's spies.*

From my peripheral, I watch as Samwell's jaw dropped and his face flushed with anger. It seemed he had been unaware as well.

Kira walked confidently across the field as she approached me. Not once did she look at Samwell. Her breath came in short bursts and I knew she had ridden hard to tell us the news.

"She's in the dungeon." My heart fell as I prepared myself. "The king is furious. He wanted her. . . " Kira's eyes brimmed with unshed tears as she looked across the dark. "He wanted her stripped and placed into one of the larger cells with other prisoners, but the prince wouldn't allow it."

Disgust and bile rose in my throat. My loathing for the insane monarchs grew to new levels.

"He has instructed the guards. . . to not treat her kindly. However, most refused."

Shock filled me. The men in the clearing ruffled with unease. Some nodded with admiration. It was unheard of for a guard to disobey the king. Then, Kira's words finally registered.

"Most?"

Kira's large chest heaved as her shoulders slumped. "They would not allow any healers in to bandage her wounds, but one. . . friendly guard guessed at least a broken rib, an arm, and maybe worse."

Fury choked me as I marched toward my horse, but Sir Johnathan's large frame suddenly blocked my path.

"There is more." Kira's voice was a whisper. I whipped my head back around as my heart pounded in my throat. "The king has decreed. Marian has disgraced the kingdom by burning the flag. She will burn too, come morning."

The world seemed to sway around me. I struggled to stay upright, gasping for breath. Jonathan's hand met my shoulder, but I shrugged him off. Now was not the time to panic. Now was the time to act.

Resolution filled me. I would get her out. I would get her out *now*. I moved once more for my horse, but Johnathan still stood between.

"You will move." I felt the venom drip from my words as I closed the distance between us. I did not care how I would take the man down, but he would not stand in my way.

"Robyn." Johnathan's voice reached out for me through the darkness. I shook my head, ignoring him. The sorrow and grief in his words were almost too much for me to bear.

"You. Will. Move," I spoke each word, drawing my sword from its sheath. Johnathan did not move. His shaggy, brown hair fell into his face as he looked down at me.

"We will get her back." He repeated my father's words, but this time, I truly heard their promise.

"She is hurt." I choked the words out. "She is afraid." Hot tears threatened to spill, but I would not cry in front of my father's men. "He wants to *burn* her."

It was his turn to choke out the words. "I know. We will get her back, Robyn. By my word, I swear it." Johnathan drew his sword. The long, silver blade emerged from the sheath. Its flat blade glinted off the light of the lanterns. The soft thud resonated through me as he stuck the end into the ground—the truest sign of fealty.

Around me, I heard the familiar zing of swords being drawn. I spun slowly as each man in the circle drew his sword. Each blade sliced into the ground as the men knelt.

This time, I did not bother to fight the tears as they streamed down my face.

There was no sound in the forest except my own bated breath. Johnathan rose before me, and I knew he was silently waiting for my instruction. I turned to Kira. Her slender shoulders straightened under my sudden scrutiny.

"You will get one of our guards, someone who refused the king's instructions, to wait outside her cell tonight. See if the guard can slip her anything for her wounds." Kira nodded as I spoke. Her face filled with new determination. I looked at the men around us. "We will wait on the very edge of the forest until morning."

Father's story about Marian's mother suddenly leapt to the forefront of my mind. "If the king makes *any* move to come to her, he must be dissuaded. Slip something into his drink, clock him over the head. Do anything to keep him from her cell."

Kira's face fell, and I knew that she knew exactly why the king might visit Marian's cell.

"Perhaps Mistress Gene could arrange a sleeping potion for the royal family. . . even the prince." I nodded, kicking myself for not considering that Asher might also want to visit.

Kira continued, a playful smile sweeping over her face. "Mistress Gene must be careful though, a sleeping potion might delay the royal family's morning duties. It would be a shame if they should oversleep."

With that, Kira climbed back atop Marian's horse. I watched the white mare disappear into the dark woods.

"We will get her back." I proclaimed to the men of Sherwood. Determination grew in my chest. I would get her back, and there was no one in all of Notting who would stop me.

Marian

The pain throbbing across my cheek was bearable. I resisted the urge to touch the wound. I knew that dirt, slime, and other unthinkable things I didn't want to consider, lined the floor of the cell and now my hands too.

Every breath had become a chore. Breathing in caused sharp pain to rack my ribs. I knew I had at least one broken rib, maybe more. My left arm was full of knives, but I could still move my fingers so I knew there must be some blood flow. There would be no way to put my elbow back in place without help, so I tried to put it from my mind.

The chill of the floor reached out to me, soaking through my clothes and burrowing deep within my skin. From the hallway, the flickering light of a torch lit the small room around me. Squeezing my knees tight against my chest, I wondered again what was to come.

At some point in the night, a guard tossed a roll of clean cloth into my cell. I watched the white cloth drop to the dirt through my clouded vision. The cuts along my arm were most likely to get infected, so I used the thin cloth to wrap my left arm as tight as I could using my teeth and my working right hand. The final product wasn't as clean as I would have liked, but I reminded myself it probably wouldn't matter anyway.

With every passing moment, I waited for true darkness to descend as the torchlight dwindled. I wondered again how long it would last. *Would the guard even bother to light another?*

The events of the last few nights, and the last few months, played through my mind on repeat. Had it only been hours ago Robyn had told me she loved me? My heart ached at the memory of the pain behind her gaze.

Why hadn't I left with her?

Tomorrow I would burn and the entire kingdom would watch it, but the only regret I would carry to the grave was the look of hurt behind Robyn's eyes tonight.

The tears were warm against my cheeks as they fell. I pulled my legs closer, burying my face between them as the sobs wracked my body.

Hours passed as I cried alone in my cell. My head throbbed and heaviness hung over my bones, pinning me to the floor. Somewhere in the distance water dripped to the floor, bringing with it the smell of mildew and mud. I listened to the steady drip, drip of the water until somewhere in the distance the thick metal entrance squeaked.

On my way down to the dungeon, I had prepared myself mentally for what I might do if someone visited my cell to take advantage of my injured state. I knew that I couldn't fight or throw any punches right now, but I still had nails and I still had teeth. The wall behind me was slick, but I managed to use it to right myself for whoever was coming to visit.

Through my blurred vision, I made out a heavily cloaked figure. When their hood fell, I could not have been more shocked than if my own dead mother stood before me.

Queen Naomi stood on the other side of the door. Her icy stare traveled over my body, examining every bruise and scrape. I was not surprised when I saw no pity in her gaze, but her look of absolute contempt shook me to my core.

I waited for her to speak while my legs shook underneath me. When she motioned to the ground, I tried not to fall too quickly.

"At first, none of this was really your fault. If not for the... problems with the common folk, I might have let you live in peace."

My jaw fell open at her frankness. Queen Naomi rubbed at her temples, suddenly reminding me of Asher.

"Why are you here?" I did my best to force my words out with confidence, but it came out more as a plea. Perhaps it was. Perhaps I truly was desperate to understand.

"As I said, at first it was not your fault. You were born like any other child—subject to the whims of your station. At least, that is what I hoped you would stay." Naomi adjusted her long cloak around her shoulders now, while my mind struggled to understand what she meant.

"You look just like her, you know that? Lady Reya and I came from the same province in the north country. We grew up together, though I was the daughter of the chief, and she just. . . nothing." Once more the queen looked up from her lashes toward me, and I knew she was trying to judge my reaction of her insults about my mother.

"Ruelle came to end the war—such was the treaty made with my father. He would marry me, I would be his queen, and bear him children, and the war would end. It was so simple."

Queen Naomi's soft chuckle filled the air as she looked up at the damp ceiling--as if responding to some great joke only she knew.

"All he had to do was bed me first. I never cared if he bedded other women. All I wanted was for our son to bring nations together." My stomach churned as she spoke. Dread filled me. Though I knew it was coming, I never dreamed I would hear it confirmed.

"Instead, he lay with your mother." Bile rose in my throat, but I fought it back. I shook my head—desperate to rid myself of my own sordid creation.

"She was my best friend. She finally told me, just three days before you were born. Do you know I tried everything? I did anything the healer said not to do. I was desperate for Asher to come early, but he would not. By the time you came, there was no other choice."

Despite the protests of my body, I rushed the bars of my cell. I clawed at Queen Naomi's cloak, but she was much faster. Fury filled me for what she had robbed me of. What she had robbed my mother of.

"When you came out that night, you looked just like your mother, but you also looked just like him. I have hated you all of these years for looking just like him."

"Why? Why not kill me too?" I spilled the words I had been wondering for days. Ever since I denied Robyn, I wondered how something so evil could be true.

"Whether your mother slept with my beloved willingly or not, it didn't change the fact that you would be his heir. Hers was a treason I could not forgive. You would be his firstborn. But I could not do it. I could not bring myself to kill you.

"I looked over your crib every night, imagining smothering your sleeping form with the blankets we had bestowed upon you. I imagined pouring poison into your food. I prayed to the gods for an ailment to come and take you away. It was my weakness. But, then the unrest started and I knew it couldn't continue. I could not allow you to jeopardize the future I had spent my whole life trying to build."

I shook my head again, but nothing could shake the lunacy of her words from my mind. Every moment I had ever had with the queen flooded through me. All the times she had attended my lessons as a child, all the times she had reprimanded me. I had had no idea the true depth of her loathing.

Then the last few days, when everything had so suddenly changed. . .

Reality dawned on me as I thought back to the night we had gone walking together through the camps.

"You knew. You knew that if we went out to the camps those men would be waiting. You wanted us to be hurt. You wanted us to die. Why? Why put yourself in danger like that?"

The queen did not respond. Her cold eyes bore into me. The flame of the candle reflected off the darkness in her eyes as she arched her manicured brow. Never before had I imagined that one person could look so conniving, so evil.

"You could have been killed too." I shook my head in disbelief.

"You still don't understand, child." She leaned closer to the bars now, speaking barely above a whisper. "It is only ever about my child. It is about Asher's future. Even if he has to marry one of those disgusting, sand-lice filth, she will bear him children. Those children will rule two kingdoms. Perhaps three if they claim their grandmother's birthright. Their dynasty will live forever. The only thing standing in the way of that is you."

My heart dropped into my stomach at her words.

"When the assassins failed, I knew something must be done before others discovered. The queen dying at the hands of the furious masses would bring the kingdom together with the cries of the citizens' sympathy and support. Asher would mourn and then marry the princess, and Notting would forget their anger as a new age was brought forth. I did not consider that your harlot might save us."

Naomi rolled her eyes in disgust, and I lunged for her again. She waved off my attempts as if I were some fly bothering her on a hot, summer day.

"All this time I have wondered what might have been, but it is too late for that now. Tomorrow you will die, and I hope you know that it is for a righteous cause. If you do not, if somehow you live, it will be at

a great cost."

The queen gathered her hood around her once more, before turning toward me again with her icy stare. "Whether it be you or my husband, I have always wondered which of you will truly be the downfall of our kingdom. . . "

I knew the King would kill me for it, but the people of Notting didn't deserve to be slaves anymore and neither did I.

I had walked this earth for barely more than twenty years, but I would burn this morning. Lord Sampson carried the torch toward the pile of wood as I struggled against the ropes pinching at my wrists. His face was filled with contempt as he approached. The nobility gathered along the stone wall of the castle high above us,

I knew if I looked up I would see the faces of the people I had spent my entire life trying to fit in with and trying to impress. I knew I would see the glimmering jewels of the royal family reflecting off the sunlight. I would see the face of Prince Asher—the man who was supposed to be my friend. How many of the Court would cry for me today? How many would mourn my death?

Would they look away or watch me burn?

I watched the torch flicker in his enormous hands. I wouldn't call to the Court for aid. I wouldn't plead for my life.

Spread wide in a circle around me, hundreds of the citizens of Notting had been summoned from their beds to watch. Many of the women were openly sobbing. Their kerchiefs pulled across their noses as they wailed. Their voices called out to me despite the wrath they might succumb from the king. My crime was treason and for that the crown believed there should be no weeping.

I refused to search the crowd for the one face I wanted to see more than any other. I knew she wouldn't be there. Robyn had made her opinion known, and my actions had come far too late.

A circle of royal guards held the people at bay.

"Free the princess!" a voice called from the crowd.

"The king murders his own child!"

I felt the tears fall down my cheeks. It seemed so many had known the truth before me. The people of Notting knew my secret. They knew that I had been born from a terrible act of violence and betrayal—and they gave me their love anyway.

If I wasn't sure before, I was now. The queen would never allow me to live as long as the people knew the truth.

The duke leaned down, placing the torch against the brittle timber at my feet. The rush of the heat from the flames reached for me as the kindling crackled. I strained against the ropes binding my chest, but each movement was unbearable. The smoke blew toward me on the breeze, and my lungs began to sting as the inferno grew.

I closed my eyes for a final time and waited for death to come.

Robyn

It almost killed me to wait. My heart ached as I watched the fire burn around her, but I knew she was strong enough. I knew that Marian could handle the flames.

We had to wait until the last minute—until the people were desperate enough to finally take a stand. We had to be sure that everyone in Notting knew just how far the king and queen were willing to go.

The king was willing to kill his own child, and the queen was willing to allow it. Prince Asher was willing to murder a friend he had known since birth. They were willing to let Marian die, all because she had the same eyes as her father. The same eyes as King Ruelle.

The crowd continued to scream and push against the wall of guards around Marian. Someone threw a rock toward a guard. I ducked as it ricocheted off his armor and back into the crowd.

I watched as a child carried a bucket toward the blaze. I immediately recognized the girl as the small child we had helped outside Colch and then again the night Danyeil was murdered. The small, brunette girl was quick as she ducked in-between legs and under the guards' swords.

"Marian!" The child called, dumping the bucket on the edge of the blaze. Most of the contents had already spilled to the ground, but a few logs sizzled as the water hit them.

"Layla! Run!" Marian screamed above the chaos.

Someone shoved against me, and I had to dip to the side to avoid being pushed into the ground. There was a commotion, and I strained to see between the sea of angry bodies.

The shouting grew, and above it all, I heard a child scream.

I pushed between two shoulders—finally nearing the edge of the ring of people. I looked to Marian first, and then watched the gray-haired man whose armor glinted in the morning sun.

Sampson stood before Marian. His mouth rose at the edge as he seemed to watch the flames. He was enjoying the spectacle, and he was reveling in Marian's agony.

The old man's wrinkled face looked out over the crowd as he lifted the screaming girl for all to see. Then, his cruel face looked to Marian as he threw the child into the flames.

The child's scream pierced the air as she was enveloped in flames. The crowd gasped in shock, but it was Marian who called for the little girl. It was Marian whose wrists dripped with blood as she fought against the ties that bound her.

As the child's screams grew, I felt bile rise in my throat and fury build in my chest. Sampson would pay for what he had done.

All at once, the crowd pushed against the guards. All around me men and women fell on the swords of the men holding them at bay. I knew it was time. As Layla's cries finally ceased, I loosed my arrow into the top of the post above her head.

The white ribbon drifted in the wind as it embedded in the post above Marian's head with a thunk that I felt deep in my chest. It was the signal for my men to make their move. It was the signal for the revolution to begin. It was time to let the capital and all of Notting fall into anarchy.

I rushed the pole holding Marian aloft as a flood of arrows flew around us. The clang of armor filled the air, and I knew without turning around that several of the castle guards now had arrows buried in their chests.

Marian fell against me as I cut the bindings on her wrists. A tremor of fear swept through me as I felt her rattled breath.

Had I waited too long to save her?

I held her tight against me as we leapt over the flames. The blaze burned at my skin, heating my thin armor to an almost unbearable level. We landed just beyond the fire. I caught my breath as the air momentarily left my lungs. I searched the crowd for a hole or gap for us to escape.

That was when I realized that Marian was no longer beside me.

A flash of blond caught my eye and I tried to follow. Gone was all semblance of order. The sound of arrows hitting bodies filled the air and I knew the king had ordered his archers to open fire.

I wondered how many of his soldiers would follow such an order. How many would refuse to kill the citizens of Notting? Many of those soldiers had family and friends in the crowd. Did the foolish king know he was giving orders that might turn his men against him?

I followed Marian, trying desperately to reach her.

Ahead I could see that the mob had surged around someone. It didn't take long to guess who it was.

"Get off me! I will have you all charged with treason!" Sampson's voice called.

Finally, I was in reach of Marian. I needed to get her out of here. It was only a matter of time until father's men stormed the castle. I needed to get Marian out of the capital before the real war began.

Silence fell around me as Marian approached the captain. I watched people's eyes grow larger as she approached. The king had forced her back into her white, healer's garb. Gone was the clean, white fabric. Instead, it had been stained black and gray from the smoke. Pieces of the hem were blackened and scorched from the flames.

The crowd widened around her, allowing me to approach her side. Marian's face was stone as she stared down Sampson. Like something from darkness, she had stepped from the flames unharmed. The heat had grabbed for her, scorched her, called to her--but she had walked away.

Her hair flowed free of its braids and fell loose around her shoulders. In that moment, when her blue eyes met mine, I knew the woman who had walked from the flames was not the same as the one who had waited for them to take her.

Marian turned from me, and her gaze settled on Sampson once again.

"I, Marian, firstborn of King Ruelle and Lady Reya of Aicias, Princess of Notting, hereby sentence you to death for atrocities against a child of my kingdom. For that, the punishment shall be death."

"You will never—"

Marian didn't wait for his response. She jammed the dagger in and out of his throat in a flash. Blood drenched the ground, spraying Marian's white dress with crimson droplets. She was silent as she turned and handed me back the blade.

Father had been right—Marian was what Notting needed. She was who would rally the people. I could see it now, and I knew everyone around her could too. We would heal Notting or we would burn it to the ground—and we would do it together.

Please Leave a Review!
Leaving a review helps in more ways than you can imagine!
Independently published authors rely on reviews for exposure.
This tells Amazon to advertise our work and, of course, helps readers
find more diverse books!

<u>Amazon</u>

**Do you want to receive notifications for sales on this book or my
other books?
Hit the yellow "Follow This Author" button by my profile image
on Amazon!**

About the Author

Morgan Perryman is a new author from the Midwestern United States. She is a true bibliophile, who has always had a love for books. Morgan has a Master's in Education and a Bachelor's Degree in English.

She is a mother of three and comes from a huge family.

Her early writer influences include a variety of classic and modern writers, including Jane Austen and Tamora Pierce.

Check out other books by this author:

Natural Born

Dear Readers,

Wow! Hello, amazing, incredible, wonderful readers! Thank you so much for taking the time to read *Of Arrows and Anarchy*.

Thank you to anyone who has purchased or received this book. You took a chance this book was worth your time and worth a space on your shelf. Whether it is a physical shelf or a virtual one, I appreciate you.

If you are interested in exclusive news, sneak peeks, excerpts from future books, and more please sign up for my romance newsletter!

Acknowledgments

Thank you so much for taking the time to read *Of Arrows and Anarchy*. I truly hope you have enjoyed reading it as much as I have enjoyed writing it.

The truth of this book is it started as a dream. Unlike my debut novel, *Natural Born*, which came out last year, this book has evolved much, much faster than I ever expected. However, it would never have been possible without my amazing team.

As always, thank you to my amazing husband Jonathan for supporting me throughout this process. You push me to reach for my dreams, but somehow help me stayed grounded.

Thank you to my alpha reader, the amazing Trema Minning. You have listened to me whine and moan and still given me such incredible, critical feedback. Trema is an amazing mother and absolutely loves reading. If you are interested in some awesome homeschool resources and lessons, or some delightful reviews on a variety of genres, please check out her blog **Coffee Wasted Momma.**

Thank you to Joyce for proofreading this book. I am so thankful for your careful eyes and critical feedback. I hope this experience was infinitely easier than looking through the last book, and that every book from here on out gets easier and easier.

Thank you SO MUCH to all my amazing beta readers. I am hoping to get book two to you as fast as possible, but I cannot describe how important your feedback for this book was.

Love & Hope,
Morgan Perryman

Trigger Warning
(Spoiler Content)

This book contains scenes that may be distressing for some readers, including injured and hurt animals, parental death, death of a child by fire, attempted sexual assault, and violence with swords, arrows, and fire.

Pre-order Book Two
in
The Banner Calls Trilogy Now!
From Fire to Ice